They Won't Let You Live

They Won't Let You Live
Simon Blumenfeld

With an introduction by Tali Chilson

LONDON BOOKS CLASSICS

LONDON BOOKS
39 Lavender Gardens
London SW11 1DJ
www.london-books.co.uk

First published in 1939 by Nicholson and Watson
This edition published by London Books 2022

The publisher wishes to thank Eric Bloomfield
and Sheba Solomons for their assistance with
this edition of *They Won't Let You Live*

London Books would like to thank Oxford Diecast
for the kind use of the cover image
www.oxforddiecast.co.uk

A catalogue record for this book
is available from the British Library

ISBN 978-0-9957217-9-1

Printed and bound in Great Britain by
CPI Group (UK) Ltd, Croydon, CR0 4YY

Typeset by Octavo Smith Publishing Services
in Plantin 10.5/13.5

For Eric and Sheba

INTRODUCTION

In 1921 Simon Blumenfeld, born to Jewish immigrants from Czarist Russia in the East End of London, left school at fourteen and went on to work long hours as a sweatshop presser and cutter.[1] Nevertheless, he still found the time and energy to publish articles, short stories and four novels, with *They Won't Let You Live,* which came out in 1939, his fourth and final book.

Blumenfeld was the forefather of an Anglo-Jewish literary revival that began in the mid-1930s. His contemporaries Ashley Smith and Gerald Kersh were also publishing during this period, and they would be joined by William 'Willy' Goldman a decade later,[2] and subsequently followed by Bernard Kops, Arnold Wesker, Wolf Mankowitz, Harold Pinter, Alexander Baron, Roland Camberton and Emanuel Litvinoff, to mention but a few.[3] These writers all had something in common. They were the first generation of Jews born in Britain to East European Jewish parents who had escaped the pogroms. Arriving in London at the beginning of the twentieth century, they were the 'poorest of the poor' of Eastern European Jewry, bringing with them no knowledge of English, possessions or skills. They came to a country that was ready to welcome cheap unskilled labour in its endeavours to better compete with the rival German market. These people were industrious and contributed to the growth of the garment trade in the back-bedroom sweatshops of Whitechapel, Leeds, Manchester and Edinburgh – with Burton and Moss Brothers among the companies that became household names.[4]

Blumenfeld, like the writers mentioned above, is likely to

have continued his education in the reading room of White-chapel Library and at Circle House, the headquarters of the Workers' Circle Friendly Society, both cultural hubs in London's East End at the time that appear frequently in the writings of most writers from the area. It seems that for these authors deprivation was not an inevitable consequence of poverty and, indeed, excellence not exclusive to the confines of privilege.

The central theme in Blumenfeld's writing concerns the individual who struggles to find a place in this world. This was due to a deeply held conviction that human beings must never be treated as superfluous, made redundant or be marginalised. In his first novel, *Jew Boy*, an international bestseller, the protagonist, Alec, is told by the wealthy and cultured Elspeth that being a Jew meant he was 'a guest in her country'. Alec's response to this was that the place one lives, works and pays tax in must be one's country. Irrespective of his being Jewish, Alec is unable to eke out a living, however hard he works. By the end of the novel Alec finds his place in what is depicted as an inclusive and welcoming Communist Party.

In *They Won't Let You Live* Blumenfeld once again addresses the subject of anti-Semitism but in a different way. Whereas in *Jew Boy* Blumenfeld touches on casual anti-Semitism through anecdote, in *They Won't Let You Live* he probes the broader epistemological question of knowledge by examining anti-Semitic tropes, the way in which they are formed and the manner in which they inform public opinion. Put another way, he is preoccupied with the question as to how our ideas and beliefs are formed and what relation – if any – they have to a truth. In order to do this Blumenfeld initiates a dialogue with a selection of English-language authors past and present who have participated in the so-called Semitic discourse. These are Shakespeare, George Eliot, Rudyard Kipling and TS Eliot.

At first glance it is all too easy to classify this book as an interwar anti-fascist novel. It depicts the rise of British fascism and the plight of middle-class small-business owners who, unlike the unemployed working class, had no recourse to public funds. One reason for this was the fact that from 1931 support from the Labour Exchange was means tested, and they did not qualify. However, a closer reading reveals that there is much more taking place. The two shopkeepers central to the plot are not just middle-class business owners: one is Jewish, the other Christian. The reader soon realises that *They Won't Let You Live* revisits Shakespeare's play *The Merchant Of Venice*. Jacob and Oscar are struggling to survive during the economic depression of the 1930s. The ubiquitous unemployment of the period occurs despite little if any loss of wealth in Britain, where, unlike the USA, no banks had collapsed.[5] Problems with credit lending meant that the ruthless presence of larger corporations led to the decimation of smaller businesses. Unemployment among professionals was especially dire, as the author Andy Croft observes:

> Out of a total 'black coated' workforce of two million, between three to four hundred thousand were unemployed in the spring of 1934. This less visible deprivation among graduates and professionals clearly caught the interest of a number of novelists. By the middle of the decade the unemployed professional was a familiar figure in contemporary fiction, like Kim Currie . . . who has applied unsuccessfully for 187 jobs since graduating.[6]

Blumenfeld 'rewrites' the Shakespearian play's plot to demonstrate that under financial duress both merchants behave exactly the same regardless of their religion or race. They take money that does not belong to them, they betray their fellow tradesmen by putting them at risk of financial ruin and they both end up in the same place. This serves as a notable departure from Shakespeare's plot, which vilifies Shylock mercilessly for being a usurer who is ultimately brought to his knees financially and, to add insult to injury, is humiliated and estranged from his daughter. Conversely, Antonio – the Christian – is celebrated as a virtuous and loyal friend despite the way he conducts himself with Shylock, a fellow merchant.

Despite the differences in narrative, there is a salient point that unites both authors in their respective literary goals. This becomes evident when we examine how Blumenfeld himself reflects on the meaning behind Shakespeare's play; what we are left with is a redeeming interpretation of a narrative that intends to subvert prejudice. In the play the only account that we have of Antonio's shortcomings is from Shylock. This decision, it would seem (to Blumenfeld at any rate), was one which Shakespeare made to probe his audience's prejudices as to whether they believe Shylock. Whether the accusations levelled against Antonio are to be believed is a matter for the audience to decide.

The question of who we believe is also a matter that preoccupies Blumenfeld in his novel. Dai Phillips, the novel's fascist party leader, for example, has no concern about the possibility that his indiscretions may be given away by his friend Benny, a Jewish bookmaker. Phillips explains to Benny that he is confident that no one will believe Benny's word over his.

When viewed through this prism, our decision then to believe the accusations against Antonio as related by Shylock recontextualises Shylock's own moving statement: 'If you prick us do we not bleed?' For Blumenfeld, it would appear that this becomes the focal point of Shakespeare's play – that is, ascertaining the humanity of the Jew and challenging a widespread dehumanisation. In Blumenfeld's view, Shakespeare's plot was a description not a prescription. The fate ascribed to Shylock can be seen as a representation of the hostility that Jews faced in Europe. This alternative interpretation may explain why Blumenfeld rewrote the plot in this novel so that both shopkeepers are not different in the ways they behave and what fate holds in store for them.

It is perhaps worth mentioning that in 1930s America there was a sea change in critical opinion. The prior notion that seventeenth-century plays such as Shakespeare's *The Merchant Of Venice* were responsible for contemporary racism and anti-Semitism was replaced by the opposing view that these plays served as a basis for contemporary humanist movements. These movements would base their 'moral claims on the humanist heritage of Shakespeare, Victor Hugo and other "cultural giants", which validated the progressive fruit of the Shakespeare legacy'.[7] It is certainly of note that Blumenfeld was familiar with the US communist literary scene, its critics and writers.[8]

Prejudice and its examination are further informed by biblical allusion. Blumenfeld – a keen Hebraist – names the Jewish merchant protagonist Jacob, whose namesake is one of the Old Testament patriarchs. The biblical Jacob stole from his elder brother Esau the privilege of his birthright. Blumenfeld's Jacob is similarly characterised in part by his sensual handling of the wad of cash that he unexpectedly receives and everything which he sees within it. Like Molière's miser Harpagon, Blumenfeld's Jacob, while looking at the running serial numbers, repeats: 'Money . . . money'. This trope is further reinforced by different characters such as Oscar the Christian shopkeeper, who states: 'A Jew will do almost anything for money.'

Blumenfeld 'conditions' his readers to believe that Jacob's character is indeed the embodiment of this anti-Semitic trope. He does so to elicit the reader's prejudices only to then cause them to question later whether Jacob's shortcomings are unique to him or, indeed, universal. As Blumenfeld's role model and later friend Aldous Huxley pointed out six years prior in his 1932 novel *Brave New World*: 'One believes things because one has been conditioned to believe them.'

The consequence of Blumenfeld's conditioning with regard to Jacob materialises in Jacob's meeting with Spencer. Oscar the Christian merchant has an estranged brother, Spencer, who is a moneylender. Spencer, we are told, stole money from the family business and coveted his brother's fiancée. Spencer refuses to lend Jacob money because, as he claims without explanation, he never lends money to Jews. At this point the reader has already been led to side with Spencer. This is a consequence of the conditioning that Blumenfeld achieves through the development of Jacob's character, which he uses as a basis for the reader's own prejudices. The reader will have to realise for themselves that they need not be predisposed towards siding with Spencer because of what they already know about his own nefarious personality.

Oscar expresses his anti-Semitic views to his son and daughter. Oscar claims he has done business with Jews for 'donkey's years' despite never liking them. In Oscar's words: 'There's something greasy and underhand about them, as if they're always on the watch to do you down. They're all opportunists.' However, Kim, Oscar's son, derides both his father's and his sister's anti-Semitic attitudes: '"Sure! Sure!" Kim repeated mockingly. "They're all Jews. Lord Beaverbrook, and Sir Harry McGowan, and George Lansbury, and the Agha Khan. Anyone who's outstandingly successful in business or politics is a Jew."'

In addition to traits, physiognomy as an anti-Semitic trope is also unpicked. For example, when Kim's college friend Coleman, a blue-eyed and fair-haired Irish lad, turns out to be Jewish, it causes much astonishment for Oscar, who believes that there is a 'Jewish look'. Unlike his father and sister, Kim does not fall for such stereotypes and realises that they are at odds with reality.

So far, the examples of the gap between anti-Semitic tropes and reality have been expressed diegetically – by 'telling' – but this gap between reality and perceived reality is also reflected in the novel's story by means of 'showing'. Within the narrative the reader will find multiple examples where the gap between reality and perceived reality is evident. For instance, it is pertinent that it is the Jewish bookmaker Benny who salvages Oscar's reputation when Oscar himself has behaved in an underhand manner. This example alone stands in complete contrast to Oscar's expressed prejudices.

Blumenfeld uses the plot to demonstrate the gap between prejudice and reality, which gives the narrative a parable-like quality. At the core of every parable there is a moral. For that moral to be timeless, parables often omit specific details concerning time and place. This might explain why Blumenfeld demonstrates a reluctance to name the streets and squares he describes, unlike in his previous novels. Instead, certain buildings, which Londoners would have been familiar with, are used as markers. These markers implicitly suggest that Oscar's shop is, in fact, situated in London's East End.[9]

With the reader's confidence in appearances shaken, even non-verbal communication becomes enigmatic and difficult to interpret. Is Jacob's smile on leaving Spencer's office the smile of a happy person who got what they wanted, as the commissionaire believes, or is it something else? The reader, who is better informed, knows all is not as it seems. The insider knowledge that the reader is granted serves as a means by which Blumenfeld makes other key points. For example, misleading appearances can also be used for political expediency. In the case of the fascist leader Dai Phillips we see how the fact that he is beaten up by a Jew is for reasons other than the political ones that the party would have others believe.

In addition to prejudice and misleading appearances, uncertainty plays a role within the novel's narrative. This is manifest in the gnawing uncertainty of Kim's biological paternity. In a time before DNA testing, Blumenfeld draws on the greater uncertainty that men had over the paternity of their offspring to serve as a foil for an interrelated question: What really decides a person's identity, nature or nurture?

The character of Kim introduces another author with whom Blumenfeld enters into dialogue. His naming alone seems a nod to Rudyard Kipling's novel *Kim*. Kipling's Kim – nicknamed 'Little Friend Of All The World', 'naturally at ease with all colours and creeds', who 'embraces the new' and 'does nothing with immense success' – is brought up to become the person he is, not by his biological father but by the Tibetan lama who mentors and nurtures him. Kipling's Kim is cosmopolitan, stranger-loving, fearless in character and seems the direct inspiration for Blumenfeld's Kim. Blumenfeld's Kim, a university graduate, is unable to translate his philosophy degree into any upward social mobility without the necessary funds and connections, which he lacks. Kim seeks employment as a taxi-driver as a consequence of his family's business going under.

Another area of uncertainty is explored through one of the characters Kim comes across. At the cab station he meets Rusty, a young working-class man and inveterate gambler. Rusty has a premonition that he is unlikely to survive the inevitable national draft for the looming war. Uncertainty, said Sigmund Freud, clouds our ability to deal properly with reality. In this novel gambling serves as a metaphor. We are all likened to gamblers in the way we attempt to get to grips with reality. Those attempts are irrational and clouded all the more by uncertainty. Like gamblers, we desire to ascertain the power of prediction in order to gain control over our own circumstances. But, in doing so, we inevitably appeal to superstition and pseudoscientific calculations. This is better known as 'the gambler's fallacy',[10] a devised system of betting which informs and instructs the gambler's choices in roulette or any other game. The system is based on statistics but mostly relies on prejudice; each go on a roulette wheel is unique. The fact that we might consider each run as part of a larger linear sequence has, under this system, little to do with any rational consideration. It is we who provide the context in which every spin of the roulette wheel or every winning racehorse can become a pattern on which base probability is judged. The relationship between reasoning and gambling is taken further in the example of Oscar, who, lacking a system entirely, decides to gamble on a horse on no account other than its name (disregarding its past racing form), and is therefore no more rational in his approach. The horse's name, Oscar feels, accurately describes his dire financial situation. The gambler sticks to his system even when it fails him, imagining that he is on the cusp of winning. Winning is not only exciting but fulfils an irrational sense of entitlement, as we see with Rusty: '[it], he felt, had been coming to him for a long while'. It is clear to see that gambling is a way for Rusty to manage his growing anxiety about imminent war, the uncertainty he feels over his personal fate and a way to boost his meagre finances in the hope of living it large before disaster strikes.

Gamblers and their grip on reality might be seen as a subset of a larger area of interest that Blumenfeld explores within his novels. This interest concerns how people's beliefs inform their actions, and the question preoccupies Blumenfeld in his novels *Phineas Kahn* (1937) and *Doctor Of The Lost* (1938). Blumenfeld addresses this question with particular reference to religious individuals and their actions in the world. In *Doctor Of The Lost* we are presented with a spectrum which stretches from the real Dr Barnardo's philanthropic activism to the fictional Oxford-educated missionary Zachariah Quelch, who believes that the class system and poverty are ordained by God. Similarly, gambling, amongst other things, in *They Won't Let You Live* serves as a way to demonstrate how the beliefs and prejudices of people may be detrimental to their own lives.

The gambling metaphor seems to have been inspired by George Eliot's novel *Daniel Deronda* (1876), in which it is a dominant metaphor. Deronda is another young man not raised by his biological father. Instead, he is, at his mother's request, nurtured by an English gentleman to become one himself. The novel would have us believe that despite his upbringing Deronda somehow still responds to the call of his 'race' even when he is unaware of his own Jewish provenance. He falls for a Jewish woman and resettles in Palestine.

For George Eliot, nature trumps nurture. Ethnicity and religion seem to be the ultimate determinants of one's identity and destiny, especially if they are Jewish. It seems that in her opinion Jews are racially different, and it is in their inherent nature to stick to their tradition and community. In her novel, Eliot expressed a common view held at the time that there was something immutable within Jewish nature that was inextricably linked to its ancestral origins in the Orient, or, as aptly remarked by Ian Thomson, Eliot's *Deronda* is considered to be 'a sympathetic proto-Zionist' novel.[11] In contrast, Alec, the protagonist of Blumenfeld's *Jew Boy*, presents the opposite view. In *Jew Boy* we learn that political movements of a nationalist nature are totally alien to the world view which forms Alec's lived experiences: '"I ask you as a Jew, have you never felt the urge, the desire, to go to Palestine, the home of our fathers?" Alec shook his head. "No! . . . I've never had the least interest of that sort in Palestine!"'

As discussed, George Eliot's dominant gambling metaphor is used to illustrate the manner in which people think about reality. This critical examination and its rationale is not applied when it comes to her own treatment of the Semitic discourse. The notion that Jews are racially different had a lot to do with Benjamin Disraeli's claim, following Matthew Arnold's two essays 'Culture And Anarchy' and 'Hellenism And Hebraism', that the 'Jew represented religion, property and natural aristocracy – the very foundation of Empire'. Jews are the embodiment of race, according to Disraeli, as opposed to those who are falsely universalised 'communist' conspirators.[12]

Within his narratives Blumenfeld is making the case for the importance that nurture and lived experience have in the formation of one's identity.

Moving on from George Eliot, Blumenfeld explores tropes themselves as a linguistic device. We see this in his examination of TS Eliot's idea of the 'objective correlative'. Kim and his new cabby friend Rusty plan an escape from the urban scene to visit the countryside. It seems that Blumenfeld is alluding to the famous Huxley quote 'A love of nature keeps no factories busy', which is why the love of nature – a working-class trait, as says the director of Hatcheries And Conditioning in Huxley's *Brave New World* – must be suppressed.[13] This particular trope is echoed by the concern of Kim's uncle Spencer that, without his financial support for Kim to train as a barrister, 'He'll get the lower-class mentality and outlook, and that's the end of him as a professional man.'

The notion of a 'working-class mentality' was something that was shared by the established Anglo-Jewry, who held Jewish East End immigrants in low regard for their proclivity to gambling and their communist sympathies. Or, as historian David Cesarani writes: 'The East End was losing its better-off population to North, North-East and even North-West London. The residue was a predominantly proletarian Jewish community which shared the working-class habits and outlook of the non-Jewish population.'[14]

For Blumenfeld, it is safe to say that any kind of generalisation based on class, race, faith or gender was wrong. However, it is not enough for him simply to subvert tropes. He goes further and examines both their inception and reception. In a conversation between Kim and Rusty, Rusty comes up with the poetic-sounding phrase 'six green trees in a row'. This phrase conveys Rusty's 'longing' for the views of the country-side. Rusty has indeed created what TS Eliot dubbed an objective correlative,[15] which is an object or event that is used to evoke a desired emotional response in the reader. It is also a trope where figurative language is employed to express emotion that cannot be communicated literally. Figurative language expresses emotion by showing rather than describing feelings. According to Eliot, it is what an elite poet creates when endeavouring to express in words their most obscure inner feelings.

Eliot's objective correlative in art is inextricably bound up with the problem of knowledge.[16] The poet's subjective feelings are thus being objectified in the poet's attempt to understand himself in a way that can be almost instinctively understood by the reader. It seems that Eliot's artistic desire to bridge the gap between subjective and objective is his attempt to pin down an ontological truth in the process. Critically, while language can indeed construct a world and impact reality, this does not mean that language can be trusted to truly describe the world as it is. To the best of our knowledge there are no 'pink elephants', yet we all understand to what the words refer.

If we take a closer look at this particular objective correlative, 'six green trees in a row', it is easily imagined as referring to six trees standing next to one another. Yet it should be borne in mind that Rusty, who is a hardened gambler, is using the language of gambling (much in the same way that *Jew Boy*'s tailor protagonist Alec tends to take notice of a person's clothing first). If so, then Rusty's 'in a row' might be a temporal rather than a spatial image, that is, one tree after the other like six lucky separate winning horses in six consecutive races. This understanding alone can explain Rusty's celebratory tone. Rusty, with his objective correlative cum literal gambling argot, creates a mental connection between going out into nature and winning. This is because winning, like going out into nature, is about fulfilling desires. What appears to be an objective correlative is really quite ambiguous, as it lends itself to two different interpretations. It is simultaneously temporal, when taken as gambling language, *and* spatial, when understood as the figurative objective correlative. Language imbued with ambiguity depicts an internal thought process and not the world itself.[17] Likewise, tropes, while purporting to describe reality, manage only to describe how we see and feel about reality. There seems to be nothing 'objective' in the objective correlative literary trope, neither in its inception nor in its reception.

In pointing out linguistic ambiguity and the importance of context in the act of communication, Blumenfeld has created what Roland Barthes called a modernist 'writerly' text where language itself is being examined, and it is made clear that language does not necessarily represent the world naturally.[18] Such text demands co-operation from a reader, who must actively participate in producing the text's meaning.

Blumenfeld's critical exploration of Eliot's objective correlative belongs with a wider critical response on his part to Eliot's writing. TS Eliot, in his 1934 book *After Strange Gods*, wrote: 'What is still more important is unity of religious background; and reasons of race and religion combine to make any large number of free-thinking Jews undesirable . . . And a spirit of excessive tolerance is to be deprecated.'[19]

'Free-thinking Jews' suggests that TS Eliot, like George Eliot and Disraeli, believed Jews belong, in fact, to a cohesive, conservative and immutable entity. TS Eliot, the anti-progressive American who settled in Britain, the Unitarian who converted to the Church of England, believed in homogeneity of communities.[20] People, he argued, should live where they were born, and a class system is an inevitable, natural phenomenon. The homogeneity of the community is necessary to preserve its culture.

In his famous 1920 poem 'Burbank With A Baedeker: Bleistein With A Cigar' Eliot strongly criticised Shakespeare's cosmopolitan vision of the Rialto (the main market area of Venice) in *The Merchant Of Venice*:

Declines. On the Rialto once.
The rats are underneath the piles.
The Jew is underneath the lot.
Money in furs. The boatman smiles[21]

Eliot seems to claim that the Jews in the Shakespearian Rialto
were actually oppressed and not part of this cosmopolitan
vision.[22] A cosmopolitan world vision appeared in Kipling's
Kim and also in Shakespeare's *The Tempest,* mentioned at the
end of *They Won't Let You Live*. It seems that yet another anti-
Semitic trope is at play, namely the cosmopolitan nature of the
allegedly unpatriotic and lacking-all-sense-of-belonging Jew.

The literary works discussed so far reveal that the cosmopolitan vision is shared by leading English authors and is not
exclusive to Jews. This brings up a question concerning the
concept of belonging. A personal sense of belonging, if not
being echoed by one's society and country, is hardly of any
significance. A sense of belonging cannot exist without a hope
of some reciprocity. For example, this is how Oscar expresses
his sense of belonging:

> the Curries had played no insignificant role in that rapid
> growth. They were part of this city, part of these streets, as
> he was. Even dead, they were still alive in the century-old shop
> that stood as a monument to their industry and perspicacity,
> while he was their chosen representative carrying on the
> same mercantile tradition.

Oscar finds out that his feeling of belonging amounts to
nothing when he becomes bankrupt. His subjective sense of
belonging is not echoed by his own society in his hour of need.

For TS Eliot, however, the 'Jew' is incompatible with the
traditions and culture of an exclusively Christian Europe.
This same Europe Blumenfeld describes in the last pages of
his novel as one 'whose fabric would never more be endangered

by one shrieking lunatic straddling Europe'. It seems this is Blumenfeld's counterclaim against Eliot's idyllic but false and exclusionary vision.

Returning to the aforementioned poem and its vision of the Rialto as relayed in *The Merchant Of Venice*, Blumenfeld seems to claim that it is easy enough to criticise someone else's symbolic vision as being divorced from reality while ignoring one's own false symbolic vision.

After the Munich crisis of September 1938, which saw the ceding of the Sudetenland in Czechoslovakia to Nazi Germany, Eliot published an essay, 'The Idea Of A Christian Society', in which he wrote: 'I believe that there must be many persons who, like myself, were deeply shaken by the event of September 1938, in a way from which one does not recover.' Eliot's shock was borne out of his belief that a Christian Europe would never sacrifice one of its own nations to appease the tyranny of another. Eliot's reaction to these events might be seen as a vindication of Blumenfeld's position that Eliot's notion of a Christian Europe was itself divorced from reality. Nevertheless, Blumenfeld himself would likely have also experienced the dashing of his ideals when writing this novel in 1938. After all, it happened shortly after Stalin's Moscow show trials, which must have served as a sobering realisation that communism was now irreparably divorced from its vision.

Arnold Wesker's communist mother, when told about the Jewish 'doctors' plot' in the USSR – the dismissal, arrest and torture between 1951 and 1953 of leading doctors, mostly of Jewish origin, who were falsely accused of plotting to assassinate members of the Soviet leadership, including Joseph Stalin; they were released after Stalin's death in 1953 and the affair subsequently acknowledged as a fabrication – commented that she did not stop using electricity just because a lightbulb had gone off. Blumenfeld, too, sticking to what might have become for him now only a symbolic vision of a more equitable world, ends his novel with another symbolic vision. This time it is his protagonist Kim's hopes for a post-war world. The novel concludes with forgiveness, when Kim reaches out to Leah, Jacob's daughter. Kim's post-war vision is of a change that will allow everyone to belong, to thrive and to use their gifts, but it does not include revolution. Kim and Leah are referred to as 'orphans of the storm'. This is also the title of a 1921 silent film by DW Griffith, who uses the French Revolution to warn about the rise of Bolshevism. The film is about class struggle and the plea for inter-class understanding. The change that Kim advocates is that 'the whole of life could flower harmoniously', very much along the lines of Griffith's plea in the film.

In 1937, two years prior to the publication of *They Won't Let You Live*, Aldous Huxley published his influential *Ends And Means*. The opening of the fourth chapter, 'Social Reform And Violence', claims:

> The more violence, the less revolution . . . To be regarded successful, a revolution must be the achievement of something new . . . no revolution can be regarded as successful if it does not lead to progress. Now the only real progress, to quote Dr Marett's words once more, is progress in charity. Is it possible to achieve progress in charity by means that are essentially uncharitable?[23]

In the final pages of *They Won't Let You Live* Blumenfeld quotes from Shakespeare's *The Tempest,* and in doing so he offers his readers the key with which to unlock his own novel. Language, art, misleading appearance, the debate between nature and nurture, betrayal and forgiveness, are all themes of Shakespeare's play.

The total effort of Prospero's magic is to lift people from the base emotional state to a more rational one. Language itself is being examined: Prospero's ability to manipulate others with words or Caliban's corrupt use of the language he has been taught by Miranda. Caliban exemplifies nature without nurture. Prospero's magic, like all magic, can be either good or bad, and so is art.[24] Art can also be constructive or destructive because it has the power to manipulate and create damaging illusions and misconceptions that may go even beyond the control of the writer. At the end of the play Prospero avows to stop practising magic. It is significant then that this is arguably considered to be Shakespeare's final play. Blumenfeld, after all, acknowledges this at the end of his novel: 'Shakespeare had a word for it, always and everywhere. The Universal Man had nailed down the situation in the *last flowering* [TC italics] of that gigantic genius.' Is it possible that Blumenfeld intended *They Won't Let You Live* to be his very own last literary 'flowering'?

In this novel the reader will discover a work that adeptly addresses many difficult topics without shying away from the perennial issue of anti-Semitism. Blumenfeld nevertheless manages to do so in a riveting, gripping and even humorous way. The plot is so suspenseful that the reader's powers of prediction are put to the test and often confounded as one plot twist after another presents itself.

It is human to have prejudice. This is after all the way we deal with a complex lived experience of misleading appearances and uncertainty. It is inevitable that our emotions get the better of our more critical and rational thinking. Blumenfeld's discourse leaves at the door the usual violence that often accompanies public debates on the subject. Without excluding anyone from the conversation or being accusatory Blumenfeld argues that prejudice must never be confused with observation and that language does not reflect reality but can nevertheless have a devastating impact on it.[25] In doing so he has laid out a blueprint for how we may wish to conduct public discourse in our own times.

Tali Chilson
Oxford, 2022

I am grateful to Eric Bloomfield – Simon Blumenfeld's son – for the help he has given me in writing this introduction. Thanks are also owed to Andy Croft, with whom I shared my first thoughts about *They Won't Let You Live,* and Paul Willetts for his helpful advice. I am indebted to the work of Ken Worpole, Andy Croft, Iain Sinclair and John King. It is thanks to them that Blumenfeld's literary corpus can be put into a wider context. Last but not least, I would like to thank Erica and Bernard Kops for the life-enhancing inspirations they are.

1. Tony Kushner and Nadia Valman (eds), *Remembering Cable Street: Fascism And Anti-Fascism In British Society,* Valentine Mitchell and Co., 1999, p. 203.
2. Ken Worpole, *Dockers And Detectives,* Verso, 1983.
3. Ken Worpole's introduction to *Jew Boy,* London Books (reprint edition), 2011.
4. This is taken from Willy Goldman's revised edition to his *East End My Cradle* (1940), which has not been published to date. My thanks to Emma Goldman.
5. Robert Graves and Alan Hodge, *The Long Weekend: A Social History Of Great Britain, 1918–39,* Penguin Books, 1971, pp. 243–4.
6. Andy Croft, *Red Letter Days: British Fiction In The 1930s,* Lawrence and Wishart, 1990, p. 104.
7. Alan M Wald, *Exiles From A Future Time: The Forging Of The Mid-Twentieth-Century Literary Left,* Chapel Hill Press, 2002, pp. 175–7.
8. As we can learn from Blumenfeld's own biography; see page 247 of this book.
9. Croft, p. 107.
10. See Jess Rosenthal, 'The Large Novel And The Law Of Large Numbers; Or, Why George Eliot Hates Gambling', *ELH,* vol. 77, no. 3, Autumn 2010, pp. 777–811. Published by Johns Hopkins University Press.
11. Ian Thomson, 'The Voice Of The Jewish East End: The Neglected Postwar Fiction Of Alexander Baron', *New Statesman,* 5 February 2020.

12. See Brian Cheyette's seminal *Constructions Of 'The Jew' In English Literature And Society: Racial Representations, 1875–1945*, Cambridge University Press, 1993, pp. 13–94.

13. My thanks go to Eric Bloomfield for pointing this out to me.

14. Simon Blumenfeld and David Cesarani, 'Jew Boy', *Jewish Quarterly*, vol. 34, issue 2, 1987, pp. 22–3.

15. TS Eliot, 'Hamlet And His Problems', in *The Sacred Wood: Essays On Poetry And Criticism*, Methuen, 1920, pp. 95–103.

16. Armin Paul Frank, 'TS Eliot's Objective Correlative And The Philosophy Of FH Bradley', *The Journal Of Aesthetics And Art Criticism*, vol. 30, no. 3, spring 1972, p. 311.

17. William Empson's *Seven Types Of Ambiguity* (Chatto and Windus, 1930) was a very influential book, and it seems that Blumenfeld had read it.

18. Roland Barthes, *S/Z*, Richard Miller (tr.), Basil Blackwell, 1990.

19. TS Eliot, *After Strange Gods: A Primer Of Modern Heresy*, Faber and Faber, 1934, pp. 19–20.

20. Northrop Frye, *TS Eliot: An Introduction,* Grove Press, 1963.

21. The republication of this poem after the Holocaust infuriated Emanuel Litvinoff, who confronted Eliot directly by reading his own poem of protest.

22. David Scott Kastan, *A Will To Believe: Shakespeare And Religion*, Oxford University Press, 2014, pp. 82–118.

23. Aldous Huxley, *Ends And Means*, Chatto and Windus, 1937.

24. Emma Smith, *This Is Shakespeare: How To Read The World's Greatest Playwright*, Pelican, 2020, p. 317.

25. '"Clarification by discussion"' was the Communist Party's alleged goal.' See Victor Navasky, *Naming Names*, Viking, 1980, p. 302.

CHAPTER ONE

Just around the corner was the West End. This was really the West End, too, but not to the woman. To her the West End meant bright shop windows and uniformed commissionaires, crowds and bustling traffic, while the sedate dignity of this Georgian square impressed her merely with the frigid unfriend-liness of some outer-London suburb. Rather contemptuously she counted the numbers of the broad porticoes that, flanked by prim bays, jutted on to the pavement. 13 . . . 15 . . . 17 . . . 19. Number 19. This was it. This was the house.

She climbed the four stone steps that led to the spacious porch and the massive, buff-coloured double doors, and passed through the chilly entrance to the hall. To make certain she hadn't blundered, she looked around the walls. Just behind the door, on the smooth biscuit paint, was a black patch, and on it, with various other names picked out in white, she read FITZROY LOAN AND INVESTMENT CORPORATION. 2nd FLOOR.

This was the house all right, although it still held a slightly unreal air. She had never been in a block of offices that from the outside – or for that matter the interior – looked less like offices than these. Films, plays and books had accustomed her to expect an atmosphere of opulence embracing the home of a big concern. She had expected to find long corridors shining with chromium, light oak and ebony, and troupes of chic stenographers chirruping down them like bright birds, while well-groomed preoccupied gentlemen, clasping sheaves of papers, opened and closed countless doors to the incessant accompaniment of clacking typewriters. The woman was disappointed. The building hadn't even the severely practical appearance of the offices she knew in the East End. Loud, brisk voices would have been out of place here, where it seemed only quiet, half-somnolent dodderers conversed in whispers. She couldn't understand it, for this bleak house was not a hundred yards from the hub of London; here, she knew, thousands upon thousands of pounds changed hands daily, and yet she might be in one of those huge, old-fashioned dwellings with which the sons of retired cotton spinners ringed the metropolis at the close of the last century.

The staircase was wide and steep, and the stairs smelt faintly of disinfectant, the stout banisters were of ornately carved oak, the walls austerely distempered a very pale beige like a hospital corridor. Still disapproving, leaning heavily on the banisters, the woman climbed the stairs. On the first floor she stopped to regain her breath. She was no longer young, but her face still retained the remnants of a more than ordinary youthful attractiveness. Her figure was plump without being gross, and her clothes, although not new or very expensive, were neat and clean. She looked, in fact, like a respectable charwoman on her afternoon off.

On the second floor she found the offices of the Fitzroy Loan and Investment Corporation. The interior of the suite was even less prepossessing than the drabness of the building had led her to expect, for the outer office was the size of a hairdresser's cubicle. Two shabby, leather-upholstered chairs stood against one wall. The opposite wall was of grey frosted glass, with a door at the side, and in the centre a wooden-framed hatch, the word ENQUIRIES written across it in block letters. The woman crossed the dingy reception room and, leaning on the narrow wooden shelf below the hatch, tapped at the window. Almost automatically it slid to one side, and a pretty blonde looked out.

'Yes?' she enquired.

'Mr Currie, please,' the woman said.

'Have you an appointment?'

The woman shook her head. 'No.'

'Hmmmm!' said the girl.

Her sharp blue eyes took in the details of the woman's appearance with a quick, practised glance of feminine appraisal. Clothes not good but not shabby, and not this year's or last year's either. And she wasn't good-looking, too stout, the girl thought. That's pastries and starchy foods. Lord! Hope I never get like that! With a rapid movement she smoothed her frock over her hips, and the gesture seemed to confirm Mr Currie's taste in women. He liked them slim and tall, young, of course, and preferred them blonde. Whatever this person's business, the girl was pretty sure that the boss wouldn't want to see her.

'. . . Well . . .' she drawled at last in a dubious tone, 'I'm afraid Mr Currie's very busy.'

'Never mind about that,' the woman answered tenaciously. 'I told you I want to see him.'

'And I'm telling you he's very busy,' the girl replied sharply. She had taken an immediate dislike to the woman. She was so sure of herself, the old frump, half-cockney, too, by her speech.

'What is the nature of your business?' she added as a matter of form.

'It's private,' said the woman.

'Must you see Mr Currie himself?'

'I must,' the woman repeated.

'Very well,' said the girl resignedly, polishing a speck from her varnished nails. 'What's the name? But you may as well know you're wasting your time. I don't think it'll be any use. Who is it?'

'Matilda,' said the woman quietly.

'Is that the surname?'

'Never mind the surname,' the woman answered. 'Just say Matilda.'

'One moment,' said the girl brusquely. 'Take a seat, please.'

The hatch closed with a swish and a click, following so closely on each other that they seemed one sound. The girl turned with an air of extreme boredom to a commissionaire perched on a round black stool like a second-hand piano accessory near her desk.

'George, there's a lady to see Mr Currie,' she announced. 'Some old dear, says her name's Matilda.'

'Mrs or Miss?' asked the commissionaire.

'Neither. Just Matilda.'

'Matilda wot?'

'Ma– tilda ground, and Pa pulled out the weeds,' the girl answered brightly, with an air of superior facetiousness.

'Come orf it, funny-cuts,' growled the commissionaire. He rose from the stool and stuffed the *Greyhound Express* into his hip pocket. 'This ain't a game, Miss Clarke,' he protested. 'This is business. Now 'oo shall I say?'

'Matilda. Matilda plain or plain Matilda.'

'Right,' said the commissionaire. 'But if it ain't, I'll tell the boss you told me so.'

He moved towards the door. 'Matilda . . . huh!' he muttered to himself. Even now, he only half-believed it. He turned with his hand on the knob. 'Matilda?' he asked again.

'Honest,' said Miss Clarke. 'And if my five years here mean anything, Mr Currie will tell you to pitch her down the stairs. You're a betting man, George,' she added banteringly. 'What's the odds?'

'No odds,' George answered, 'but I'll always gamble ten Player's on a long shot.'

'Done,' said the girl. 'Small Player's.'

She watched him enter Mr Currie's room. He wasn't a bad sort of fellow, George, but a bit dull, and she felt she had taken rather a mean advantage of him. Betting on certainties was not very sportsmanlike. A shabby man might stand a chance of seeing Mr Currie, but a shabby woman, never. She'd go as far as to let George buy the cigarettes, but then she would give them back to him, although, of course, he would insist on giving her five. Miss Clarke prided herself on being a smart girl, she knew what was going to happen. It needed something more than good looks to hold down a job like this, it needed a knowledge of psychology as well. She was Mr Currie's first line of defence. If she didn't choke off half the seedy beggars who tried to buttonhole him, the boss would never have a moment to himself. She could imagine him playfully pinching her arm and saying, 'Nina' – he never called her Miss Clarke when there were no clients in the office – 'Nina, you're my right-hand man.'

The door opened, and George came out.

'Well?' she said, smiling. She knew very well what the answer would be, but it would give her additional pleasure to put the waiting woman in her place with boss's own words.

The commissionaire's face wore its usual bored expression. He had learned to keep his eyes open and his mouth shut, but his demeanour advertised the fact that he never saw anything Mr Currie didn't want him to see, and that he heard nothing but Mr Currie's orders. Slowly, George crossed over to Miss Clarke and stood gazing at her cryptically.

'Well?' the girl repeated impatiently.

George sat down on his stool. 'I'll tell you a story,' he said with maddening deliberation. 'I goes inside an' ses to the boss just like you told me. "Mr Currie," I ses, "there's a woman outside by the name of Matilda." "Matilda?" ses the boss. 'Is face goes sort of white fer a minute. "Matilda?" "Yes," I ses, "an' Miss Clarke seems to think she ain't the sort you'd care to see." "Indeed!" 'e ses. "You tell Miss Clarke to keep 'er thoughts to herself, an' George," 'e ses, "show her in right away."'

'R . . . really . . .' fluttered Miss Clarke, rolling her *r*'s like a telephone operator. 'He really wants to see her?'

'And 'ow!' George replied. ''E jumped at the name like she was 'is long-lorst maiden aunt.'

Puzzled, the girl crossed over to the hatch and slid back the panel. The woman was sitting in a chair, fidgeting with her handbag. Seated, she seemed even more dowdy than when she was on her feet, as though she were a blob of jelly poured from a shapeless mould. Automatically the girl's hands passed again over the svelte line of her hips, and she half-shuddered. Miss Clarke gave it up, she simply hadn't the faintest idea of what a gentleman like Mr Currie could see in this drab old crow. Suddenly the woman looked up, meeting the girl's critical gaze. Immediately Miss Clarke's face softened, although her eyes still bore that malignant glint, and she put on the usherette smile that she reserved for Mr Currie's favoured clients.

'This way, please,' she said, waving a well-tended hand. 'Through the door on your right.'

She closed the hatch and sat down before her typewriter. Only the very rich could afford to dress like that. In the course of her employment she had run across several of Mr Currie's aristocratic clients who looked like touched-up nineteenth-century scarecrows, but they were protected from sartorial criticism by their lineage, and it was obvious from the woman's speech that she had no pretensions to 'class'. And yet she couldn't be one of the 'new rich' either, or she would never have dared to show her face in this place. Miss Clarke would have given a great deal to know what was going on at this moment in the inner office. She wondered what this Matilda had to say to the boss, but as her fingers drooped pensively over the keyboard, George rudely interrupted her reverie.

'Ain't yer forgotten something?' he asked.

Miss Clarke looked up. 'Have I?' she said.

George stretched out a large, calloused palm. 'A tanner,' he demanded. ''And it over, an' I'll send the kid out fer some fags.'

'Oh – I *am* sorry!' she apologised. Her slim fingers dipped into her handbag and brought out a sixpence from the purse.

'George,' she said, as she dropped the coin into his hand, 'who d'you think she is?'

'Dunno,' George answered, rising from his stool. 'Mebbe she's 'is old woman.'

'Nonsense,' said Miss Clarke. 'You know Mr Currie hasn't got a wife.'

'Ain't 'e?' grinned George, moving to the door. 'With these 'ere millionaires, you never can tell!'

CHAPTER TWO

Spencer Currie rose from his chair as the woman entered the room. He was a short, dumpily built man with a thick, fleshy nose, small grey eyes and a wide, thin-lipped mouth. Although not at all good-looking, his appearance was striking – and this was not entirely due to the faultless tailoring of his clothes. There was a brisk, magnetic quality about Spencer Currie. His personality was never wholly submerged under any circumstances. He could never slide anonymously into a crowd, a fact which had pleased him and inflated the vanity of his younger days, but which he no longer regarded as an asset. Where previously he had constantly sought to catch whispers of 'Who's that distinguished-looking man?' he now knew that his name and presence were sufficient to evoke remarks envious and contemptuous like 'That's Spencer Currie, the money-lender' or 'Spencer Currie, rich as Croesus'. It was no longer fun being Spencer Currie, he didn't want to be 'different', but an unmistakable air of distinction helped to set him apart from strangers, and wherever he moved amongst friends and acquaintances, he was irrevocably branded by his wealth. His own individuality was dead, he had become a glittering symbol – *the* Spencer Currie.

Face to face with Matilda, the financier could almost feel the rigid barriers of wealth dropping away. She had always had that effect on him, made him seem warm and human, a normal man without any specious trappings. He walked over to her and clasped her outstretched hand.

'It's good, real good to see you again, Matilda,' he said. 'I haven't been so close to you in years. And what's more, my dear, you're still as good-looking as ever.'

As his strong hand curled round her palm, the woman felt herself blushing furiously, while her heart gave a sudden upward lilt. It was all wrong, of course, at her age. She should have shed such emotions years ago, a married woman with grown-up children. But it was the way Spencer looked, the way he walked, the genuine warmth that throbbed in his beautiful, deep voice. Gently Mr Currie pushed forward a high leather-backed chair for her, and even the critical Miss Clarke would have had to admit that the woman sat on it with commendable grace. Her eyes sparkled, and with her flushed cheeks she became much younger, much more attractive. She looked, in fact, quite a different person from the woman who had waited so patiently in Mr Currie's outer office.

'Thank you,' she murmured, crossing her hands demurely over the handbag in her lap. Then she looked up at Currie, and again the colour rose in her cheeks as she noted the unconcealed admiration in his eyes. 'The same old Spencer,' she uttered half-challengingly. 'The same pretty speeches. You haven't changed a bit.'

He grinned with boyish frankness. 'Why should I?' he demanded.

'You're rich,' she answered soberly. 'You're a success. Everyone's heard about you. Why, I've even seen your picture in the papers, hobnobbing with lovely actresses. And yet you still say I'm pretty. No, Spencer,' she said with a sigh. 'To a man looks don't matter, he's always the same, always a man, but I'm an old woman – I won't see forty any more.'

The financier perched himself on the edge of the huge, dark-mahogany table facing her, his short legs swinging several inches clear of the floor. What she said was true – she was no longer young, but he didn't see her like that, she would never be middle-aged or old for him. He seemed to see in her another Matilda, the idealised unchanging Matilda of his youth who had made such an impression on him that the vision seemed more real than the flesh-and-blood person on the chair.

That vision did not exclude a middle-aged or even an old Matilda. They were contained one within the other, with the radiant girl Matilda indelibly superimposed upon them all. He leaned over and gently pressed her hand.

'You're wrong, Matilda,' he said softly. 'You'll always be the same to me. Always as you were twenty years ago.'

As if the conversation had gone far enough on those lines, the woman withdrew her hand and sat up more stiffly. Sensing the change, the financier slid to the floor and stood with his back to the table. He was becoming again *the* Spencer Currie; the humanity was draining away. Even the tone of his voice altered. When he spoke again it seemed strangely matter of fact.

'Tell me,' he said, 'how's Oscar? Are you happy with him?'

'Your brother is the best husband in all the world,' she answered.

'But are you happy?' Currie persisted.

Matilda made a little gesture with her shoulders, as if she saw no point in such foolish questions. 'In this world,' she said, 'a lot of things go to make up what we call happiness. Oscar's struggling for a living. It's hard to be happy when there isn't a minute free from worry.'

'Oh! . . .' he muttered. 'I suppose you're right. And Kim? How's the boy?'

'He's fine,' she answered. 'And Pamela's fine, too.'

'I'm not interested in Pamela,' he interrupted. 'It's the boy. Has he got a job? Is he working?'

'He is – and he isn't.'

'What d'you mean by that?' the financier asked sharply.

'Well, he's working,' said Matilda. 'He goes out every morning and comes back at night, but he hasn't got a job yet. He's learning to become a taxi-driver.'

'What!' Spencer Currie exploded. 'A taxi-driver?'

'That's right,' she repeated. 'A taxi-driver.'

'You can't know what you're talking about!' the financier

protested. 'With a BA degree and a university education! Tell me, Matilda, are you trying to pull my leg?'

'I wish I were,' she answered seriously. 'Since he left the university he's applied for a hundred and eighty-seven jobs. Don't laugh. That's the exact number. I know, because he's kept a careful tally. Now he's given it up. In future, he says, they'll have to apply to him, and while he's waiting, he's learning to drive a taxi.'

Spencer Currie shook his head commiseratingly. 'Poor kid,' he remarked. 'I don't feel like laughing. Neither does he, I should imagine. It must be breaking his heart.'

'Not at all,' Matilda answered. 'He likes it. He's only sorry he's wasted all those years at school.'

'Then it's not Kim you've come to see me about?' the financier said regretfully.

Matilda shook her head. 'No.'

Currie's face dropped, as though the news came as a bitter disappointment. 'I was hoping you'd come about him,' he brought out reluctantly. 'There's so much I could do for him,' he said. 'The boy's got brains. I could train him to become a solicitor, a doctor or a barrister, send him back to the university or abroad somewhere to continue his studies. Why should he waste his life on the driver's seat of a cab? Once he's done that he's lost. He'll get the lower-class mentality and outlook, and that's the end of him as a professional man.'

Mr Currie was gradually working himself into a passion, and his words increased in vehemence as the full implications of Kim's behaviour sunk in, until at last he burst out angrily, 'It's a disgrace! I won't allow it! The boy was born to be driven around in cabs, not to be a driver. I tell you, Matilda, I won't allow it – I won't! Of all people, my son a taxi-driver!'

'He's *not* your son,' the woman said.

'Ugh,' grunted Currie disgustedly. 'You don't have to talk like that to me. According to birth certificates and marriage lines, he isn't, but that's for everybody else. You know and I know, he's mine.'

The woman's lips closed in a firm line. 'I'm married to your brother,' she insisted obstinately. 'That other thing happened more than twenty years ago. It's time you forgot it. Kim is Oscar's. Once and for all you've got to understand. Kim is Oscar's son.'

Currie hoisted himself back to his perch on the edge of the table in silence. There was a hurt, sulky look in his eyes, as though he were a small boy deprived of some cherished toy. Matilda felt sorry for him. In spite of his wealth, she pitied him for his loneliness. Without a word, she bent towards him and put a soothing hand on his knee, while he turned his head away as though he were ashamed the weakness might break through in tears.

'Well . . . what is it you want me for?' he said at last.

'It's about Oscar.'

'What's the matter?'

'He's in trouble. He needs money.'

With an effort, Spencer Currie became himself again. The subject was money, and he was an expert in every branch of finance. He gathered the conversation tightly in his capable hands and took control of it. He was on his own ground now, not a suppliant but a dictator. 'I advised Oscar to give up that tuppenny-ha'penny business years ago,' he grumbled. 'There's no room for the small trader any more. In Father's time that little shop was a goldmine. Nowadays it's nothing but a liability.'

'You're right,' Matilda answered. 'It *is* a liability. The strain of running it is driving Oscar crazy. Sometimes, if it wasn't for Pam's wages, we wouldn't have enough to meet gas and electric bills.'

'Ummmmm! . . . I'm sorry to hear that,' the financier commented. 'But if it's really so bad, why doesn't he pack it up?'

Matilda gave a wry smile. 'Do I have to answer? He's your brother, *you* ought to know.'

'I do know,' said Spencer. 'A Currie. Proud and pig-headed. Head of the House of Currie, Established 1841, Ladies' and Gents' Hosiers. Ugh! The tradition of combinations and ladies' undervests and triple-spliced socks. Oscar needs a charge of dynamite up his pants. That's what he could do with badly. He's too honest, too easy-going. Nobody can afford those luxuries in business these days; they're two more liabilities.'

'What's the use?' said Matilda resignedly. 'Even if he wanted to, it's too late for him to change now.'

'I know,' Spencer retorted, 'I know.' He slipped off the table and walked round to the other side. Seating himself, he drew a cheque-book from the drawer. 'That's why he's got to suffer,' he continued, giving a quick glance over the counterfoil stubs. 'And it's no more than he deserves. But it's hard for you and Kim. How much do you want?'

'A hundred pounds.'

'All right.' He unscrewed the top of his pen without changing his expression, as if such a trifling sum were beneath his serious consideration.

'One moment,' Matilda interposed. 'Not a cheque, please. Cash, if you have it.'

'No difference,' said Currie. 'I'll give you cash.'

The financier closed the cheque-book and returned it to the drawer. Crossing the room to a huge, black safe in the corner, he unlocked two doors, plated like dreadnoughts, and drew out a thick sheaf of banknotes. He wetted his thumb and forefinger, and from the opposite end of the room Matilda could hear the brittle crackling of the new notes as he counted out a hundred pounds.

'Sure that'll be enough?' he threw across his shoulder, the larger sum still poised in his hand.

'Yes, Spencer,' said the woman.

With a nod, the financier replaced the wad of money that was not appreciably slighter, and locked the safe. Turning, the twenty five-pound notes in his hand stuck out like insignificant scraps of crisp, white paper, he crossed over to Matilda and put the money deferentially in her lap.

'There, madam! One hundred pounds.'

'Thank you, Spencer,' said the woman gratefully.

'It's nothing, Matilda. For God's sake don't thank me,' he answered, pulling himself on to the table's edge again. 'It's for you and the boy. If it were ten or a hundred times as much I wouldn't miss it. Tell me now, truthfully, did Oscar send you?'

Matilda sat up sharply, as if the mere suggestion had startled her. 'Good heavens, no!' she ejaculated. 'If Oscar found out, I believe he'd cut my throat.'

There was a discreet tap at the door.

'Come in,' said Mr Currie.

The commissionaire entered without seeming to note the woman and passed a slip of pasteboard to the financier. He glanced at it and nodded.

'All right, George,' he said. 'I'm engaged for the moment. Tell him to wait.'

He balanced the visiting card quizzically on his fingertips and with an amused smile dropped it into the woman's hand.

'Look at that, Matilda.'

There was a tiny coronet on top of the rectangular slip and beneath it an address in Mayfair with the name of a sporting peer. Had Matilda followed the racing news, she would immediately have recognised it as belonging to one of the shining lights of the turf. Currie watched a look of incredulity creep over her face and felt at the sight all the pride of a primitive male exhibiting his strength and warlike trophies before the captive sex.

'A lord? A real one?' she asked.

'Real enough,' he said lightly. 'Title goes back almost to William the Conqueror.'

She half-rose from the chair. 'You mustn't keep him waiting, Spencer. I'll go.'

'Nonsense!' He waved her back to her seat. 'It's all right. He won't run away. It's just someone else wants to borrow money.'

'But, a lord!' she protested.

Spencer Currie smiled. 'I get dukes as well – and duchesses. Half the people in *Debrett's* and *Who's Who* come to me, and, between us two, there are some I wouldn't trust with a fiver.'

'You seem to know all about them,' she remarked. 'So Spencer Currie's moving in high society now.'

'Only during business hours,' he chuckled. 'Those same paupers would love to pass me by in the street. I'm good enough when I lend them money on security that a bank wouldn't spit at, but socially, I'm just another low-class bourgeois, a shopkeeper's son. It might be different if I got myself elected to a couple of exclusive clubs or bought a safe seat in Parliament or wheedled a title with a hundred thousand pounds' worth of charity, but who wants it? They're not my sort. I'd sooner roll up my sleeves for a game of poker or solo with some pals than spend the afternoon at a tea party in a lord's mansion any day of the week. And that's what I shall do when I retire,' he continued in a dreamy voice, his face softening as though a lifetime's ambition were rising up before him. 'Take a little house in the country or in a nice residential suburb with someone like you to look after me. I'll lead a quiet, solid, middle-class existence, and if I go to the city once a month, that'll be once a month too often.'

'Well, why don't you do it?' she asked. 'You've got enough money to retire. What's stopping you, Spencer?'

'Kim,' he answered abruptly, 'and someone like you.'

As if she hadn't heard, the woman folded up the banknotes

and put them carefully in her purse, then, brushing her skirt down with plump, work-worn hands, she rose to her feet.

'Thank you again, Spencer,' she said. 'I'll go now. I hope I won't have to come to you on such errands any more.'

The financier slid to his feet and stood facing her. He almost looked for the moment like the youth she had loved twenty-odd years ago. Her 'threepenny piece', chubbier, but still tiny, and in spite of his cunningly built-up heels, half a head shorter than Matilda.

Suddenly he gripped her hands tightly against her body. 'One thing you must do for me,' he said.

'What's that?'

'You must send the boy to see me.'

She shook her head. 'It'll be difficult. I don't know how to manage it. What shall I say?'

'Say what you like, only send him,' he insisted. 'Promise?'

'All right,' she said. 'I promise. I don't know when, but I'll send him.'

'Thank you, Matilda.' He kissed her lightly and humbly on the cheek. 'Now remember. It's a promise. I've got to see Kim.'

No sooner had the door closed behind the woman than Miss Clarke entered, and it seemed as if an alien personality had obtruded itself in the room that was still warm with the presence of Matilda.

'Well, what is it?' he asked irritably.

'That gentleman,' said Miss Clarke, 'he's still waiting.'

'Let him wait,' snapped Spencer Currie. 'I'm in no hurry to give him money.'

'There's another matter,' said Miss Clarke. 'You wanted to write Mr Smedling.'

'Young Smedling? . . . Well, you don't need me for that. Send him the usual letter . . . Hmmmmm! "Dear sir" . . . and don't forget the "Honourable" on the young skunk's envelope . . . "Dear sir . . . so many months behind in your payments. Unless you fulfil your legal obligations . . . etc. etc.'' Well, you know the rest. I'll sign it when you're done.'

He stopped and seemed to be watching Miss Clarke very closely. Soon, she felt, he would pinch her cheek familiarly or chuck her under the chin, or something like that, and call her 'Nina'. The girl was sure he was weighing up her looks against those of the woman who had just left. It was rather an uncomfortable scrutiny, but Miss Clarke was quite confident she could stand the test. She placed her head to one side, and, with one hand on her hips, stuck out her bosom and poised one leg behind and a little apart from the other to display the best points of her figure. It was coming . . . after five years it was coming. One of these fine days, and it might be very soon indeed, he'd come out with a proposition, and that would mean a mink coat at least.

Miss Clarke was right, for since Matilda's visit Spencer Currie was seeing her physically in quite a different light. She was undoubtedly pretty, but her body didn't act as a whole, it never rippled with one movement. It seemed bound into watertight compartments, each working independently on a well-oiled ball and swivel. Her face now, it was attractive, but it ended so abruptly at her chin, and her breasts, they were compressed into an unwavering tautness by some fancy, figure-forming brassieres. There was a sort of hiatus round her waist, and her hips and thighs were a barrel-curve to the knees. Shapely enough on the whole, but she was never truly a whole. Just her hips moved or her legs or her face, well-controlled like disciplined soldiers – but it was always only part of her, her entire body didn't flow. That was the trouble with these young women and where Matilda was different. When Matilda spoke, you could almost see the words rippling right down her, and when she moved, all her body moved at once. That was so much of her fascination. She was getting on in years, putting on weight, too, but her body was in one piece – it was alive.

He smiled, and Miss Clarke thought this was an opportune moment to redeem her error about Matilda.

'Mr Currie, I'm awfully sorry about that lady,' she apologised.

She smiled as she awaited his reply. Almost certainly it would be 'Nina' – with a playful pinch, and maybe not in such an innocent place either. But, to her surprise, Mr Currie's tender smile faded, and he became the boss again.

'Never mind, Miss Clarke,' he said uncompromisingly. 'You'll know for next time. Whenever she comes, don't ask any questions. Send her in right away!'

CHAPTER THREE

On the bus, Matilda climbed to the top deck and chose a back seat, right against the glass emergency exit. It was a long time since she had held a hundred pounds in her bag, and it made her feel rather nervous. Although her visit to Currie had been quite private, she was half-afraid that some super-criminals had sensed the banknotes in her handbag by some occult means and might be following her. She hugged the bag tightly. She dare not lose the money, for it meant so much to Oscar. One or two people joined her on the top deck, but there were any amount of seats vacant, so she was left alone at the back, her nearest neighbour being towards the centre of the bus. As it jolted along, she opened the bag to assure herself that the money was still there and closed the clasp against her hand so that the tips of her fingers rested comfortingly on the notes. Every time the conductor ran up the stairs, his heavy footsteps, the jangling of his accoutrement and the loose coppers in his leather pouch disturbed her and caused her to press the precious bag more tightly against her imprisoned hand.

She knew her behaviour was foolish. Nobody was following her; nobody in the world apart from Spencer even suspected that she carried a large sum of money on her person, but her nerves were on edge, and that made her unusually timorous. She supposed it was meeting Spencer again after all these years and being so close to him. And Matilda had not lied when she had said that she believed Oscar would cut her throat if he knew she had gone to his brother. Spencer had always been unscrupulous, the spoiled one, and Oscar swore that he had laid the foundations of his fortune by frequent dipping in the till when they had worked together in the shop. That may have been true, but Oscar had never caught him in the act; what had made her husband his brother's deadliest enemy was when he had seen him kissing Matilda the night before their marriage. That had so infuriated her fiancé that she dared not tell him the truth, that she loved his brother and that the kiss was the most innocent in their whole relationship. And then Spencer had disappeared, and the boy was born, then the girl, and she had settled down to be Mrs Currie – Mrs Oscar Currie – and had almost forgotten about Spencer until Oscar's need had driven her to him.

She sighed as she alighted from the bus at her journey's end. Things might have been so different had she run away with Spencer as he had urged. She would have been spared the harrowing experiences of the past few years, with the shop steadily declining and Oscar seemingly breaking up with it. And yet it had been a good life, she had no complaints on that score; she had learned to love her husband, and the children had bound them more completely together. Only the shadow of Spencer ever came between them; the mere mention of his name could turn the equable-tempered Oscar into a quarrelsome grouch. But there was only one kiss that he knew about, or was it, as she sometimes wondered, that he understood much more than that? She dismissed Spencer from her mind, he had served his purpose. She had the hundred pounds Oscar needed so badly in her bag, and once she passed it on to him she could sink back safely into the old, placid life. Placid after a style, and only comparatively because she had become completely accustomed to money worries; in these unsettled times they were as much part of their normal existence as the morning bacon, whereas Spencer was a new and disturbing feature. What was the use even of thinking about him? He had probably forgotten her already, while she had quite enough to contend with in the daily domestic round. She told herself again not to act like a fool, she was an old woman, a mother and a housewife, and Spencer Currie was an entanglement she could ill afford.

Being early-closing day, Rothstein's shop was shut when Matilda arrived there. Mrs Currie knew Jacob Rothstein's habits. After lunch he usually pottered about in the shop for a couple of hours, putting things straight before he left for the city on one of those more and more infrequent buying expeditions when he had stock to replace. Mrs Currie knew how it was only too well; it was exactly the same with Oscar. Week by week he sold less and bought less. When he went to the city now, it was more from force of habit, just to go round the old firms and exchange a few 'hellos' with the salesmen and grumble about what things were coming to. A light in the stockroom on the first floor told her that Jacob was home as she had expected, so she made her way to the side door and pressed the bell.

A pallid woman with staring eyes and an emaciated face answered the door, a woman who looked as though this mask of perpetual fear were the permanent expression of her features.

'G-good . . . good afternoon,' she stammered nervously. 'I . . . I'm afraid Jacob isn't in.'

'Nonsense,' Matilda answered firmly. 'I know he's in, and I want to see him.'

'But, Matilda,' the woman protested, 'you know how things are, dear.'

Mrs Rothstein screwed her lean, pale face into a pleading, piteous expression, the large, frightened eyes still sharply fixed in their intensity, but Matilda remained adamant, refusing to budge. She had come to see Jacob, and she knew he was home. She was sorry for Mrs Rothstein and hated to load her mind with even the semblance of fresh troubles, yet it was essential for Matilda to talk to her husband, and she knew that the continued iteration of her errand would gain her admission to the house.

'It's important,' Matilda insisted. 'I must see him. There's nothing for you to worry about, dear,' she assured her gently. 'It's just a private matter between me and Jacob.'

'All right,' said Mrs Rothstein resignedly. She beckoned Matilda into the passage and closed the door behind her. Under other circumstances Matilda would have been shocked at her appearance. She remembered her as a beautiful, slim girl. Now Mrs Rothstein looked like a witch out of *Macbeth*, with her dishevelled grey hair, her dirty overall and the stooping figure that slummocked past her on twisted, heelless leather slippers. At one time Mrs Rothstein had been a paragon of smartness like most Jewesses of her type, and Matilda had often envied her figure and her bearing. She had not gone like this all at once; her trimness had worn off gradually, but the last year or so had completed the change with such startling suddenness that while a few months ago the old beauty still shone in odd places, she looked now a complete caricature of someone old enough to be her own mother.

Mrs Rothstein led the way down the passage. She was used to creditors knocking the doors down – it was about time, too, but God alone knew how it would all end! Running a business these days was one continual trapezing on the tightwire. The tiniest slip, and they plunged into bankruptcy. And yet she had hardly expected the Curries to clamp down on them this way. They were supposed to be friends, and as friends they should have understood . . . Friends! . . . Huh! . . . The best friends were one's own pockets, and when they were empty, everything else was dead.

At the foot of the stairs she halted. 'Jay-Cobb,' she bawled in a high, screechy voice, a shrill, wavering scream that seemed part and parcel of her prematurely aged and crooked metamorphosis. 'Jay-Cobb! Mrs Currie's here to see you!'

A small figure appeared at the head of the staircase, a slim, sallow, middle-aged man with a thin black moustache and a neat black beard. From the top of the stairs a hall light diffused a misty radiance round his wide, bald head and gave him the malevolent appearance of a conspirator in a melodrama.

'. . . Mrs Currie? . . .' he said, puzzled, then, recognising the woman behind his wife, his voice took on a note of unforced cordiality. 'Come right up, Matilda. I'm in the stockroom if you don't mind climbing the stairs.'

He disappeared again, and Matilda set foot on the staircase. That was all she seemed to be doing today – climbing stairs to Spencer; up and down buses; and now here, more stairs for a change. Puffing exhaustedly, she reached the stockroom and found Jacob busily boxing some hose. Near the door there was a well-worn armchair, the horsehair padding oozing from the torn upholstery like hay from a well-filled nosebag. The chair stood out invitingly, as a foaming glass of beer might to a thirsty farm labourer, and sighing with relief she sank between the welcoming arms.

'. . . Ah! . . . Take a seat,' said Jacob without turning as soon as he heard her shuffle in.

'Thanks. I've already got one,' she replied, stretching her legs luxuriously.

'That's good,' Jacob said. 'Make yourself comfortable. Sorry to keep you, Mrs Currie, but I won't be another minute.'

'That's quite all right,' she answered, fanning herself with the handbag. 'Take your time, Jacob, take your time.'

Matilda watched his nimble fingers smoothing out the hose, grading them against the powerful electric light and packing them into marked boxes. He was a man now, with a beard, dignified and respectable, but in her mind there was still a clear picture of him as a child when his behind shone between the desperate patches of his threadbare trousers. She and Jacob's wife had played together in the same street, and years later, when Oscar had gone in for the wholesale side of hosiery in a small way, Jacob had been one of his first customers and one of the best – that was, until little over a year back.

Then his account had gone up and up, and in spite of his repeated promises to reduce the bill had remained at a figure far too high to be healthy for Oscar.

At last Jacob piled the boxes on a high shelf and, pushing the ladder in a corner, perched himself on an empty packing-case opposite her.

'Now, what is it, Matilda?' he said.

'It's about Oscar,' she replied. 'You owe him a lot of money. He could do with it.'

'So could I,' said Jacob, 'if I had it. And really, I've got the money, but it's all in stock. The trouble is, I can't sell the damned stuff. Just now, I can't shift a thing.'

'That's no excuse,' Matilda insisted. 'You've had the goods, you ought to pay for them.'

'I will,' said Jacob. 'I promise you I will. I'll pay back every penny, only he's got to give me time. After all, I've known Oscar since he was a kid. Of all people, I wouldn't catch him for a brass farthing. Now would I?' he pleaded.

'I . . . don't know,' Matilda answered hesitatingly. 'I don't know about anyone or anything these days.' A disturbed look spread over Jacob's face. She had not intended to hurt him, so she hurried to placate his feelings. 'Yet somehow, I don't think *you* would. But isn't there something you could do?'

'Nothing at the moment, I'm afraid,' Jacob said. He leaned forward confidingly. 'Now put yourself in my position,' he suggested. 'Supposing all your husband's creditors pounced on him at the same time and demanded payment in full, would he be able to settle with them? Of course not! They'd have to wait. It's the same with me. I'm placed exactly like that. Everybody wants money just now, everybody, but I'm not taking enough to pay expenses.'

It seemed quite a reasonable explanation, but Matilda was not to be deflected from her purpose. 'Look here, Jacob,' she said. 'I do my husband's books. You owe Oscar a hundred and thirty pounds. Give him fifty, and we'll forget the rest.'

'I'm sorry,' Jacob replied, spreading his hands in an impotent gesture. 'I can't.'

'Twenty-five then?'

'Not even that. If only he waits a little longer, I'll be able to pay him back in full.'

Matilda sat in silence for a moment. This was precisely what she had expected. Now, she braced herself to broach the real subject of her visit.

'Jacob . . .' she said, uncertain how to continue, 'I've managed to borrow some money . . . If I let you have it, will you give it to my husband?'

'Certainly,' he assured her. 'Why not?'

'You don't understand,' she said. 'The money must come from you in part settlement of your account. I don't want Oscar to know I had anything to do with it.'

'All right,' Jacob asserted. 'But I'm telling you beforehand, I don't know when I'll be able to pay you back.'

'Never mind about that,' Matilda answered decisively. 'He's terribly short of money. I want you to see that he gets this hundred pounds.'

★ ★ ★

As Matilda's slow tread descended the stairs, Jacob, left by himself in the stockroom, stared silently at the money on the table. This was the most peculiar experience of his whole business career. He had never been in any doubt that he would be able to persuade Matilda to see his point of view, but he had hardly expected to be presented with a hundred pounds. It wasn't a dream; there the money lay before him, black and white; whorls, signature and watermark all complete; twenty sheets of paper, the equivalent of a hundred English pounds sterling. He got up and walked to the window and was just in time to see Matilda crossing the road. He watched her disappear round the corner, then went back to the table and sat down and looked again at the twenty five-pound notes.

When the Jews hungered in the wilderness, Jehovah sent them manna from Heaven; now this woman came to his house and brought him a small fortune, just when he found himself with no place to turn for a penny. He stretched out his hand and fingered the white crispness of the notes, then pressed them tightly together in his fist. Crumpled, they looked like discarded scraps of tissue paper from a stocking-box, and yet they were still money, still labour power, still hose and lingerie and rent and food. Carefully, he smoothed them out again, with the impressive, shiny black ink uppermost, and looked at the numbers that ran consecutively as though they were fresh from the bank. Tokens of freedom, tantalising him, crystallised wafers of sweat and blood to be passed on to someone else.

Absorbed in his contemplation, he hardly heard his wife climbing the stairs to the stockroom. When she came in, she found him curiously silent and hunched up over the table. She guessed the cause of the trouble; Currie was going to foreclose. Matilda, with her sympathy, her honeyed words, her glib 'You've nothing to worry about, dear' had brought home the ever-hanging threat, 'Pay up, or else!'

'What's happened, Jacob?' she enquired in a dull voice.

Her husband sat up as if he had just woken from a trance. 'Money . . . money,' he repeated.

'All at once?' said Mrs Rothstein. 'The whole lot?'

Troubled, anxious words tumbled from her thin, querulous lips. 'Does Oscar want everything right now? Didn't you explain the position? Surely, he won't be so hard?'

'It's not that,' he said. 'It isn't that at all.' The words stuck in his throat; the simple fact seemed so difficult to explain. 'She brought *me* money to give to him,' he brought out at last.

'To give to him?' Mrs Rothstein uttered incredulously.

Jacob nodded. 'To give to him,' he repeated, knowing how fantastic his words must sound. He picked up the money and spread it out on the small table. Each individual note fluttered from his shaking fingers, curling over the stained oil baize till in front of his hands there rose a froth of white paper. 'A hundred pounds,' he said. For the first time he turned and looked at his wife. 'A hundred pounds. Think of what *I* could do with a hundred pounds.'

Mrs Rothstein's earliest emotion had been inquisitiveness about this peculiar transaction, but her husband's strange manner of speaking swung her sharply to the offensive. She didn't like what he was thinking about. He mustn't do it! She had enough trouble already.

'Forget it, Jacob,' she protested acrimoniously. 'For heaven's sake! The money isn't yours.'

'I know it isn't,' he answered wearily. 'I was only day-dreaming. But just you think . . . supposing it was . . .'

'Well, we'll suppose,' she grumbled bitterly. 'We'll say the hundred pounds was yours. Thirty-five pounds would go to this one that's pressing you, thirty pounds to stave off one writ, thirty pounds for another. Then you'd have five pounds left, and what could you do with that – except weigh yourself twelve hundred times? Would *we* get anything out of it? Would the children get some clothes, would you get a suit? Not a bit of it! The hundred pounds would vanish down your creditors' throats. For a week you'd sleep peacefully, then the week after that you'd be in the same hole again. I tell you, Jacob, it isn't worth it.'

Rothstein looked at her steadily, as if he had not heard a word of her vehement argument. 'Leah's school fees are payable in a few days,' he said quietly.

'I know,' she answered.

'And next week there's a month's rent due, and payments on the radiogram and the vacuum cleaner.'

'I know,' she repeated with growing apprehension. She felt as though the walls of the room were closing round her, as if the low ceiling were dropping lower. This hateful business life, with its debts, worries and more debts, had entrapped her. It had changed her from an attractive woman who took a pride in her appearance to a stooping slattern. She had become a cheat, a bare-faced liar, and as if this wasn't enough, Jacob was driving her into something far worse. She wouldn't have it. Just a little more pressure could make her scream with hysteria, and yet it wasn't Jacob's fault either. He was a good man, an honest man, but in shackles, and his desperation was forcing him into this dreadful thing. Her husband's quiet voice was hypnotising her as she knew it was being wrung from him. She was helpless and imprisoned, while these soft, evenly spoken words were breaking her will and her resistance.

'Spencer Currie's a millionaire,' Jacob continued relentlessly. 'I haven't any millionaires in my family. Matilda can get more hundreds where this one came from.'

With an effort, the woman gathered the shreds of her self-respect for revolt. 'That's enough, Jacob,' she burst out, and even as she spoke, her voice seemed harsh and unnatural, as if it didn't belong to her – as though she were listening to someone else talking out of her mouth. 'What you're thinking of is robbery,' she continued rapidly. She had to get those ugly words out fast while she could still say them, before this new-found resolution left her. 'It's robbery!' she repeated mechanically. 'I've stood everything till now without complaint, and I'll do anything else you ask me, but I won't be a thief, and I won't let you steal either! You hear me, I won't let you!'

Jacob collected the banknotes in a tidy pile, only the heightened colour of his face suggesting that her tirade had been directed at him, and calmly snapped an elastic band round the money. 'It wouldn't be stealing,' he replied, turning his head away from her. 'Just borrowing. My need is greater than Oscar's. I'd pay Matilda back. Every penny.'

'Jacob!' his wife panted, as though she had just undergone some strenuous physical effort. 'You'll get us all into trouble. Don't do it!' she warned him tensely. 'The money isn't yours!'

With a sigh he thrust the precious little package into a pocket set in the lining of his waistcoat and carefully buttoned the flap. When he looked at his wife again, he seemed subdued and chastened and, having regained his usual pallor, appeared to have suddenly grown years older. It seemed to her that the walls had been pushed back into proper perspective again; as though a shaft of sanity had pierced the dark hysteria of the room.

'You're right,' he said at last, caressing the pocket regretfully with his fingertips. 'The money isn't mine!'

CHAPTER FOUR

At the stroke of eight, Oscar carefully rolled down the blinds that shut off the interior of the shop from outside view. Thank heaven the day was ended! He went into the street and gave a final glance at the windows. Didn't look *too* bad, but the front could do with more light to brighten it up a bit, a new coat of paint – some slick fittings. Across the road, about twenty yards down at the corner of the main street, ran the rectangular two-storeyed building of the Empire House Traders. It was closed, too, but even in the dark, and at this distance, the bold neon lights above the entrance and the vivid splashes of chromium across the black-marble façade shone with bright defiance. He looked again at his own display and was suddenly struck with its paucity, as though there were nothing to back it up in the shop – something was wrong with it, but he didn't know just what. When he put a lot of goods in the window it looked overcrowded, and when he chose only a few leading lines, the impression was one of poverty and stagnation. The truth was, he admitted to himself, that he was a shopkeeper and not a professional window-dresser, and in these days you had to be both. He needed more of the right sort of stock, a bigger variety of goods, a couple of smart assistants, better fittings and a more attractive front; in fact, all he was short of was quite another shop.

Fashions changed so quickly in shop fronts. You had one put in as the latest thing, but, by the time you'd finished paying for it, it was as out of date as last year's dance frocks. The public were sheep. They couldn't understand that what they ought to buy were service and quality, and that value was what counted. But no! Everything had to be smart, stuck on top of a lopsided cardboard barrel in the window and, after purchase, wrapped up in cellophane, with fancy labels. Honest value didn't seem to count any more, and Currie's had given them honest value for close on a century. In a year or so would be the centenary of the shop's founding. A hundred years of honest value. That would be a fine slogan to play up; he would paste it in large letters right across the windows – if he lasted that long!

He looked at the weather-beaten sign, in old Gothic script as it had first appeared in Grandfather's day. It made him proud to think that Currie & Son had been a familiar landmark in this neighbourhood for nearly a century. The founder had imagined that the shop would carry on to perpetuity, that Currie & Son would endure like Hitler's fabulous Third Reich for at least a thousand years, but Oscar knew what a miracle it was to survive week by week, and as for the '& Son', that was already a misnomer.

He closed the door behind him and walked thoughtfully into the shop. Automatically he took off his long, grey alpaca coat and hung it behind the counter in its traditional place. The movements were so much part of him that he hardly noticed them any longer. He had no conscious idea that he had divested himself of the outer garment. Then there came six steps to the till, the old scooped-out oak square of his grandfather, but now scraped so thin by countless coins that he could almost feel the bottom of the counter beneath the worn, hollow base. Years ago he had discarded the old till for a cash register and kept this valueless chattel only for sentimental reasons. Now the cash register stood neglected in a corner, and he used the till. What was the use of making a fool of himself? He no longer needed to ring up the purchases; there was no point in saving time when all he had was time. It would be childish to keep on pushing up the brass shutter to check the number of customers and the takings when he knew exactly who had come into the shop, and to a penny how much they had spent.

He picked up one ten-shilling note, a handful of small silver and some coppers. The note he placed carefully in his wallet, and glancing over the silver thrust it into his trousers pocket with the coppers. Just two pounds – Friday's takings, and that the Friday before Easter, one of the two peak weekends of the year. He remembered when he had grumbled at taking that much on an ordinary Wednesday, notoriously the worst trading day of the week. Now two pounds was Friday's income, and he had to be thankful for that. Still, this bad patch wouldn't last for ever, things would improve as they had always done before, but Oscar knew very well that neither in his father's day nor in his grandfather's, had trade ever been so obviously on the down grade for so long a spell. It couldn't be that he was finished, as Kim so confidently asserted, finished along with all the other small shopkeepers of his class. That was only the bombast of opinionated youth. There was life, plenty of life yet in the long-suffering middle-class, although Kim held that they were a decaying order, sentenced by modern industry and commerce to be squeezed out of business by trusts and combines. That was simply university talk, more of the rubbish he'd picked up in college. A little knowledge was a dangerous thing. It would have been better for Kim to have started behind the counter at fourteen as he did. It would have been a wonderful day for him when he could have handed over the keys to his son. Didn't like being a draper – ugh! And look where his education had landed him, if he was lucky enough to pass all his tests – in a cab rank!

The idea stirred uneasily in his mind. Maybe the boy was right, only when Oscar grumbled about trade, Kim ought to realise that he was merely asserting his inalienable right as an Englishman to grumble, and there was no cause to start proving by statistics and economics that he was headed inexorably for extinction. He didn't believe it. Anyone with a glib tongue and a head for figures could prove anything by statistics, and no group of pundits was ever more consistently wrong than these same professors of economics. There was a resilience in his business that the youngster didn't understand, couldn't, because he hadn't been born to it; this business that he and his father and his grandfather had spent their lives on was not doomed, it had a metabolism of its own – when it seemed most quiescent it was gathering new life, finding fresh roots. That was what he liked to believe, what he wanted to believe, was embodied in Currie & Son; but on days such as these Kim seemed justified in the harsh things he said. Oscar, although he hated to admit it, was afraid to face the situation. He kept pushing things back, waiting, refusing to look squarely at the future. That an account would have to be struck one day he knew, and he dreaded it, but until the final summing-up was unavoidable, he refused to think about it. Bad enough to worry about this week's bills without breaking your head about what would happen next week or the week after that. He had faith. In the long run, Currie & Son would survive as it had survived for a hundred years.

Oscar patted his few hairs to one side in front of the large mirror and straightened his jacket before he entered the shop parlour, carrying out each of the tiny rituals hallowed by years of performance. He was wearing well. In spite of his business worries he didn't look much on the wrong side of fifty. His carriage was still erect, a relic of his army days, and his broad shoulders, another Currie inheritance, still squared manfully without hint of a one-sided slope or a stoop. He was of average height, with a florid, round face, its only touch of character being the thick mouse-colour moustache, tobacco stained just above the upper lip with wings of a deeper reddish brown. Everything about him was average, nondescript, except for his voice that seemed to come in a strangled wheeze from the top of his skull – a strangely unsuitable vocal medium for a man of his physique, but not congenital to him, being the aftermath of laryngitis following on a gas attack during the war.

He tried to reorientate his mind before he stepped into the parlour, to appear at least outwardly cheerful beyond the strict confines of his business, but it was a metamorphosis that was daily becoming more and more difficult to effect, like attempting a once easy sleight-of-hand trick with fingers gradually stiffening with age. Stepping into the cosy room, and closing the door carefully behind him, he saw the whole family gathered in the little parlour. Unusual, the thought struck him at once. I ought to be honoured, the gang's all here . . . Unusual for Pamela and Kim to be staying in together any night, but there he was, large as life, those big glasses perched on the end of his nose, with another of his blasted fat books at the table, and Pam titivating herself in front of the mantelpiece mirror. Matilda sat in her favourite corner on a low stool, knitting. Her hands had always to be occupied with something. When she wasn't knitting she was sewing, and when she was doing neither of these things, she was washing linen, or making beds, or polishing a gas stove that shone as brightly before she started as when she had finished. He dropped into the adjustable fireside chair that was reserved for him in the evenings and bent down to unlace his boots.

'How was it today?' asked his wife.

'Not bad,' Oscar answered off-handedly, wriggling his stockinged toes with a sigh of sheer physical pleasure. 'Not too bad, Matilda.'

Kim looked up from his book, shaking a long, wavy lock of brown hair from his forehead like a frisky colt. 'Not bad!' he commented sarcastically. 'Don't tell 'em, Dad. You've had about two-and-a-half customers in all day.'

Oscar pushed his feet into the slippers and stretched himself back in the armchair as far as it would go. He would interfere, the young know-all, and Oscar was beginning to resent it. It was time he was taken down a peg or two.

'How do *you* know?' he enquired. 'Have you added telepathy to all those other things you've learned about, but can't earn a sausage from? You haven't been here *all* day.'

'No,' said Kim. 'But I was around best part of the afternoon, and I didn't hear the bell go once. I probably overestimated your trade, Dad. I doubt whether you had even two customers.'

'Well, if you want to know,' Oscar lied, 'I had ten times two, and I took over four pounds, which isn't too bad, considering the beastly weather we've been having – and the Crisis.'

'Crisis, my aunt!' Kim returned, unimpressed. 'You've always got some excuse. It's either too hot, or too cold, or it's raining, and when it isn't the weather, it's a Crisis.'

'It doesn't seem to have affected the other shops,' Pamela broke in, still busy with her cosmetics at the mirror. She stuck her tongue out at her reflection and carefully licked the line of her lips. 'I passed by the Empire House Traders this evening on my way home. They were pretty crowded, I'd almost say mobbed out.'

'Lookers,' grunted Oscar. 'Lookers, not buyers.'

Pamela poked her lipstick back in her handbag. 'Buyers,' she insisted. 'I went in myself, I even bought something, too.'

'What!' Oscar exclaimed.

'Don't be angry, Dad,' she said soothingly. 'I did it just to give you an idea of what they were selling.' She took a flimsy scarf from her open bag and tossed it across to her father. 'How much?' she asked.

Oscar spread out the diaphanous square critically. In spite of his prejudices, the pattern met with his unqualified approval. He held it up to the light, but there were no flaws, and the fabric remained unbroken between the strain of his two tensed thumbs.

'Printed georgette,' he said. 'Art silk, of course.'

'That's right,' Pamela answered. 'But how much?'

'Well . . .' Oscar stroked his moustache thoughtfully. He didn't want to appear foolish before his own children, he wanted them to have at least some respect for his business acumen. 'Well,' he commented, 'wholesale, they're about sixteen and six a dozen' – undercosting them intentionally by at least three shillings – 'but buying bulk, they could probably get them for thirteen to fourteen bob, rock bottom. Working on the very minimum profit, I should say they could be sold for one-and-three to one-and-six apiece.'

'Rock bottom?' Pamela asked uncertainly, as though she had paid a great deal more than that.

'Absolutely,' Oscar assured her, smirking with satisfaction at having pulled a neat little trick over these youthful connoisseurs of value.

'Well,' said Pamela, about to drop her bombshell and watching closely for the effect, 'I'm sorry to disappoint you, Dad, but these are a shilling each.'

'What?' Oscar ejaculated, sitting up tartly. 'That's impossible! Unless they're a job lot, or damaged, or unless they've been stolen.'

'You examined one for yourself,' Pamela pointed out. 'They're not job stock, and they're not damaged, and I doubt whether they can be stolen. All the girls at the office bought them weeks ago, and they've still got loads coming in, plain and printed, dozens of different designs and colours.'

Oscar looked at the scarf again, relaxing uneasily back in his chair. The raw material alone, and there was about a yard of it, must have cost at least a shilling to manufacture, apart from dyeing, spraying and overlocking the edges. It was a bargain, and he had to admit it. At last he shook his head. 'I don't know how they do it,' he brought out grudgingly.

'There you are,' Kim jumped in. 'It speaks for itself. And I'll tell you how they do it. They may not be better businessmen than you are, but they've more money to play with. Retailing now is not for the man with a capital of a few hundreds but for strings of stores with hundreds of thousands, even millions of pounds to speculate. That's what you're up against, Dad. You haven't a chance!'

Oscar nodded vaguely. He felt too depressed to argue, even with Kim. This scarf was like the writing on the wall. And yet possibly it was just a 'call-bird' to attract custom to the other counters. A big firm could afford to sell certain items at a loss and more than recover it on different merchandise. But, whatever it was, it boded him no good. His depression gave way to a feeling of half-inarticulate resentment. He was angry, but he didn't quite know whom to blame.

'Let them get on with it,' he growled. 'It won't be for ever. I'll carry on my way, they can go theirs.'

'That isn't how to look at it, Dad,' Pamela protested. 'You've got to hit back. You can't just sit still and let them take away your living. They're a lot of foreigners anyway, the Empire House Traders, probably a bunch of Yids with names like Polsky, Slipcovitch and Slumpcovitch,' she spat out disgustedly. 'Those slimy Jews don't deserve any consideration, they don't play fair, the price cutters and chain stores, they're all run by Jews.'

'Including, say, Woolworth's?' Kim suggested with a grin.

'They're Jews, too,' said Pamela shortly, with a challenging toss of her head.

'Sure! Sure!' Kim repeated mockingly. 'They're all Jews. Lord Beaverbrook, and Sir Harry McGowan, and George Lansbury, and the Agha Khan. Anyone who's outstandingly successful in business or politics is a Jew.'

'I don't know that that's so far from the truth either,' Oscar asserted. 'I've done business with Jews for donkey's years, but I've never really liked them. There's something greasy and underhand about them, as if they're always on the watch to do you down. They're all opportunists. That's why they all get on so well.' He had never been an anti-Semite, couldn't recollect having spoken outright this way before, but Pamela's accusation had aroused a subconscious resentment. It must have been there, dormant all the time, or it couldn't have come out so easily this way. Still, it was off his chest and he felt the better for it, and his words seemed to have the authentic ring of experience and authority. 'Mind you' – he felt impelled to qualify his remarks – 'some of them are quite decent fellows, yet there's just that *something* in the way. I can smell a Yid a mile off. If one of them comes into a room when I'm there, my spine seems to tingle as if to put me on my guard.'

'Always?' asked Kim.

'Always.'

'That's very interesting,' said Kim. 'I'll tell my friend Coleman about it – if I ever see him again.'

Oscar raised his eyebrows. 'Why Coleman?' he asked. 'I remember him. Surely he's that Irish boy you were friendly with at college. What's he got to do with Jews anyway?'

'Nothing much,' Kim answered, 'except that he's a Jew himself, in spite of his blue eyes and fair hair and his "Oirish" brogue. Shows how absurd your prejudices are and how much your spine-tingling race-detector is worth. Be truthful, Dad, imagine it's "so-help-you" in a court of law. Has any Jew ever done you down so badly?'

Oscar shook his head. 'I can't say that. But it's because I've always been too smart for them,' he added smugly.

'Then what exactly is it?' Kim pressed.

'I don't know,' said Oscar. 'It's people like these House Traders and the little price cutters in the market that get my goat. For a hundred years we've managed to keep this business going; now it looks like only the Jews are doing any trade.'

'There's your friend, Rothstein,' Matilda interjected quizzically. '*He's* a Jew, but he doesn't seem to be doing any too good either.'

'I don't know,' Oscar answered. 'Somehow I've never thought of Jacob as a Jew. Going to school with him, and doing business together all those years, he's seemed to me

64

just like any ordinary Englishman. But he's a Jew all right, and, I suppose, like the rest of 'em a bit of a rogue, too, on the sly.' He nodded, as though the memory of Rothstein's account emphasised the truth of his words. 'Still owes me a hundred and thirty pounds,' he continued ruminatively. 'And swears every time I see him that his business is going to the dogs . . . I wouldn't be surprised to see him go bankrupt any day, but I wouldn't be surprised either to find he had a tidy pile stacked away some place where his creditors couldn't reach it.'

'Neither would I,' said Pamela acidly, snapping fast the clasp of her handbag. 'Of course, he'll go broke and open up somewhere else and swindle some more poor Englishmen.' She drew herself tautly to attention, as though she were a soldier on parade. 'That's what we True Britons are fighting against,' she announced proudly. 'Our Party, with Lord Harkness, will put an end to all that.'

'*Our* Party?' said Kim. 'That's news.'

'Maybe to you,' Pamela replied. 'You've always got your nose stuck in a book, so how do you expect to see what's going on?'

'Well, what *is* going on?' Kim asked. 'And what's that little bunch of comedians to do with it?'

'Never mind,' she returned sharply. 'But the True Britons are not a little bunch any more, and they're not comedians. We're deadly serious – and you'll know all about it soon enough.'

'Really?' said Kim banteringly. 'What are you going to do? Blow up the House of Commons?'

'Better than that,' she replied. 'We'll take it over, and then we'll get rid of all those damned foreigners!'

'I wish you luck,' said Kim. 'Only remember me when you're in the Cabinet.'

Pamela picked up her gloves and moved towards the door. 'I won't get anywhere near the Cabinet,' she admitted.

'At least I *know* I haven't the brains. We've got people in the Party much cleverer than me.'

'Really?' said Kim sarcastically. 'That's surprising.'

'Anyway,' Pamela answered, 'a woman's place is in the home.'

Kim grinned. 'Well, why don't you stay there?'

She looked at him angrily for a moment, then shrugged her shoulders. She knew she was no match for Kim in an argument, but if Dai Phillips were with her, he'd be able to silence this smug superiority with a few well-chosen words. If only she could talk like Dai! One day she would bring him home, and then Kim would discover whether they were comedians or not. For a moment a tart reply hovered on her lips, but she thought better of it. Kim wasn't worth the trouble, best to ignore him, for he'd only twist her remarks into something grotesque or ridiculous. Pointedly ignoring her brother, she bade goodnight to her parents and left the room, defiantly slamming the door behind her.

'Why don't you leave the girl alone?' said Oscar when she had gone.

'Me?' Kim replied. 'I wasn't even aware that I'd touched her. Still, if it comes to that, I don't think a spanking would do any harm, and, as her father, I think you're the one to administer it.'

Oscar hid a smile behind his big briar pipe. Whatever the merits of the case, it didn't do to side too openly with one child against another, especially when they were both of them just a little mad. Matilda went on placidly with her work. She was used to these family squabbles; if they weren't about politics, they were about something equally silly, and besides, she was preoccupied now with a much more important matter – she was waiting for Jacob and a hundred pounds.

There was a slight scuffle at the front door, as if the cat had tripped over the strip of coconut matting just inside the shop. Kim pricked up his ears. That would be the postman,

and every post was an adventure. Why, it might even be a job
– ironically enough just now, when he had given up all hope
of an academic position and was practically in line for his
cabby's badge. He walked out of the parlour down the narrow
lane between the two massive counters to the door and picked
up a pile of correspondence. Rapidly, he scrutinised the
envelopes. Several unmistakable circulars he threw unopened
on the counter; there was nothing for him tonight. The rest
of the mail he brought into the parlour.

'Here, Dad,' he said, holding the letters towards his father.
'All for you.'

'No thanks,' Oscar replied, without moving from his seat.
'I'm far too comfortable just now. What's the good of opening
them, they're only bills – I'm fed up with the blasted things.'
He blew a great cloud of smoke contentedly from his pipe.
'This evening,' he said regretfully, 'I thought I was going to
have a rest – at least one night without a headache, and here
they are again to plague me. You read them, Kim, or throw
them away – I haven't the heart!'

The young man leaned against the mantelpiece, his tall
figure poised slackly and accentuated by the looseness of his
sports jacket and flannels – his customary garb, the university
uniform he hadn't yet been tempted to discard. Brushing
back the recalcitrant lock that always escaped like a small
boy's over the wide Currie forehead, he removed his glasses,
for he could see quite well without them, and opened the
first letter.

'Rates,' he announced. 'Final notice.'

'Tear it up,' said Oscar. 'I shan't think of paying till I get
a summons. Even then, I won't!'

'Why not?' Kim asked.

'Quite simple. Because I haven't got the money. I'll offer
to pay in instalments.'

'But you haven't paid off last year's,' said Kim.

'That's nothing,' Oscar replied. 'They know *I'm* all right.'

The Currie & Son complex seemed to be enveloping him again. 'Look at all the years we've been here, all the years I've been paying rates. They won't do anything to me,' he argued, blusteringly. 'And what *can* they do anyway?'

Kim smiled. 'Nothing much, Dad,' he said drily, 'except stick you in clink. Local government officers are funny people to start with – I can see me and Ma and Pamela having to visit you in jail.'

'Suits me,' grunted Mr Currie in his hoarse, strangulated croak. 'I'll have a rest there anyway.'

'But, joking apart,' Kim interposed, 'what are you going to do about it? Rates have got to be paid.'

Oscar's face fell. He had been fighting against the nightly dose of depression that he usually managed to hide from Matilda. Around closing time it fell on him like a pall, and tonight he had been trying to choke his brain with flippancy, bolstering up his spirit with rosy remembrances of 'the days when', but the situation was worrying him, and confronted by the coldly analytical attitude of his son, he could no longer conceal the state of his mind. Bills poured in like a never-ending stream, and in his efforts to meet his obligations, to maintain the Currie commercial reputation, he felt like a worm burrowing beneath the earth to escape the groping, alien fingers that probed ever closer, ever deeper below the surface.

He made a hopeless gesture, bringing his pipe in a wide arc through the air. 'When the time comes,' he wheezed, 'I suppose I'll find the money. I'll put somebody else off and pay the rates. Now for God's sake,' he muttered angrily, 'throw the blasted thing away!'

Kim tore up the notice and threw it into the grate. He always seemed at loggerheads with his father, but it really hurt him to see the way the older man struggled. Overburdened with debts that he would never be able to liquidate, he dragged one foot half an inch out of the mud only to sink six inches deeper with the next step. Oscar had been accustomed to handling money, to making a good living. He was proud of his status as a businessman, as a Currie, and Kim by this time knew that it was useless rubbing in that in many respects he was worse off than the low-salaried worker. He worked longer hours than any union would allow and drew less in real wages in return at the end of the week. He was not entitled to any form of state insurance, no sickness benefit, no unemployment pay. His only asset was an endowment policy that had ten more years to run and for which he had difficulty in keeping up the payments – apart from the fact that its current value was held in mortgage by the bank. Kim knew all these things, as Matilda did, and the ostrich-like behaviour of his father usually irritated him. But looking at Oscar now, he felt only compassion for a cornered, harassed, shrunken little man.

'Well, that's settled the rates,' said Oscar, breathing more freely and squaring his shoulders again as though he had just thrown off a heavy encumbrance. 'It'll be weeks, maybe months, before anything happens. Meanwhile, son, you've got some more love letters. Read them. Just a word or two. I'll know the rest.'

Kim slit open another envelope. 'Rayling Interlock Co. . . . Account overdue . . . Please remit.'

Oscar lay back more comfortably in his chair and relit his pipe. Ah! That was better. 'Who did you say that was from?' he enquired.

'Rayling Interlock.'

Oscar dismissed them airily. 'They're all right,' he said. 'They'll wait. Next!'

'Henlock's Hosiery . . . New lines if you'll call.'

Oscar chuckled. 'They don't want me to call. They want some cash. Well so do I! Next!'

'Gunther's . . . Fifty-seven pounds . . . Please remit – remit, in red ink, Dad, and underlined – otherwise we shall be reluctantly compelled . . . etc. . . . . etc. . . .'

'Gunther's, eh?' mused Oscar. 'In red ink, too. They're a tough bunch all right. I'll have to send them something . . . Any more?'

Kim put the bills on the mantelpiece. His mother would file them later, that was her job. Only one typewritten letter remained in his hand.

'Just this,' said Kim, 'but it's marked "Personal". Maybe you'd better read it yourself.'

'No, no!' Oscar replied hurriedly. 'It doesn't sound half so bad this way. And "Personal" is a bad sign, too. It usually means that someone's turned very nasty and insulting or that solicitors are on the job.' He braced himself in the chair against this fresh assault. 'Go ahead, Kim,' he said. 'Tell me the worst.'

Anxiously, he watched his son's eyes travelling down the letter. Kim seemed surprised at something it contained. He carefully folded up the missive and looked inside the envelope.

'Well! What d'you know about that!' he exclaimed.

Oscar jumped to his feet, unable to restrain his impatience any longer. Whatever it was, he must see for himself.

'What is it?' he demanded.

'From Old Rothstein,' said Kim. 'Funny we should have been talking about him just before. Well, he's actually paying up his account!'

'No!' uttered Oscar incredulously. In two rapid strides he stepped before his son. 'Give that to me,' he said peremptorily.

He opened up the letter again. Matilda, tense on her stool, watched him. The moment she had been awaiting all day had arrived. Her needles clicked at an excited tempo, automatically following the intricate pattern of the jumper. So Jacob had sent the money on instead of coming over in person. Perhaps it was better that way; it made the whole thing more private, confined the joy of deliverance within the family circle. She saw a wide smile spread over Oscar's face, the smile of someone who has suddenly come into an unexpected fortune; but Matilda knew that the money meant only a few weeks' respite at most. Oscar's fingers dipped into the envelope, and he extracted a neatly folded cheque. Carefully, almost reverently, he opened it out and read it. Only now did he quite believe the evidence of his eyes, and his exuberant expression became a little more restrained, although still touched with a warm mobility.

Matilda smiled. Officially, she still knew nothing about this windfall. She had to assume the pose of a mystified housewife, or he might become suspicious.

'What's happened, Oscar?' she asked. 'Must you keep me out of it, dear?'

He turned his beaming face on her and waved the letter excitedly in the air. 'You'll never guess,' he said. 'This is what you can call a real piece of luck. I owe Jacob an apology for the things I said about him after all. He must have developed a conscience or something. Here have I given up his account as lost for ever, and out of the blue he sends me a gift – a cheque for twenty-five pounds!'

CHAPTER FIVE

Jacob wearily closed the ledger. Figures . . . figures . . . figures . . . His head was aching, and his eyes smarted. For the best part of the night he had been poring over his books, but they all told the same story. He was in an impasse. Trapped, with no hope of extricating himself. He had run his full course. Now he had come to a dead stop. Ruined!

Next week he had to meet so many bills that the mere thought of them made him sick. He had finally given his creditors cheques, and the first batch were due for payment in five days' time. Forty pounds to Green's for goods he had bought in order to realise cash to meet an earlier and smaller bill. After a struggle, that had been settled; part of Green's goods lingered on his shelves, and forty pounds was due next week. He couldn't put them off any longer; he should have paid them within four weeks, now nearly three months had elapsed. And that wasn't all. There was another cheque for seventeen pounds, and several odd fivers, and against those pressing liabilities his assets were a shopful of dead stock, and at the bank an overdraft of seventy-five pounds.

There were a good many like him, Jacob knew, but at the moment that was small consolation. Working without capital, he manipulated post-dated cheques, getting goods from Peter to pay Paul and credit from some other trusting Jew to meet his obligations to both. For fifteen years the system had worked. He had managed to live well all that time, and even occasionally to put by a little money, but the last few years had eaten up all his savings and piled debts on his business till breaking point was reached. He was at a loss to explain it. There was a slump, true enough, but that could be only half the story;

he was a keen buyer, yet apparently whatever he bought was not keen enough. The weather had turned topsy-turvy: it was hot in October and freezing in July. Dictators were rampant over Europe, grabbing hunks here, chunks there. Nothing was reliable any more, not even geography. His best customers owed him money, and those to whom he gave a little credit, he never saw again. He had paid back another twenty-five pounds to Matilda, but the rest of the money he had 'borrowed' from her had vanished weeks ago; he had lost a good friend and was another fifty pounds in debt.

Three hundred pounds was all he needed to get himself straight. It wasn't a lot of money, really, not more than a rich man could spend in one evening at a night club, yet that amount could save him from bankruptcy and put him on his feet again. Or even two hundred pounds, or a hundred. A hundred pounds could restore his credit. If he met the cheques for Green's and the others, he would be able to get fresh goods and carry on for a while longer. How much longer he didn't know and really didn't care, so long as he managed to put off the evil day for a spell. He had to carry on, since there was nothing else he could do. He couldn't become a workman because he had never learned a trade, and as a shop assistant he was too old, too slow and too shabby. A hundred pounds! He wracked his brains for someone he could approach for a loan. A hundred pounds . . . Where could he get a hundred pounds?

He climbed the stairs to his bedroom on the top floor. Going to bed was an empty formality: for weeks he had been unable to sleep. He undressed in the dark in order not to disturb his wife, and slipped beside her beneath the sheets. As he snuggled closer to her body, he was half-repelled by her nearness. He shifted away and lay on his back, staring at the ceiling. Even his wife was no longer any comfort with her emaciated figure and cold, stringy flesh.

Night after night he undressed the same way, put on his

pyjamas and got into bed, but when, dog-tired, he thought his brain should be numb as well, the details of the day's business and the morrow's cheques would still revolve in his head, robbing him of sleep. Tonight he was determined to rest. If he worried any more, he would go crazy. He was ruined. Utterly and irretrievably ruined. There was nothing he could do about it unless somehow, from somewhere, he could raise a hundred pounds.

Having rationalised his position, he felt much better. Now he had faced the worst and knew that there was no escape, it didn't seem so terrible after all, and he began to wonder why he had been driving himself frantic all those weary months. I'm broke, he repeated to himself, almost with satisfaction. Dead broke. I'm not the first, and I won't be the last. Nothing can save me now, unless . . . He dismissed the thought as ridiculous; hundreds of pounds didn't grow on trees. He was broke. Broke. He refused to think about it any more. Let the others worry, the onus was now on his creditors. Let them do just whatever they pleased!

He slept well and woke up feeling refreshed. He was a different man. A curious sense of optimism permeated him; something would turn up today, he was sure, he could feel it in his bones. He went downstairs into the shop and found three bills waiting for him on the mat. Carelessly he stuffed them into his pocket without bothering to tear open the envelopes. Three or three hundred, what did it matter now? Humming to himself, Jacob dusted the counters and put some goods on display, then he opened the shop and waited for customers.

The day wore on. A few people made minor purchases. Nothing happened. No more bills, no summonses, no judgements. No writs, no bailiffs. Not yet anyway. Soon his position would become known, and all his creditors would descend on him like hungry mastiffs. He didn't care. Let them all come. He was still in his shop, and something might yet turn up.

Mrs Rothstein was amazed at the way he got through his dinner. Usually he left half the food on his plate, yet today he had wiped up his helping without difficulty and even asked for more. Something must have happened. She had not seen him looking so well for months. He smiled and cracked jokes at the table, and that hadn't happened for years. She only hoped his high spirits would keep up, for she hardly recognised in this jesting man opposite, her morose, perpetually worried husband.

After the meal, Jacob washed his hands, murmured a pious grace with unusual deliberation and went down to the shop. His wife was still in the dark as to the reason for this sudden change. Jacob had noticed her curious glances across the table and knew what she was puzzled about, but she hadn't asked him any questions, and for that he was thankful, since he wouldn't have known what to reply. Let her think he had had some good news. It wouldn't do her any harm either to stop worrying for a day, and maybe his optimism would become infectious, and he could catch it back from her when this miraculous spell wore off.

The shop bell tinkled, and a short, thick-set man entered. Jacob looked up. As soon as he saw his prosperous-looking visitor he knew why he had been feeling so cheerful. Years ago he had got from the library an odd book by a man named Dunne that told about experiments with time. Of time moving in a continuous stream, of the past, present and future being co-existent and sometimes encroaching one on the other. Something like that could explain the newcomer's presence. He was a distant relative, hitherto hardly accessible, and reputed to be rolling in wealth. Jacob's subconscious mind must have picked up an inkling of this visit and communicated the message in some curious way. Why hadn't he thought of him before? If there was one person left in London he could tap, Morris was surely the man.

As Jacob moved towards his visitor, he noted the stylish,

dark clothes, the broad expanse of waistcoat with the thin platinum chain strung between the pockets. From the curled brim of his continental velour to the smoothly polished uppers of his handmade shoes, Morris exuded an unmistakable prosperity, the sort of blatant affluence that raises a restaurant porter's hand to his cap or induces an obliging constable's 'sir!' together with the quickest way to the nearest cab-rank.

'I was passing by,' said Morris casually, 'so I thought I'd drop in.'

'You're welcome,' Jacob replied. 'I can't tell you how welcome. Take a seat.'

He dusted a tall, three-legged stool and pushed it towards his visitor, but Morris waved his hand, he preferred to stand. Two podgy fingers dipped in the capacious waistcoat, and a cigar appeared.

'Have one of these,' said Morris.

'No thanks. I don't smoke.'

'Take it all the same,' said the rich man genially. 'Give it to someone who does.'

'Thanks,' Jacob answered.

'How's business?' said Morris, glancing round the shop with a critical eye.

'Not too good. And you?'

'Also not. Nothing doing at all. Nothing.' Morris grinned and blew out a cloud of aromatic smoke that formed into wide, nebulous rings near the ceiling. 'I don't suppose you know of anyone with a couple of thousand pounds to spare?' he asked, half in jest.

'Thousands?' said Jacob, answering him in the identical cheerful manner. 'And hundreds wouldn't do?'

'Even hundreds would do,' Morris replied, a trifle too eagerly, still with the same, semi-bantering grin. 'Not for long, though. A couple of months at the outside. And I could pay good interest, up to twenty per cent. What do you say, Jacob?'

'Well,' said Jacob. 'If I knew where I could lay my hands on some money, I'd borrow a couple of hundreds myself.'

Morris laughed good-humouredly. He took out a gold dress-watch from his pocket and glanced at the time. 'I'm late,' he said, shaking his head. 'I've got to be going.' He flicked a scrap of cotton from his lapel. 'Shows you how hard it is to get hold of a few quid, even from relatives.' The rich man sighed philosophically. 'Thank heaven I don't need it!' he remarked, as though he had merely been testing Jacob and had found him sadly wanting.

He shook Jacob's hand and walked with him towards the door, holding his palm all the way down the shop in a warm, sweaty clasp. Jacob was not deceived by his jests or apparent hurry. He himself had more than once tried this same method of approach. First with a joke and then, if his proposals were taken seriously, asking for a loan outright. But if the grin were answered by a smile, then it was no use pursuing that tack any further. Morris knew it and was retiring as gracefully as possible, imagining he left behind intact his reputation as a plutocrat.

At the door he pumped Jacob's hand again and let it free reluctantly, as though he got pleasure from the moist, fleshy contact. 'Got an appointment,' he said with a smug show of regret. 'Otherwise I'd like to stay. By the way,' he added as an afterthought, 'how's the wife?'

'Very well,' Jacob answered.

'And Leah, and the boys?'

'Fine,' said Jacob. 'How's your family?'

'All right . . . Well, goodbye!'

'Goodbye!'

So Mr Dunne was wrong after all. Jacob watched Morris's broad back pass down the street; he seemed all body, with nothing to speak of in the way of legs. Morris, the rich man of the family, coming to him for a loan! It always gave him a certain amount of satisfaction to learn that things were not going too well with others, that he wasn't the only one in trouble. Today he felt more bucked than ever, and it didn't seem just a momentary satisfaction but something permanent, following on the optimism he had inherited with the morning. Morris, too! And not so long ago he had been a rich man, really rich, with cars and property and a fat bank balance. Thinking of Morris, he forgot about himself. A man like that, solid as a rock, safe as the Bank of England, and now he was broke – like Jacob. It showed you what the world was coming to; you could be as rich as Spencer Currie one day and the next as poor as – well, as poor as Jacob Rothstein. He couldn't think of anyone worse off.

Spencer Currie . . . Whatever had brought *him* at this moment into his mind? That gave him an idea. He knew that Matilda's money must have come from him, although she hadn't mentioned it. Spencer and his brother were on bad terms. Jacob knew the whole story, but since schooldays the financier had always looked up to him, the top boy, as a paragon of all the virtues. He would get hold of Spencer Currie. Desperate straits needed desperate measures. It was a hunch, foolish, fantastic perhaps, but he would play it to the limit.

CHAPTER SIX

The following afternoon Jacob had no difficulty in getting in to the financier. A few moments after leaving his card with the girl at the enquiries hatch, the commissionaire came out and escorted him into Mr Currie's room.

'Why! Hello, Jacob,' said Spencer Currie cordially, rising from his chair behind the table, the shortness and squareness of his stature carrying the illusion that he was still seated. He extended his right hand over a litter of documents and welcomed the visitor. Almost with the same movement, his left hand slid to his waistcoat, producing a large cigar.

'Smoke?' he asked.

This was the second cigar Jacob had been offered in two days under somewhat similar circumstances. 'Thanks,' he said, accepting it with the fervent hope that it would prove a more successful prelude than the first.

Spencer Currie waved him into the chair opposite and leaned across the table, clicking an automatic lighter into flame. 'Light?'

'Thank you,' Jacob said again.

The financier smiled at Jacob's clumsy attempts at lighting up. It was obvious from the way he pursed his lips and screwed his eyes together that he had seldom, if ever, smoked a cigar before in his life. He inhaled gingerly, suspiciously, and exhaled with short, sharp puffs, blowing vigorously as though to expel the very minutest trace of nicotine from his mouth. As soon as a thin grey line of ash formed round the dimmed red, smouldering point, Jacob judged that he had smoked enough, and with an expression of relief took the cigar from his mouth. Looking up at Currie, he saw that the financier's deep-set grey eyes were twinkling, the thin lips twitching to repress a grin. Excellent, he thought. Thank heaven he found it funny. If getting a loan depended on being funny, he would turn cartwheels about the office, or jump through paper hoops, or tell him some of the dreary, determinedly dirty stories the travellers left behind in the shop instead of goods.

'Well?' said Currie, seating himself again.

'I want to borrow some money,' Jacob announced without any preliminaries.

The financier's fingertips rapped gently on the edge of the table, then he levered his legs against it and scraped his chair back a little distance along the floor.

'Money, eh?' he said thoughtfully. 'Well, how much do you want?'

This was real business. Jacob could see now why Spencer Currie was so successful. Straight to the point and no humbugging. 'You want money – How much?' . . .Well, how much? What could he ask for? A hundred seemed too paltry; five hundred pounds too much. He decided to compromise on two hundred and fifty. He hadn't actually counted on asking for more than a hundred before he came here, but his reception had been so warm that now twice that amount did not seem a ridiculous request. Might as well be hanged for a sheep as for a lamb. And what was two hundred and fifty pounds to Spencer Currie after all? He could flick a dozen times that sum down the sink and not notice it. Besides, Jacob was an old friend, a schoolboy hero. It was quite on the cards that Spencer might give him the money as a gift. But he wouldn't take it like that. Oh no! He would accept it but only on the condition that he repaid it later in full.

Jacob sat up and spoke confidently, without a tremor.

'I need two hundred and fifty pounds,' he said.

'Two hundred and fifty, eh? That all?' Currie answered. 'Hmmmmm! Now supposing you tell me all about it.'

Jacob leaned forward; if the financier had not been on the

other side of the table, he would by this time have held him familiarly by the lapel. Currie was prepared to listen; that meant he was interested, and if he was interested, the salesman in Jacob would cajole the money out of him. Eagerly Jacob traced his difficulties while the financier nodded sympathetically, the thin lips pressed together like a colourless fissure in the flesh. He left nothing out, put nothing in; the facts as he told them were sufficient to warrant a loan from anyone.

As Jacob stopped talking, Mr Currie rose from his chair, walked round the table and, hitching himself on to his usual perch, leaned forward pontifically.

'I . . . I don't quite know how to put it, Jacob,' he said, 'but I'm very sorry.'

Jacob's face fell. He could hardly believe his ears . . . 'W-what?' he mumbled.

'I'm sorry,' Currie repeated incisively. 'I can't do it. For three good reasons. First, because I don't handle anything less than five thousand pounds; second, because all my money is tied up; and third, because I don't deal with Jews.'

Jacob felt a sudden surge of anger. He forgot why he had come here; his personal affairs no longer seemed of any interest. Three good reasons, Spencer had said, three, and good! Why, the first was swank, the second a fairy tale and the third an implied slander. Currie shrank before him to mannikin stature; he seemed no longer an imposing figure, no longer the millionaire, the man with the money bags and dispenser of largesse, but a snotty little boy showing off before an older schoolfellow – an insulting, spiteful little boy at that.

Jacob controlled himself with difficulty. 'If I were the man I ought to be,' he flung at him, angrily, 'I'd punch you right on top of the nose for that!'

'Oh?' Spencer slid to his feet. 'Well, why don't you try it on?' he challenged, bristling like a fighting bantam cock.

'You don't deserve it,' said Jacob quietly. 'You haven't any sense, you don't know any better. With all your money, Spencer, you're a blockhead; you've no manners and no culture, and if I hit you I'd only be degrading myself to your level.'

Spencer pulled himself back on the table while Jacob watched him quizzically. His anger had almost evaporated, and it seemed that a new relationship had been established between them in which Jacob occupied the superior position, exactly as in the days of their youth. Spencer was suddenly stripped of his fabulous wealth. Spencer was no longer rich, neither was Jacob poor. They were both children again, with Jacob the senior, the object of envy and adulation, enjoying all the liberties of speech and action that seniority implied.

'I don't see why you should get so excited.' Spencer protested.

'Don't you?' Jacob replied sarcastically. 'Well, think! Now if I'd come to you and said I wanted money, and you said "No" right away, I would have answered "Thank you very much", and we'd have parted friends. But to draw me on like that, make me tell you all those intimate things about myself and my business and then to say that you don't deal with Jews . . . Why . . . Why . . . *Zoll dir shtinken fin kopf!*' he exclaimed, as though only those particular words could convey his exasperation and contempt.

As Currie raised his eyebrows suspiciously at the string of foreign gutturals, Jacob smiled. 'You're right,' he said. 'It isn't very complimentary. It means "May your head stink", only it sounds much better in Yiddish.'

Spencer hardly knew whether to be angry or take his remarks as a joke not quite in the best of taste. He, too, had fallen under the influence of their old relationship, and, in spite of himself, he tried to humour his visitor as though Jacob's regard were of value to him.

'Listen, Jacob,' Spencer urged soothingly, 'when I say I don't deal with Jews, that isn't meant to be insulting. It happens to be one of my principles not to lend Jews money, that's all. Some of my best friends and business associates are Jews, but I wouldn't loan any of them a penny. Would you like to know why?'

'No I wouldn't,' Jacob answered. 'It's probably some crazy anti-Semitic notion that's stuck in your head, and an anti-Semite won't listen to reason, so he's not worth arguing with anyway. I don't hold a brief for Jews, and I don't speak for anyone but myself. All I know is that I'm sorry I came here. When I came to you, I needed a hundred pounds so badly that I'd have done anything for it – short of murder. Now if you gave me a thousand I wouldn't take it for nothing.'

'Be reasonable, man,' Spencer insisted. 'You've come here on business. Well, I'm talking business. I can explain my attitude about lending Jews money, but you won't let me. And it happens to be as I say,' he lied shamelessly, 'that all my money's tied up, and two hundred and fifty pounds isn't worth the bother of raising. If you'll take my advice, you'll go to the Scottish Discount Trust in St Agnes Square. You'll get the money without any trouble – all you need is one good personal surety.'

Jacob rose to his feet. 'Thank you,' he said dryly. 'If I had one good personal surety, I wouldn't have to come to you or go to St Agnes Square either, my own bank would have been as pleased as Punch to oblige.'

Spencer thrust his hands in his pockets. 'So that's how it is,' he mused. 'And you've come to me just for old time's sake. Well, Jacob, let me give you a word of advice –'

'No thanks,' Jacob broke in curtly. 'I don't need your advice.' Ceremoniously he deposited his cigar on the ashtray. 'And I don't need your cigar either. I don't want anything from you!'

'But, Jacob, you won't let me finish,' Spencer grumbled, his attitude softening still more. 'If you'd only listen, I might be able to do something to help you.'

'You're forgetting,' Jacob retorted with quiet dignity, 'that I'm a Jew, and a poor Jew at that, and you don't do any business with Jews – yet I wouldn't change places with you for all the money in the world. A man's character, I've found, still counts for something, after all. I knew your father; he was a gentleman, and your brother wouldn't talk to me as you've done, although I owe him money. Oscar hasn't got half your brains, or a fiftieth of your cash, but you're not fit to lick his boots!' He moved towards the door, the insult still rankling. 'As for you, Spencer Currie,' he threw a parting shot over his shoulder. '*Zoll dir shtinken fin kopf*, that's all!'

Triumphant, he slammed the door behind him and, straightening his shabby coat in the outer office, put on the black trilby hat that he wore only for special occasions. With a cheerful nod to the commissionaire, he passed beyond the grey frosted partition to the corridor. George mustered enough interest to look after his jauntily departing figure. The commissionaire recognised the symptoms.

''*E's* all right naow,' George commented to Miss Clarke, cocking a finger in the direction of the hatch. 'Must 'ave copped a packet orf the boss!'

On the way down, Jacob felt strangely exhilarated, as if he had scored a tremendous moral victory over the financier, although, with Currie's refusal of a loan, the last faint hope of even temporary solvency had vanished. He had been sentenced. It was the business equivalent of the judge's black cap, and yet he was unaccountably happy. He supposed some murderers must behave in a similar fashion as they wait for the trap to drop; after the agony of the trial and the condemned cell, the scaffold must come as a relief. The trap had been sprung beneath him, too; there was no way out. He was a swaying skeleton, strung up between earth and heaven; released from one world yet not quite ready for the next.

He took the bus to Aldgate and, as it ran down from the city, watched the crowds streaming along the High Street. He got off at the station and drifted down the broad pavement, carried with the impetus of the crowd, yet apart from it, feeling aloof and superior, above all this petty, earthly striving and bustle, like an amused visitor from a much more civilised planet. What did it all amount to anyway? Behind the bright lights, the attractive windows, Jacob knew what was going on better than most. Ninety per cent of these traders – comfortable-looking, paunchy men, peroxided, polished and manicured women – were on the brink of ruin. They couldn't fool Jacob Rothstein, not this tremendously alive Jacob Rothstein who knew that they were hanging on to solvency only by the grace of patient creditors. Still in his role of an extra-terrestrial tourist, he would like to have a few words in a corner with the owner of that glittering gown shop, for example. He would curl the man's tie jovially round his finger, and 'Tell me, as man to man,' he would say, 'how much money do you owe?' And if the other were truthful, he would name a figure high enough to make the earthly Jacob's troubles sound like a children's game.

As he drew closer to his home and left the thronged main thoroughfare, Jacob gradually felt his spirits sinking. Away from the crowds his anxieties started to press on him again, singling him out as an individual, those same, ruthless problems that he still had to face. They had them in the High Street, too, that was the way business went on. Everybody owed money, everybody worked on credit. The higher you went up the commercial scale, the more money you owed. The retailer owed the wholesaler money, the wholesaler was in debt to the manufacture and the manufacturer was tied up to the bank. It was a vicious circle, and, when the banks rafted in their credits, the small man got the worst deal of the lot; his tiny credit dried up first. There was no room for him any more, the bigger people were squeezing him out. They wouldn't let you live, not even a starvation existence. You were in the way and had to be liquidated. They wouldn't let you live.

The shop was closed when he arrived home, and there was a note for him on the kitchen table. His wife had gone to visit her sister, and the boys were at a movie and would not be back till nine. He put the kettle on the gas and sat down on a chair. The exhilaration had evaporated completely and left him too depressed even to think. There was nothing to think about. He felt like a piece of mechanism with the vital parts removed. The wheels had stopped, there was no motive force to propel them any longer. So in his business, and so in his head.

He picked up a teaspoon from the table and held it for a moment in his hand. It seemed to be something more than a piece of base white alloy, it bulked larger, seemed to have a significance wider than that given it by its normal domestic function. The whole room appeared to have swelled in relation to Jacob, all these inanimate objects, the stove, the kitchen cabinet, the sink, the taps, they loomed about him forbiddingly with terrifying solidity and permanence. Beside them he felt frail and of no account, as though they controlled his destiny and not he theirs.

His nose caught the whiff of escaping gas. He looked at the stove and saw that he had omitted to put a light beneath the kettle. Wearily, he rose from the chair and, almost unwillingly, turned off the gas. Everything seemed too much effort now, even making a cup of tea. He wouldn't bother, just sit still and wait for supper – not that he'd be able to eat anything when his wife did return.

The odour of gas lingered in the room. It was not an unpleasant smell, like a clean, mild antiseptic. From the back of his mind he conjured up hints from a government gas-precautions booklet he had read some time ago. Quite simple: you had to retire to an air-tight room, take a warm bath and smoke a pipe. But supposing you didn't smoke and didn't have a bath? Ah, then you could make a room gas proof by sealing the edges of the door and windows with cellophane or wide adhesive tape and hanging a damp blanket against the threshold. Those were hot tips, straight from the government laboratories, and it worked the other way, too – it kept gas from coming in but also prevented it from seeping out. He had no gummed tape in the shop, but there was plenty of adhesive brown paper. That should do the trick just as well.

He went into the shop, and from a drawer in the counter drew out a roll of adhesive brown paper. That was something from the good old days, when he had needed it to keep the bulky purchases of customers together. The roll was nearly two years old, and three-quarters of it still remained intact. There would be enough for his purpose, and to spare. Unhurriedly he went about his task. First, he locked the kitchen door from within and closed the windows. Mechanically, he cut the paper into lengths, working accurately according to exact measurements, for he hated slipshod work, and fixed a double layer over the cracks round the door, and tightly sealed the windows. Even the keyhole he blocked with a crisscross pattern that covered the tiniest holes in the lock. When he had prepared the room to his complete satisfaction, he opened the door of the gas stove, and turned on all the taps.

He sat down on a chair while the gas hissed all round him. Soon, he felt as though his head were swelling. In the distance a telephone bell rang insistently. That would be one of his creditors. Thank heaven none of them could reach him where he was going now. Mingled pear-drops and carbolic – the odour of gas was sickly sweet, and there were cracked bells jangling in his ears. He thought of his wife, of Leah, and his two sons, his two boys. Sturdy-limbed, they would be tall and strong – if they grew up, if enemy bombs didn't smash their young lives to pieces – and they smiled like angels, their laugh was purest music. He would like to hear them laugh just once again. Rosy apples of faces, split with white teeth. Just to hear their laugh once more . . . It wasn't too late yet, he still retained all his faculties. He tried to rise to his feet. If that movement succeeded, maybe he would turn off the gas, if not, then it didn't matter.

He held on to the side of the table and stood up. It was as

though he were floating on air. Suddenly his knees buckled beneath him, and he flopped back on to the chair. The gas hissed musically like an orchestral diminuendo, and the whole room swayed in a mist. His head sagged down on his chest. Out of life in a dream, in a dream . . . Better that way. Painless . . . Like a tooth out under anaesthetic. Goodbye! . . . Only one regret, not to see the boys again . . . Goodbye, goodbye . . . He felt puffed out like a misshapen balloon. In a moment his ungainly, bloated carcass would wobble up to the ceiling without pain . . . His head sank lower on his chest. Even if he had a chance to save himself now, he wouldn't move a finger. Why should he go back to the old dogfight? He didn't stand a chance. It was useless . . . They wouldn't let you live.

CHAPTER SEVEN

'There's no need for you to be so cut up about it, Ma,' said Kim. 'Your manner's so doleful, anyone would almost think you had something to do with Rothstein's death.'

'Maybe . . . maybe I have,' Matilda answered uncertainly, screwing another reluctant tear from the corner of her eye. She felt that she had to defend herself, although nobody was bringing any charge against her. Somehow, she imagined that she was deeply implicated in Jacob's death, and all that morning she had brooded over the dark secret. Only now was it coming out with Kim, who had intuitively sensed what was wrong. Pamela, although she had the whole day off, was as usual too busy with her personal appearance to notice anything strange about her mother, while Oscar had so many urgent problems to face in the shop that nothing less than a thunderbolt could have jolted him from his preoccupations. 'I . . . I shouldn't be at all surprised,' she said.

'Nonsense!' Kim expostulated.

'It isn't nonsense,' she returned, as though she found it vitally necessary to pin at least some portion of the blame for the tragedy on to her shoulders. 'Why . . . I was threatening to sue him for the money he owed us the day before he died.'

'Everybody was suing him,' Kim replied nonchalantly, 'although you had less cause to than most. After all, he was paying us back. Fifty pounds in a couple of weeks is good going – too good, if you ask me. Old Jacob was cracking up. Only a lunatic would have sent along great chunks of cash like that.'

'Only a lunatic,' said Matilda, 'or a thief.'

Kim took off his spectacles thoughtfully. They seemed

out of place on a member of the Currie household. Nobody else in the family wore glasses, and, except when he was reading, it seemed, even to him, that the large horn-rimmed lenses were a studious affectation. There was something about his mother's attitude he didn't fully understand, and he felt it essential to get it quite clear, for Matilda was usually the most level-headed person in the house.

'Jacob was no thief,' said Kim with an air of finality, slipping his spectacles into the outer breast pocket of his sports coat. 'No. He was no thief, unless every businessman who doesn't pay all his bills promptly is a thief, which makes Dad one, and ninety-nine per cent of the others. Jacob had nothing to fear from being sued by you or anyone else. It would just be another civil action. Dash it all! They can't hang you for owing money! It's only after a hell of a lot of trouble that they can even send you to jail.'

'That's just where you're mistaken,' Matilda replied. 'If I'd sued him, he'd have gone to jail without any trouble.'

'I don't understand,' said Kim.

'I didn't think you would,' Matilda answered dryly. 'That money Jacob sent along was mine, and fifty pounds was only the half of it.'

Kim uncrossed his legs and slid them aimlessly along the floor. 'I see,' he commented. 'But where did you get a hundred pounds?'

'Guess . . .' said Matilda.

Kim nodded. He rose to his feet and, pursing his lips, walked across to the mantelpiece. 'Uncle Spencer?' he asked.

Matilda was hurt by the look on the young man's face, as though he as well as Oscar had been betrayed by her action. Hurriedly, she tried to justify herself. 'Oscar needed the money so badly,' she murmured apologetically. 'I knew he wouldn't have touched it if he thought it came from his brother, so I arranged it that way with Jacob.'

Kim shook his head. 'You shouldn't have done it, Ma,' he

protested gently. 'You might have known something like this would happen. I'm not superstitious, but it seems, somehow, that there's a curse on Uncle Spencer's money. It appears to me just as if it's tainted.'

'Rubbish!' said Matilda, her attitude stiffening, almost her old self again, the unsentimental, efficient housewife. 'I'm surprised to hear *you* talking like that, a clever, modern young man like you . . . After all, what have you got against your uncle?'

'Nothing . . . that is, nothing I can explain.'

'Well, why don't you go and see him?'

'What for?' Kim burst out. 'So's he can laugh at me and act the condescending rich uncle to the poor relation?'

Matilda smiled. 'Listen, Kim,' she said, soothingly. 'I'm quite certain he wouldn't do anything of the sort. He wants to see you. It won't hurt you to go up to his office one day.'

'No!' Kim shook his head obstinately. 'I don't want to go up there. I can't bear the sight of him anyway. It's such a terrific . . . terrific . . .' He groped on, floundering for words. 'I don't know . . . revulsion . . . Yes, that's it, revulsion . . . I suppose I inherited it from Dad – if that's a rational explanation,' he finished up more quietly.

'It isn't,' Matilda replied warmly. 'It isn't, and it can't be!'

'Dad hates him for something,' Kim went on stubbornly. 'I don't know what it is, and I don't care, but it must have been pretty bad to have had such an effect on an easy-going fellow like Dad.'

'So you won't go?' she asked again.

'No,' he said, firmly.

'But I promised I'd send you!'

'Well, you've kept your promise,' said Kim. 'You're sending me, but I'm not going to go.'

He reached up for his hat and made for the door, then, halting, he turned and crossed over to his mother and, putting his arms gently on her shoulders, kissed her repentantly.

Matilda's head was still lowered over her knitting, but the hand that reached up for and caressed his wrist was steady once more, as though all memories of Jacob Rothstein had been relegated to their proper place as something quite impersonal – regrettable, but outside the sphere of her intimate existence.

In the street, a few paces from the side door, Kim stopped. Where should he go? The weather was too fine for the pictures and too uncertain for any long jaunt in the country, and yet he had intended to celebrate, for today, he felt, he had good cause for celebration. He had passed the last of the gruelling 'knowledge' exams at the 'Yard'. All he had to get over now was the minor hurdle of a driving test, and he could take out his first fare. And how nearly he had messed it up at the 'Yard' – stumped by a question about the situation of an institution right next door to his old college, a building he had passed almost daily for years. Luckily, the inspector was a good old stick; a quizzical wink, a tap on the shoulder and a word in the right place, and he had remembered. But all the fellows weren't so lucky, nor were all the inspectors such sports. Some of them took a fiendish delight in sending the same men down week after week for trivial inaccuracies, as if it were necessary to know exactly how many blocks it was from Piccadilly Circus to the Lambs' Club in order to be an efficient driver of a London cab. He saw the pale faces and furrowed brows that came down from the inspectors' rooms; for the inquisitors it was merely routine, usually a bore, sometimes a joke, but for all these men every mistake was a tragedy, punishable by postponement of their jobs for yet another week.

Still, he was past that now, and he had to reconcile himself to the knowledge that his academic career had ended before it had really begun. He had to forget that he had once been a university man and had a degree. That roll of parchment had looked very nice in his hand at the photographer's, but it was apparently only for decorative purposes. Tonight it would disappear from its frame in his room, and with it would vanish for ever Kim Currie, Esquire, Bachelor of Arts, with honourable mention in five subjects. He was now a cabby – a number on a licence plate – almost. There were one or two more formalities, but they were only formalities. He had received his diploma from Scotland Yard, but, unlike the university degree, it entitled him to a job, and he could walk straight into the next garage and get one.

He ought to be thinking of that right now. There was a large garage a few hundred yards down at the back of the clock tower. That would do as well as any since it was conveniently situated near home. That would be his destination. He was striding off into a new life, and, even if it wasn't creative, it was useful. He served the public, but, more important still, he was no longer an educated parasite; he would be able to make a living.

In the midst of his triumph, he felt a twinge of compassion for the failures. He was sorry about Old Rothstein, but it had been inevitable, and what disturbed him even more was that he could see a similar process driving his own father down into the gutter. All Oscar's bastions were gradually being undermined. Every excuse he had given for his languishing business had proved a fiction, and he had given every excuse but the right one. First it had been dogs. The public spent too much money on greyhounds, and the shopkeepers suffered. Then there were tote clubs, but they had been declared illegal, and yet the shopkeepers still suffered. After that the fruit machines and pin tables and war fears and, most serious menace of all, the football pools. The 'something-for-nothing disease' Oscar had dubbed it, an affliction that took sixty million pounds a year from the public's pockets and out of the traders' tills. And the huge chain stores went merrily on their way, increasing their profits year by year, by thousands, by millions of pounds, giving fantastic dividends, so large that they had to disguise them as bonus shares, yet they made it all from the same public, half-moribund, in the money sense, from dogs and pin tables, war scares and football pools.

One day Oscar would find out that he, Kim, was right, and if he did, what then? It was too late to do anything about it now, so it would obviously be of less use later on. He wished he knew the answer to all these problems. Kim was clear up to a point. He could prophesy with pragmatic exactitude Oscar's decline, but for the life of him he didn't know how to prevent it. It struck the young man that he held precisely the same position as his father, except that his standpoint was the reverse side of the medal. Kim insisted that Oscar was doomed to failure, while the older man pooh-poohed the suggestion, and between them they could not offer one constructive proposal. Kim couldn't get a solution out of his books nor Oscar from a century of inherited trading experience. How desperately Oscar was searching for a way out Kim had discovered last Thursday. In the luncheon hour, when he usually closed the shop, Oscar had dallied behind the counter, and Kim had come across him filling in a football coupon. That was the last straw of a drowning man. It showed the virulence of the epidemic, if the 'something-for-nothing' craze had struck down one of its stoutest adversaries, one, moreover, immunised against it by constant injections of anti-pool serum over a period of years. Oscar had been terribly ashamed. He backed horses very modestly, to the tune of a few shillings every week, and took a sweep ticket a couple of times a year, but all that he regarded as a legitimate flutter, while the pools, he asserted, were nothing but a gigantic swindle. Yet, in spite of his convictions, he knew that some people were lucky, and if *he* happened to be one of the lucky ones he could get thirty thousand pounds for sixpence, so why shouldn't he have a shot, even if he knew practically nothing about football? Kim, diplomatically, had not enlarged upon the incident, because he knew his father must feel rather like a prize scholar discovered using a crib at an important exam.

Outside the garage, a tall, red-haired young man in a suede jacket was flicking some specks of dirt with a silky chamois from an immaculately sprayed and polished cab, a new green Austin. Kim looked at it admiringly. Before very long now, he would be in charge of such a glistening chariot himself.

'Nice bus,' he remarked.

'Yeah,' said the young man unenthusiastically, with a slight nasal drawl. 'But it ain't mine. I only drive it.'

'Got a new fleet in this garage?' Kim asked.

'Near enough. They're weeding out most of the old crocks – and about time, too!' He looked at Kim quizzically. 'Why? You thinking of buying up the joint?'

'Not exactly,' said Kim with a grin. 'I was thinking I'd like to work here.'

'Well, you could do worse,' the cabby admitted. 'The boss here ain't such a bad guy. Got your plate?'

'Not yet,' said Kim, 'but I've got over the worst. I've passed all the "knowledge".'

'Good!' the young man replied, and impulsively he stuck out a large hand. 'Well, if you're going to work here, we may as well be buddies. My name's Alf, only I'm usually called "Rusty" on account of the colour of my hair.'

'Mine's Kim.'

'Short for something?' the cabby asked.

'No. Just long for Kim.'

The young man chuckled. 'Well, I suppose you can't help your name. It's non-committal anyway. Better than having to be a Clarence or a Ferdinand all your life.' With a grand gesture he indicated the running-board. 'Take a seat, pardner,' he invited him.

'Thanks,' said Kim, sitting down beside him on the running-board. 'Have a cigarette?'

The young man shook his head. He had a frank, open face, with large, mobile, freckled features. Everything about him was on a big scale, slightly larger than life. Kim was tall, nearly six feet, but Rusty was a good head taller; his hands were the tough and leathery paws of a manual worker, even his snub nose was broad and plastic, seemingly boneless, and his supple, thick-lipped mouth jerked about his face with smooth elasticity as he talked, showing yellowish front teeth, thick and strong as the teeth of a bull.

'No thanks,' he remarked, as Kim lit up. 'I got a more expensive vice – ponies.'

'Had any luck with them lately?' said Kim.

Rusty's loose lower lip swung downwards in a rueful grimace. 'Nope,' he answered regretfully. 'I never have any luck with anything. I'd better warn you, buddy, I'm a hoodoo. Whatever I touch turns out a flop,' Rusty sighed. 'They told me things was fine in the States,' he continued ruminatively. 'But when I worked my way over in 'thirty-one, all I found was breadlines. And winter was coming on, and I didn't have an overcoat, and believe me, buddy, you need an overcoat in New York in December. So they told me to go West, and when I enquired how, they said hitch-hike. But the guys with automobiles wasn't biting that fall, so I wore out three pairs of shoes getting to California, and when I arrived at Los Angeles half the studios had closed down, they wasn't even making movies any more –'

'Excuse me saying so,' Kim interrupted, 'but you don't look a bit like a film star, Rusty.'

'No!' the cabby ejaculated in mock surprise. 'Well, you're the only guy who's ever said so. Anyway, I wasn't figuring to have my classic features immortalised in celluloid. I'd heard that there was always plenty of work for a handyman around the studios when they're in full blast, and I can do most things with these hands of mine except' – with a chuckle – 'except make a darn good living.'

'Well, you got to California – and what then?'

'Well,' said Rusty, 'then I gave myself up to the cops as an illegal immigrant, and they found they had enough bums of their own to look after, so they put me in jail and shipped me back home.'

'Well, you're all right now anyway,' Kim remarked.

'Oh, I get by,' Rusty admitted. 'But that's because I'm the only one I got to support. This game ain't what I thought it would be, though. I'd heard the boys was knocking up ten, twelve quid a week, easy as pie, so I figured that'd be Jake for old Rusty, but as a hackie I've found my limit's been three, except one bank holiday when a drunk gave me a pound and told me to keep the change. I sorta feel it's been my fault. If I hadn't become a hackie it might have still been OK for the rest, but no sooner do I get my badge than they starts bringing out private-hire luxury cars on the streets. No "knowledge" needed to drive one of them, no "Yard" tests, not even trade-union rates of wages. You ring up the firm and book a car, they pick you up at your doorstep, take you to the theatre and bring you back again for an all-in fee that's not much more than cab rates. No rushing, no scrimmaging, no waiting in the rain, and everything's hunky-dory for the customer, for the car proprietor, for everyone except the cabby – that's me – and you, too, now, buddy.'

'Still, it can't be too bad,' said Kim hopefully. 'Anyway, it's better than doing nothing, and it may improve.'

Rusty shook his head. 'Not while I'm in it, pardner. All my life I been flogging dead horses. Why, I guarantee if I went in for making baby carriages everybody would stop having kids, and if I became an undertaker they'd all live longer than Methuselah.'

Kim grinned. 'It strikes me,' he commented, 'there'll always be Rustys knocking around right until the millennium, yet your sort always manages to stay cheerful about their troubles. You remind me of Browning's Ibn Ezra, way back in the Middle Ages. He journeyed from Spain to Cairo to see Maimonides, but as usual was disappointed. Yet he didn't sit down and cry, he wrote a poem about it:

>   '"I call on my Lord in the morning
>   But am told that on horseback's he's sped,
>   I call once again in the evening
>   And hear that His Lordship's abed.
>   But whether His Highness is riding,
>   Or whether My Lord is asleep,
>   I am perfectly sure disappointment
>   Is the one single fruit I shall reap."'

Rusty laughed out loud and brought his hand down on Kim's knee with an appreciative slap. 'Boy, you said it! There's a guy right after my own heart.' He stopped and looked at Kim admiringly. 'You spout poetry pretty well,' he complimented him. 'How d'you know all them things?'

'Well,' said Kim apologetically, 'I hate to admit it, but I went to college once, and I learned a lot of things for my degree – most of them not so useful as poetry – out of books.'

'So you like books,' Rusty remarked. 'Well, brother, you've come into a profession where books plays a big part. Out there in the cab ranks you'll have plenty of time for reading books, and if you was any good at writing you'd find plenty of time for that, too.'

Kim shook his head emphatically. 'No thanks. I've done all the serious reading – and writing – I'm ever going to do, I'm learning to use my hands from now on.'

'Good for you, buddy,' Rusty said with a commendatory nod. He rose to his feet and stretched his arms lazily. 'Well, I guess I'd better start using my hands, too.'

'Oh! I'm sorry,' Kim apologised. 'I hope I haven't kept you.'

'Me?' said the cabby. 'Not a bit of it!' He craned his long, freckled neck towards the heavens. 'Look at that sky! Blue as an Aryan's eyes. Not a cloud for miles . . . And I got to take the bus out cruising in the dusty city! Now ain't that my luck? It can't be raining, or dull, or blowing like blazes. No!

It's got to be fine. Every day this week it's been like that, because I've had to work, just when I'd give half my takings for the sight of six green trees in a row.'

'But you're not forced to go out, are you?'

'Sure I'm not forced.' Rusty grinned wryly. 'But we'll say it's advisable when there's only ten bob between me and starvation – and when most of that belongs to someone else.'

A sleek, dark, high-powered sports car snorted past them to the filling station on the opposite side of the road. Rusty followed it enviously with his eyes to the pump and, judging from his expression, he obviously recognised one or both of the occupants.

Kim was intrigued by this little episode, for, although the young man at the wheel was a stranger to him, the girl was his sister, and a very chic and attractive Pamela she appeared, too. For the first time he found himself regarding her as a woman and not just his sister. If he passed her, unknown, in the street, he would certainly stop and turn to admire her figure and the line of her calves and ankles, yet he had seen her washing her hair wearing nothing but a short underslip and she had seemed merely part of the furniture. But then she was his sister, and he would never think of her as other than his own flesh and blood, although there had been strange and furtive moments in early adolescence when they had both tremulously regarded each other in a peculiar light that neither could quite understand; but they had outgrown that twilight interlude of temporary embarrassment, they were part of the family now, just Curries. He supposed even husbands and wives lost all sense of bodily differentness after they had lived together long enough. It always amused him to watch staid married men craning their necks to catch a glimpse of something higher than a pair of stockinged knees above carelessly crossed legs in a tube or a bus while their own wives had far more attractive limbs that they seldom bothered to glance at. This wasn't quite the same thing, but it was interesting to look at his sister for once through the eyes of an outsider.

'That's the life,' Rusty broke in on his thoughts. 'Take Dai Phillips there. All he's got to do this afternoon is take a skirt for a ride in the country.'

'Who's Dai Phillips?' Kim asked.

'Don't you know? I thought everyone round here knew him. He's the local Fuehrer of the True Britons.'

'Hmmmm!' Kim nodded. That explained a good deal of Pamela's sudden conversion to politics. 'Do you know the girl, too?'

'Can't say I do,' Rusty replied, 'though I've seen 'em together quite a bit, lately. He lives in my street, above the Party offices. A reg'lar ladykiller, but he's got hold of a peach there – he certainly knows how to pick 'em!'

'Glad you said that,' Kim remarked. 'The girl's my sister.'

'Really?' Rusty guffawed loudly. 'Good job, then, I stopped where I did.'

'Why? Is there anything else?' Kim asked suspiciously.

'No . . . no,' Rusty assured him hurriedly. 'Don't get me wrong, buddy, only you know the way some guys shoots their mouths off when they spot a good-looking dame in a car.'

With a petulant belch, the Bentley started off and shot round the corner, Pamela's shilling scarf that covered her carefully waved hair billowing its painted flowers in the wind over her shoulders.

'Well, they're off,' said Rusty. 'I guess I'd better be off, too. Where *you* going, Kim?' he asked.

'I don't know,' Kim replied. 'But they're probably off to the country where you'd like to go, and, now you mentioned it, it's some time since I've seen six trees in a row myself. I think I'll take a trip down to Richmond. I owe myself a celebration.'

'Me, too,' said Rusty suddenly, his mind jerked into action.

'Wait!' He flung down the chamois square on the bonnet of the car. 'Buddy, I'll go along with you. I got a celebration coming, too.'

'Really?'

'Sure!' Rusty rubbed his hands briskly together. 'Sure I got a celebration. I'm going to celebrate I'm still alive. Too old for peacetime conscription but nice and dandy for the firing line. As soon as the guns start popping they'll yank me "over there" pronto by the scruff of the neck, and no excuses. I'm strong and healthy, no family to support, why I'm just the right guy for bullets to push over. Sure I'm going to celebrate while I'm still in one piece. Hang on a tick, buddy, I'll have a few words with the boss, then I'll be right back, and we'll take a jaunt up the river together – OK?'

Kim grinned and shrugged his shoulders. 'OK,' he said, imitating Rusty's nasal twang. 'OK, buddy, I'll wait.'

CHAPTER EIGHT

As they walked down the main road, Kim became acutely conscious of a smouldering rebelliousness bubbling over in his companion. Gradually his resentment grew audible, and every few paces Rusty glanced up at the sky and swore beneath his breath as he noted dark clouds, materialised from nowhere, creeping ominously towards the sun. They quickened their pace, but several drops of rain pricked them maliciously as if to mock their progress, and as a leaden, wintry glaze crept across the heavens, the slight wind dropped, and a few moments later a torrent of hail swept down on them, soon giving way to a steady, relentless downpour. Fortunately they had almost reached the Underground station, and they rushed for the protection of the booking hall, together with dozens of other pedestrians caught on the streets by this trick of the weather without mackintoshes or umbrellas.

Kim's hat was turned down all round, the limp brim of the cheap felt slopping wet, each undulating curve glistening with moisture at the laden tips. It had afforded him some measure of protection, but his companion was hatless, and, as Rusty shook himself, the red ringlets, plastered by the driving rain across his forehead, stood away from his face giving him the appearance of a wet and shaggy St Bernard. Under cover of the vestibule, a few inches from the deluge, Rusty scowled at the cascading rivulets that rushed across the pavements like boiling water, shooting from roof-top drains to gutters. At last he flung out a hand dramatically with a gesture like Ajax defying the lightning.

'There! Look at that,' he muttered disgustedly. 'Didn't I tell you I was a hoodoo?'

'You flatter yourself,' said Kim. 'Do you think that the clerk of the weather harbours a special grudge against a cabby named Rusty?'

'Maybe not,' growled his companion, 'but it certainly looks like it.'

'Are you going back?' Kim asked.

'To the garage?' said Rusty. 'Not on your life! I was only too glad of the chance to get away. We'll have to make the best of it now, buddy, that's all.'

'Suits me,' Kim answered. He grinned at his friend's woe-begone expression. To look at him one might have imagined that he had just suffered an irreparable loss. 'Never mind,' he consoled him. 'It's not summer yet – there will be plenty more fine days.'

'Sure!' said Rusty. 'But what's the good of them to me? I'll always be working, and when I won't be working, I'll be broke.'

'Supposing we go somewhere and have a bite when this gives over a little?' Kim suggested. 'You'll feel lots better after a spot of food.'

'OK,' Rusty agreed. 'I'll tell you what, it ain't far from here, let's go up to Mossy's spieler, they sell some first-class chow.'

'Why a spieler?' Kim asked. 'Surely we don't have to go to a gambling den to eat? There are any amount of respectable restaurants within walking distance.'

'Heck! I don't feel comfortable in them,' Rusty grumbled. 'Clean white cloths and tuxedoed waiters always give me the willies. Come to Mossy's,' he urged. 'Mossy is a pal of mine. He ought to be,' he added. 'The money I blued in that place, I could own the joint.'

As soon as the tempestuous flood subsided to what was a comparatively moderate drizzle, they left the shelter of the station and doubled down a labyrinth of side turnings to a narrow alley. Rusty stopped outside a dilapidated house stuck incongruously in the midst of a block of deserted factories.

He winked to a burly man lounging in the doorway and, followed by Kim, climbed the stairs to the third floor.

The spieler was a large room that, judging from the rails near the ceiling and the huge, rusting iron rack against the wall, had once been a tailor's workshop. One of the two full-sized billiard tables was being used by a couple of middle-aged men in shirtsleeves, playing snooker, and there were three others drinking coffee at the bar. The setting was not distinguishable from the usual drabness of an ordinary men's temperance club, but people kept going into an off-room and hurriedly coming out, and unseen telephones rang shrilly without cessation.

The men at the bar shifted silently to make room for Kim and Rusty, and the corpulent attendant leaned one elbow on the counter and, with a bored expression, rubbed somnolent circles with a dishcloth as he waited for the order. He wore a grease-spotted, collarless shirt over grubby flannels and a large check-tweed cap pushed back from a domed, perspiring brow.

'Two coffees, Rube,' said Rusty, 'and two cold-meat salads – with plenty of cow.'

'No cow,' replied Rube indifferently, paying far more attention to swabbing the counter. 'Pig.'

Kim nodded in reply to Rusty's questioning glance, and the cabby turned back to the barman. 'Ham, then – and don't spare the slices.'

'OK,' Rube answered without the flicker of a smile. He turned his broad back on them, a roll of fat encircling his hips like a blown-out pneumatic tyre, and his right elbow moved in a gentle curve as he commenced slicing the gammon.

Kim took some silver from his pocket. 'This is my treat,' he said.

'Oh no!' Rusty replied indignantly. 'You're my guest. I ain't that broke!'

'You'll pay another time,' said Kim.

'No.'

Kim felt very uncomfortable. 'I'll tell you what,' he suggested, 'let's toss for it?'

'Right!' Rusty agreed immediately. He was always eager for any sort of bet on practically any chance. If the guardian of the Heavenly Gate were ever dubious about letting him through, Rusty's first reaction would surely be to search his shroud for a coin and offer to toss St Peter for it. He brought out his lucky farthing and spun it on the counter. Kim saw it fell head upwards and called 'tails'. Rusty's face lit up. He grinned triumphantly when he removed his hand, as though he had brought off some spectacular coup. Carefully, he spat on the coin and tucked it away in his ticket pocket. This was the first bit of luck he had touched for weeks; it was a good omen for future operations. He picked up his knife and fork and attacked the salad as though it were a choice five-course meal at a banquet.

The room was gradually filling. Both billiard tables were now in use, and some smaller card tables had been set up and were occupied by serious men intently studying the sporting editions. Rusty glanced at his watch and, as though he had suddenly reached a decision, pushed away his empty plate and drained his coffee to the dregs. He stood up and stretched himself.

'Come on, Kim,' he said.

'Where to?' Kim asked as his companion moved towards the off-room.

'The inside spieler,' Rusty explained, his eyes glistening moistly with excitement 'My luck's changed. I can feel it. I've got ten bob. Now watch me, buddy, I'm going to make it do things.'

'Wait a minute,' said Kim restrainingly. 'That money's supposed to last you over the week, isn't it?'

'Sure! But what's the odds? I'll be borrowing on Monday with this dough or without it.' Rusty was straining at the leash.

'Come on, Kim,' he pleaded, wrinkling his snub nose appealingly like a spoiled baby. 'Come on! Don't be a spoil-sport.'

He elbowed his way to the room and opened the door. As soon as they entered, Kim, although moderately addicted to cigarettes, was half-choked by the fog of tobacco smoke and temporarily blinded. It seemed incredible that these pungent, poisonous clouds could be blown from a few men's lungs. He coughed and rubbed his smarting eyes till he could pierce with less discomfort the bluish haze.

Two clerks were seated before telephones, taking bets as they came through and noting them on long slips of paper. Several groups of men were playing poker at one end of the room, and at the other a game of faro was in progress, as much as twenty pounds being wagered on the turn of a card. In the corner, Mossy sat by himself at a table. He was in his shirtsleeves like most of the other gamblers, wearing a grey hat so light in colour that it was almost white against the jet-black ribbon. He kept chewing at a ragged cigar, his beetle brows giving his coarse, blue-jowled face a cut-throat aspect like that of a Chicago gorilla. When his telephone rang, as it did the moment the young men entered, he completed the picture of a gangster. The cigar swung over to the side of his mouth, and a finger flicked back the spotless brim of his hat as he clutched the mouthpiece.

'Yeh?' he barked. 'Yeh . . . Yeh . . . Yeh . . . OK.'

He hung up the receiver, made a note on a slip and tossed it over to one of the clerks. He looked up as Rusty and Kim came towards him.

''Lo, Rusty,' he said laconically.

Rusty nodded. 'I'm in form,' he announced. 'I'm going to wipe you up.'

Mossy grinned. 'That'll be terrible, won't it?'

'The first favourite,' said Rusty. 'Ten bob. On the nose.'

Mossy took the note and carelessly slipped it into his

trousers pocket. He looked at his watch; it was half past one. Almost at the same moment the tape machine started to run, its slick, lubricated ticking cleaving like a juggernaut through the heart of the smoke and the noise.

'No more for the one thirty,' said Mossy.

Several of the games were immediately suspended, and a bunch of sweaty men gathered excitedly round the ticker. One of the clerks collected all the slips for the first race, packed them in a large envelope, sealed the flap and wrote '1.30' across it with a thick blue pencil. Rusty perched himself on the edge of Mossy's table, supremely confident. He had picked up a paper and was already making his choice for the next race.

The favourite romped home at two to one. Mossy moved away from the ticker, and, taking out a huge wad of cash, started paying out the winners. He peeled off three ten-shilling notes and offered them to Rusty. The cab-driver shook his head.

'No,' he said. 'I told you I was going to give you the works. Stick it on Ladbroke Filly.'

Ladbroke Filly won at threes. That meant Rusty had six pounds to play with. He was lucky again on the two thirty and after the three o'clock found himself fifteen pounds ahead of the book. Somehow he was not at all excited. This, he felt, had been coming to him for a long while. But the next race was a puzzle. His brow lined with the effort of concentration. He bent over the paper, unable to decide between two horses that both seemed to have an equal chance. Form was the same, jockeys were both triers and handicaps were about level. It irritated him to be brought short like this when he had practically smelt the other winners on sight. At last he handed the paper to Kim.

'What do you think's going to win?' he enquired.

Kim shook his head and returned the paper without even attempting to glance at it. 'No use asking me,' he answered, 'I wouldn't know a mule from a horse's foot.'

Rusty's face broke into a delightful grin. He clapped his huge hand jovially on Kim's shoulder. 'You said it, buddy! You said it! It ain't what I fancied, but I'm going to stake your luck.' He turned to Mossy. 'Colt's Foot for the three thirty.'

The bookmaker nodded; the bet was on. Kim edged his way to the ticker and waited, his heart in his mouth as though his own money were at stake. The runners lined up. They were off . . . Running . . . The first bend . . . The home stretch and, miraculously, Colt's Foot had won!

The SP prices came through. Colt's Foot, four to one.

Kim pushed his way over to Rusty. 'Four to one!' he exclaimed excitedly. 'Four to one!'

Rusty nodded. He picked his teeth nonchalantly with a whittled matchstick. 'I heard, I heard . . . That means seventy-five smackers to come.'

'Don't you think you ought to finish now,' said Kim.

Rusty seemed quite surprised. 'Why?'

'Surely, you can't expect your run of luck to last all the time . . .'

'Not all the time,' said Rusty, 'just for today. The last race, and I'm through.'

'Be satisfied with seventy-five pounds,' Kim urged.

'No,' said Rusty obstinately. 'I've got to get at least a century. I made up my mind.'

'But supposing you lose?'

'If I lose, I lose,' Rusty answered composedly. 'Even then I'll only be ten bob to the bad after all. But I won't lose – I can't!' he insisted. 'I'm dead on form.' He tossed the newspaper aside. He had made his last selection. 'Hey, Mossy!' he called. 'On the favourite. Shoot the works!'

Again the favourite snatched a head victory at evens. Rusty had run right through the card. Kim felt sick and slightly dizzy as a reaction from the excitement of following the horses and being cooped up for so many hours amidst the heady atmosphere of this unaccustomed concentration of tobacco smoke. Mossy paid out the money without turning a hair. He did not worry overmuch. It was a freak loss, but he would get it all back soon enough – with interest. Rusty leaned over the table, checking up the notes with moistened thumb and forefinger, then carelessly tossed a pound to each of the clerks. That was the usual procedure after a big win, and Rusty enjoyed distributing his largesse on the grand scale.

They escaped from the press of envious well-wishers and returned to the comparative peace of the bar. Only now was Rusty beginning to feel the strain of the previous few hours.

'Two coffees,' he said to the bartender, 'and make 'em strong and black.'

'OK,' Rube answered, turning away from them as though he attended even the most unreasonable requests with just the same unhurried acquiescence.

Rusty mopped his brow. He had just discovered he was dripping with perspiration.

'Phew!' he muttered. He shook his head, and passed the handkerchief slowly round his neck, poking it beneath the constricting band of his collar. 'Phew! Darned hot in there!'

Kim nodded. He felt slightly limp himself. 'Well, what now?' he asked. 'You've got more than your hundred pounds. What are you going to do with it?'

'Spend it,' said Rusty. 'What the hell's money for?'

'All the lot?' Kim asked incredulously.

'Sure! The whole darned lot!' he repeated.

'But don't you think you really ought to put some by?'

'What for?' Rusty demanded. 'Supposing I do put it by. I get ill or fall out of work, so it keeps me going for a few months – and then what? Why, I'm just as bad off as before except I'll be regretting like hell I didn't spend it while I had the chance. What else shall I do with it? Open up a little business? I can see what's happening to most of the other business folk I know. That's out! While if I invest it in gilt-edged securities, and even they ain't safe these days, it'll fetch me an income of around three-and-six a week by the time I'm ninety. No. None of *those* things, but I've not quite decided what I am going to do. Maybe I'll go to America for a trip, just to look up my old buddies and see the World's Fair. Say! That's an idea!' He broke into a sudden chuckle. 'And won't those bums be surprised to see me again!'

'Two black coffees,' Rube interrupted, setting the cup before them on the counter. 'That'll be sixpence, please.'

Rusty flicked over a ten-shilling note. 'Here,' he said. 'Keep the change.'

Rube's sparse eyebrows lifted just a trifle, and a reluctant smirk hovered for a brief instant upon his fleshy lips. 'OK, Rusty,' he replied, thrusting the money into his hip pocket, a slight nod conveying at the same time his thanks. 'Had a good day?'

'Yeah!' said Rusty triumphantly. 'Cleaned up a packet. You know, Rube, I'm usually the unluckiest guy on two legs, but this is one time when it's played my way. I can't go wrong. Why, even if Last Chance was running today I'd put my shirt on him, and guarantee he'd come home.'

'That's a pity,' Rube answered, 'because he's running tomorrow.'

'Last Chance?'

'That's right. In the Torrington Stakes. And starting near favourite as usual.' The ten-shilling note was making the silent Rube expand a little. He propped his elbows on the counter and leaned forward confidentially. 'A real mystery, that horse,' he elaborated. 'Won his first three races in smashing style as a two-year-old, and since then he's been God's greatest gift to Mossy, six times nowhere, off the reel.' He shook his head solemnly. 'Can't understand it,' he said, 'unless they're playing him for a big job.'

'That's just what it is!' Rusty brought out, slapping his fist decisively on the counter. 'He'll win tomorrow as sure as this is my right hand. Six times nowhere, and seven is my lucky number. Boy, my shirt's going on Last Chance, and this time it's a damn expensive piece of laundry!'

'You mean it?' said Rube. 'Seriously?'

'I was never more serious in my life!'

'OK,' Rube shrugged his shoulders. 'OK', he repeated, then added in the identical mild tone, 'But just the same, I think you're crazy.'

Kim noticed that the moist, feverish glow was burning once more in Rusty's eyes and knew that it was useless attempting to check his friend. He himself had felt for the first time at the tape machine the devastating madness of gambling, and it seemed at that moment that money had no value beside that overpowering thrill. Rusty slipped off his stool and made his way quickly to the off-room. In a very short while he was back again, and together the two young men descended the stairs.

'Well, I've done it,' said Rusty. 'A hundred and thirty pounds on Last Chance.'

'Each way?' Kim asked.

'No. Not even for a place. It's win or bust – and I got six to one.'

'Phew!' Kim whistled. 'Is Mossy all right for seven hundred pounds?'

'Seven hundred? Mossy's good for seven thousand. Why, I once seen him pay out three thousand pounds as if it was cigarette pictures.'

'That's if the horse wins,' said Kim, his caution returning as they neared the ground floor. 'But supposing it doesn't?'

'There's no question of doesn't,' Rusty asserted with finality. 'It's got to win! In any case, I'm still nearly twenty pounds to the good – more than I could earn in a month,' he chuckled. 'But what's the use of worrying about money anyway? Even if I win, the odds are that I'll get sent across to the Maginot Line before I can even think of America.'

When they reached the street they found that the sun had reappeared, and the pavements were steaming, the stones mottled with rapidly drying moisture like gooseflesh.

'There!' said Rusty. 'It's turned out fine after all. Still, I'm not sorry now. All I need, buddy, is one more break to make everything complete. I just want that horse to romp first past the post.'

'So do I,' Kim returned and, as the cabby looked at him questioningly, 'I'm converted, Rusty,' he explained. 'Just for once, I'll chance a gamble myself. I'm going to put two bob on Last Chance.'

CHAPTER NINE

Oscar opened his eyes as the first faint rays of dawn filtered through the window. Another day. More and more he hated every morning that dragged him from bed to the futile struggle below in the shop, more and more he was beginning to dread what had been for him once the unalloyed adventure of commerce. It wasn't his fault, he was quite certain of that; he felt the power within him to do things, to rush about buying goods all over the city, to put them on display, to persuade customers to spend, to serve, to wrap up, to say, 'Thank you, come again,' to tie parcels, to ring a brisk tune on the cash register; it wasn't as though he were worn out, incapable of doing any or all of those things. The trouble lay outside of him. He was a good workman, yet he had to watch impotently while his fine tools rusted for lack of the raw material – customers.

He had to face facts as they were. Carrying on in this way meant inevitable failure, if not this week, then next month or the month after that. Without comprehending or appreciating Kim's theoretical reasoning, he had blundered down the hard, empiric path to reach the same bitter, undeniable conclusions himself. Times had changed, for better or for worse depended how one looked at it. In the old days every shopkeeper had had a chance of making a living, but the business layout had altered, the machinery for distribution had lagged behind the mode of production and the multiple retailers had stepped in as the ones to fill the breach. Now the small trader found that his competitor was not the little man round the corner but the huge store in the same street . . .

Saturday. Another day and the end of another week. In

his mind he passed over in review the previous seven days, and one incident stood out, rising before him again so realistically that even in retrospect he could not restrain a cold chill running through him at the memory. The telephone bell was ringing. It had been ringing all the morning. Enquiries from creditors and promises in return. He was beginning to detect a note of sarcasm in some usually subservient voices, and in others a hard, impatient, fretful tone. But this time the bell rang on a different pitch, at least so he imagined it now, a week later, and he could still feel the echo of its reverberations right through his head. 'Hello,' he had said resignedly, and he was repeating that same 'Hello' again, it was going through his brain exactly as it had transpired a week ago, as if he had made a wax record of the conversation and was playing it over softly to himself.

'Hello . . . Currie speaking.'

'This is Gunther,' that oily, unctuous voice.

'Good morning, Mr Gunther. What can I do for you?'

'Well . . . there's a little matter of eleven pounds three and six, outstanding since December.'

'Eleven-three-six?' Oscar had to laugh. 'Why, I sent you off a cheque for the exact amount four days ago.'

'Well, I'm sorry,' Gunther, the suave, slinking, heartless robot. 'I suppose there's been some mistake. It's come back from the bank . . . RD . . .'

'No! That's impossible!' It was as though someone had slapped him with startling suddenness and left the shameful impress of fingers in deep, red weals across his face.

'I thought there must be some mistake.' Gunther could surely see him from the other end, for he could see Gunther as plainly as though he were at arm's length, and he could almost feel physically the nasty bite behind each carefully chosen word. 'So, I've put it back in the bank . . . I hope it will be all right now . . .'

'Why, certainly, Mr Gunther, of course!'

There must have been a wealth of feeling in his tone, for Gunther had become more obsequious than ever. 'I'm so sorry,' he apologised again. 'I understand. There's no need to get so upset about it, Currie. There's probably been some mistake. Come and see us soon, we've some exceptional lines . . .'

Of course, Gunther was lying. He didn't want to see him, he didn't want him to buy new lines. At this moment he was probably praying for the cheque to go through all right and concocting some scheme for revenge if it didn't. Oscar detested Gunther, had always disliked the man, although all their business transactions had never been other than satisfactory. He couldn't stand that perpetual stage-performer smile and the oleaginous undertaker's voice, and he had the uneasy feeling that a pair of spiteful claws were only just concealed beneath the velvet cloak of his words.

So the cheque had come back RD. He felt once more a hot flush of shame creep over his face. In a hundred years of trading that had never happened to a Currie before. Certainly, cheques had been returned on several occasions, but they had always been queried by reason of faulty endorsements, or an illegible signature, a mistake in the date or some such innocuous defect. Never, never, 'Refer to Drawer', bearing the laconic inscription that meant insufficient funds, a stigma almost fatal to a man whose sole capital was his credit.

His first reaction had been to rush over to the bank and beg the manager to accommodate him, but on second thoughts he dismissed the idea. If, after the thousands of pounds of business he had done through the bank he was no longer good for a measly eleven-odd, then it was time he finished with banks, finished with business altogether . . . But that Gunther was an ugly customer, and he needed him, he owed him money, too, apart from this eleven pounds. Hurriedly he thumbed the counterfoil stubs of his cheque-book. Yes. They were right at the bank, he had passed the limit of his overdraft.

He couldn't expect it to expand for ever after all. He had exceeded his limit three times, and on each occasion had wheedled an extra accommodation of fifty pounds. It had been so easy for so many years that he had somehow taken it for granted that they would continue to honour his cheques indefinitely. The possibility of one of them ever coming back had never even crossed his mind. It had come as a terrible shock, but, from the perusal of his counterfoils, there was no error. It was an unmistakable warning. They were standing no more monkey business from him at the bank, no more jockeying up the limit. The line was drawn now, finally, and this was an intimation that he was expected to toe it strictly in future . . . But a Currie cheque had come back. For the first time! He felt like a forger discovered obtaining goods by false pretences and convicted by a self-righteous prig like Gunther. False pretences, that was what it amounted to, and forgery was what he had been practising now for months.

He didn't know quite how he had got through that day or the succeeding two days. Time after time he had felt an almost irresistible impulse to swallow his pride and rush over to the bank, but he had somehow restrained himself and managed to sit tight. For three days he had waited for something to happen, and on the third day it had happened. A telephone call, from Gunther again. Those few moments while he was waiting for him to speak seemed like a hideous nightmare and still made him feel uncomfortable. But the cheque had gone through. More apologies, more buttery invitations to buy fresh goods, but Oscar had scarcely listened. The receiver had remained in his hand while the smooth voice droned on and on until, with a relieved 'goodbye', he had returned it to the hook. Yet all was not well that had ended well. The whole incident remained fixed in his mind like a core of suffering and humiliation and ranked, even in the final outcome, not as a victory but as his first major defeat. He would never forgive Gunther. No . . . And he would never forgive the bank either. If they would only have warned him that they were about to send the cheque back, he might have raked up the money from somewhere – at least it would have spared him the torture of that sudden shock. It was his first experience of the sort, but if he carried on he knew now that it could hardly be the last.

Meanwhile, the Currie name was not entirely besmirched, but that didn't solve any of his problems. He had merely postponed the inevitable for a spell. What had happened to him? What had happened to the business? What had happened to all his money? The stock in the shop must have cost him the best part of a thousand pounds, but most of it was hopelessly old-fashioned and for trading purposes could not be regarded as stock at all. He doubted if any job-buyer would give him more than a hundred pounds to clear the lot, and he had a suspicion that a really shrewd dealer would offer him no more than fifty. These job-buyers were a tough breed; they were as hard as moneylenders if you had to come on to them, squeezing the marrow out of a man . . . As recently as six years ago he had had money and a freehold house and a flourishing business. Now he had nothing but debts. The title deeds of his house and shop were held by the bank against loans, and he had surrendered his endowment policy for the same reason. He was like a gambler starting off at strip poker with a fur coat and a Savile Row suit and ending up in a tattered undervest. But he had never been a gambler – his tiny weekly flutters could hardly be called gambling – and he had never run his household on a lavish scale; why there wasn't even a maid, only a daily char. He didn't drink to excess, smoked a reasonable amount and went to the movies with Matilda once a week and to a show perhaps twice a year, while Pamela had practically kept herself ever since she left school. That was the credit side. Under debit he had to write his disastrous attempt at wholesaling, some hundreds of pounds spent on shop fronts – and Kim. But it still didn't balance.

There was a large discrepancy somewhere. Lately he must have been losing several hundred pounds a year. It didn't add up; juggle as he could, it was now evident to him that in a few short years he had eaten up, apart from a quantity of cash, an endowment policy and a freehold house.

Well, all that was clear enough now, but was it still possible to salvage something from the wreck? Certainly not as he was going on at present, but the Curries were never like that, they didn't just lie down and die. Something *had* to be done about the shop, even if it involved a radical departure from precedent. But what?

A big store usually rounded the week off by having the executive heads of departments gather together in conference. That was a good idea; he had all his departmental heads right here with him in bed. Mr Currie, the proprietor, had the chair, of course, and the question was now open for discussion. What was to be done about Currie & Son? Well, Oscar was the buyer, what had he to say about it? Hadn't he been buying right? Out with it, Oscar, or for ever hold your peace! . . . But the buyer insisted that he had been buying right – after all, he'd been buying for more than a quarter of a century, but there was no longer the money he used to have at his disposal. That, however, didn't strike the proprietor as a valid excuse. If he hadn't the money now, that was partly Oscar's own fault. What had the head salesman to say? Obviously the answer was that if he didn't have the stuff he couldn't sell it.

Deadlock. Oscar started again, and immediately, by a flash of inspiration, laid his anger on the crux of the problem. The old trading methods had failed. He could no longer hope to compete with the big stores, running a number of lines, as hitherto. The only solution was to concentrate on one essential commodity. He was like a general in command of a small army; he couldn't fight on too many fronts. He had to marshal his forces and, when confronted by a powerful adversary, to strike with his whole strength at his opponent's weakest point.

It was impossible to grapple successfully with the stores backed by their huge resources unless he turned his shop into the equivalent of one of their counters, which would at once narrow down the field of battle and, with his personal experience and supervision, give him a decided advantage. Specialisation. That was the word. This was an era of specialisation, and his last hope of survival lay within that sphere. Now, on which branch of drapery could he best concentrate? Menswear wasn't much good, the trade was too slow and the range too wide, and in any case, a number of women bought their menfolks' garments, so it was necessary to please them first. That was the pointer to the whole situation. It was a woman's world, and the feminine buyer was the commercial prize – so the question resolved itself into what should be the bait?

At once an answer suggested itself. Stockings. Salesman, buyer and proprietor were immediately in accord. Ladex ladderproof hose were an excellent example. Customers bought them and came back again and recommended them to their friends; yet he had never run a fully comprehensive range as the traveller had constantly urged him because of the necessity for spreading his purchases over the whole shop's requirements. The profit was good, and nobody else in the neighbourhood appeared to run them. It seemed strange that he had never thought of this before. He should have done it years ago, but it wasn't too late even now. Ladex would prove his salvation. Gradually he would clear out all the junk, flog it at any price, get rid of the brassieres and corselets and old-fashioned combinations and concentrate on stockings – women wore so many of them these days, so many shades and qualities. It would be a bit of a wrench, but it was the only way out, and he had to do it now while his credit facilities were still unimpaired.

Every businessman found himself faced at one time or another with the necessity for carrying out radical innovations, but the basis of a successful business was precisely this quality of speedy readjustment to the changing demands of the market.

He had stuck too long in the same old rut – ninety per cent of his trouble was the dead hand of outmoded tradition. Why, he still wore a nightshirt himself, when everybody else his age had given them up long ago for pyjamas. But no more. From today everything was different, even the nightshirt would be discarded for a pair of pyjamas from stock, while Currie & Son, ladies' and gents' hosiers, would rise from the ashes again as the stocking shop. For a moment he even toyed with the idea of a new name altogether to herald his complete break from tradition, but he quickly dismissed it as blasphemy, lese-majesty . . . patricide almost. Currie & Son would remain, but he would have a sign placed beneath it, 'The Stocking Shop' or, better still, 'The Stocking Box', as a sort of subtitle.

Well, that was all settled. He glanced at the clock; it was nearly seven. He could snatch another half an hour or so in bed until his usual time for rising, but he was not a bit sleepy; on the contrary, he felt marvellously alert and clear-headed. It seemed a pity to waste this resuscitated ebullience in bed when he could be out and about making a start on his new plans, getting them out of the blueprint stage into practical operation. His wife stirred lethargically as she felt him move from her side and step on to the carpet. Her face rosy with the warmth of sleep, she opened her eyes and looked first at Oscar and then at the clock. Somnolently, like a flushed, contented cat, Matilda turned to him again and stretched her arms luxuriantly.

'What's the matter?' she asked, stifling a yawn. 'You up already?'

Oscar smiled down at her. He was suddenly imbued with the lofty virtuousness of habitual early risers, regarding with disdain the world of laggards, still slumbering while they had completed half-a-day's work.

'Already?' he replied briskly. 'I've been at work since five. And let me tell you, Matilda, it's the best day's work I've ever done in my life!'

CHAPTER TEN

Oscar could hardly be bothered much about anything other than his new reorientation all that morning in the shop – this incredulous reincarnation of a businessman. He was already engaged in devising a new layout for the windows, sifting schemes for altering the counters and showcases. He served one middle-aged lady with an underset, but that had not required any conscious effort of will on his part, for he had sold her the same sort of lingerie for so long that he could have picked out what she wanted with his eyes closed. Soon after, two young women had to go away empty-handed, yet he was more pleased about the two customers he had failed to serve than the one whose requirements he had attended. They wanted stockings and had specified Ladex – recommendations, too. No other brand would do, and price, within a certain limit, was no object. If he had had the shades they required he could have charged three-and-eleven a pair with impunity, allowing a good profit for himself and yet knowing he had given them the best stocking value in the road. It merely proved the contention he had so arduously elaborated that morning and gave added point to his newfound determination.

He kept glancing at his watch, impatient for the appearance of Mr Lumley, the traveller. He usually called around lunchtime, the first Saturday of the month, and he was a week overdue already, so Oscar expected him to show up today without fail. He would have an order for him that would warm the cockles of Mr Lumley's heart. Every line he had begged him unsuccessfully to try over the two years they had been doing business together would go on order, everything from eighteenpenny 'seconds' to eight-and-elevenpenny sheer silks.

Ladex were a small firm, they couldn't afford to advertise extensively; probably that was why the smart shops and the large stores gave them the cold shoulder, but Oscar had given their products a thorough test. Ladex was what the public wanted, and what the public wanted was just what Currie & Son would give them in future.

About half past twelve the bell rang timorously. Oscar had his back to the door, but he recognised Mr Lumley's diffident approach. Each of his travellers had his own technique. There was the dignified type, who condescended to take orders, not as though his living depended on it but with a half-aloof air, like a retired City stockbroker doing it just for fun; the aggressive type that bullied you into buying something you didn't want; the boisterous sort that did business in between jokes and race-course gossip; the wheedlers, the dialecticians, always two steps ahead, who had an answer for your argument almost before you had formulated it; and the Lumleys, who sidled in apologetically with a sorry-to-bother-you-but-I-hope-you-have-a-minute-to-spare expression and seemed relieved to slip away when the business was done.

Oscar carried on with his job, as if he were still unaware of the traveller's entrance, until a hesitant cough announced officially that he was no longer alone. Slowly he placed the stocking box on the counter and turned, presenting a formidably stern appearance to the traveller, as though, now he had recognised him, Mr Lumley's presence was not at all welcome. It amused him to see the way the traveller shrank back into his shell, as if apprehensive of a vitriolic attack. He was a small man, Lumley, smaller than Oscar, and very slight, yet he adopted the most incongruous clothes. They were in the best of taste and well-tailored, but they simply weren't for him; his pale, ascetic face was surmounted by blond hair clipped close like a boxer's, and that bristly crop was usually covered by a rustically befeathered pudding-basin hat. He never wore anything but stout brogues, tough, welted leather shoes that were more suited for mountaineering than pounding smooth city streets, and heavy, hairy tweed suits, a 'he-man's' get-up. In winter it was completed by a bulky raglan; yet this whole affectation of muscularity merely served to accentuate his inherent weediness.

'Good . . . good afternoon,' said Lumley timidly.

'Good afternoon,' Oscar replied. 'I didn't expect you today . . . I thought you were supposed to call the first Saturday of the month?' he added severely.

'Well . . . well, you see, Mr Currie . . .' Lumley foundered ineffectually at the rebuke.

'Yes, I see,' Oscar interrupted. 'And I had a whacking order ready for you, but now I'm in two minds whether to let you have it or not.'

'Really! You mean that, Mr Currie?'

Oscar couldn't quite make out whether his voice conveyed relief or apprehension, but, whatever it was, he decided that the pretence had gone far enough. He twisted the ends of his piebald moustache and allowed a reassuring smile to break across his face. 'All right,' he said, disarmingly. 'You win. Lumley, this is your lucky day!'

He motioned the traveller to a seat and perched himself on the edge of the counter facing him. There was no hurry, even though it was Saturday. First, they would have a little chat, and then, out of the blue, he could spring his big surprise.

'How's business?' he asked.

'Where?' said Lumley. The traveller seemed uncomfortable, as though he couldn't quite find his bearings.

'Outside,' Oscar answered impatiently. 'You get about, Lumley. You of all people ought to know what it's like.'

'Well,' said Lumley, apparently having gained some confidence from the compliment. 'That's a matter of comparisons. If you mean the big stores, I don't really know, yet I'd say pretty good, but if it's fellows like yourself you're enquiring about, then the answers in one word – lousy!'

'I'd use another word myself,' Oscar wheezed. 'Something a damned sight stronger. What's happened to the customers? What's the matter with everything and everybody? Why isn't anybody buying any more?'

Lumley put his briefcase on the floor and spread himself comfortably in the chair. He seemed now to be entering into the leisurely spirit of the discussion. He appeared somehow much more at home. The timorousness had been temporarily shelved, but the querulous droop of his thin lips still maintained slight vertical creases at the corner of his mouth and made his habitual despondency even more marked. Yet he was different, there was an aggressiveness about him as he stretched out his arm argumentatively that Oscar had never noticed before, an air when he spoke again that was almost didactic.

'I'll tell you what's the matter,' he announced in his thin, tremulous voice. 'It's this war fever. Everybody's got it. They can't help it when the mothers get new evacuation forms from the schools every week, when one page of the paper tells you to store food, another to build shelters, a third to join the ARP and a fourth to join the army, while right in the middle you find that if you won't join voluntarily, and you're young enough, they'll come and fetch you. They've all gone mad. The whole world's mad, Currie, and how can anyone expect to do business in a lunatic asylum?'

'It'll blow over,' said Oscar. 'There won't be a war.'

'I wish *I* could believe that,' Lumley answered gloomily. 'If I had all the tea in China, I'd bet it on a war – and not in the very distant future either.'

'Nonsense!' Oscar grunted. 'You're simply being a pessimist.'

'Quite right,' the traveller agreed. 'These days, surely, it's difficult for any sane man to be other than a pessimist. Consider the situation. We're building more battleships, more aeroplanes, more tanks, more guns, more submarines, calling up schoolboys, training women and children, and all over the

Continent they're doing the same. Why are they spending all those billions if not for a war?' Lumley shook his head morosely. 'It's all a jockeying of forces, fencing for position before the storm breaks, and when it does we'll all be in the same leaky boat. What's the use of worrying about business – or anything else for that matter? It's bound to come. I don't care any more, I've still got my tin hat from the last war to end war, and they'll give the missus a tin dog kennel to bury in the garden. That's how it is, Currie, that's the line-up, my boy, and in face of that, if anyone can still be an optimist, he must be crazy!'

'Not crazy,' Oscar insisted, 'just level-headed. Last September,' he added slyly, 'you promised me a war before Christmas, now it'll soon be next Christmas, and we're still at peace.' He slipped off the counter and stood before Lumley. The conversation had taken quite an unexpected turn. At all their previous meetings Oscar had usually monopolised it, laying down the law and scarcely listening to the traveller's mumbled affirmatives. He had hitherto regarded Lumley as a weak, spineless creature. Now that amorphous individual had suddenly developed a backbone before his eyes and, even more, was impressing his own sombre outlook on Currie. He had to shake it off quickly, for his grandiose plans did not admit of such a defeatist mood. He gathered the wind back into his sails; of course, business mattered, everything mattered to Oscar, for he was determined to make a go of it. The vital decision he had readied that morning came to his aid and swept all thought of failure aside. He leaned over and slapped Lumley encouragingly on the shoulder.

'Cheer up, man,' he said. 'I've got some good news for you. Before you leave the shop, I guarantee you'll be converted to optimism yourself.' He straightened his back and threw out a hand embracing the room, taking in, in his mind's eye, the windows, the shelves, the counters, everything. 'I'm going to become the best customer your firm's ever had,' he continued expansively. 'I'm going to fill the whole shop with stockings

– with Ladex. I'm going to run every one of your lines exclusively, and when I say every one, I mean it. Nothing's too cheap and nothing too dear; there'll be something for everyone in Currie's Stocking Box, to suit the most moderate purse or the most expensive taste.' Oscar suddenly felt very proud of his peroration, the smooth words still ringing in his ears as if he had just read them from an illustrated brochure. 'How does that strike you, Lumley? Is it an idea?' he demanded.

The traveller nodded. 'I suppose it is an idea,' he answered reluctantly.

'Then get your pencil out, man,' Oscar croaked dictatorially, 'your pencil and your order book. Hurry!' There was no stopping him now. Impatient at Lumley's slowness, he paced about before him like a lion behind bars waiting for a hunk of bloody meat. 'Come on, Lumley! Out with them, man . . . That's it . . .' He composed himself for the order. 'Now, the cheap stuff. I'll need a big dab of "seconds", at least a couple of gross assorted shades, and then . . . then . . .'

Oscar stopped. Lumley was seated before him with the order book on his knees, unopened, while the blunt end of the pencil rapped a gentle tattoo on the stiff cover.

'What's the matter with you?' Oscar grumbled irritably. 'I haven't all day. It's Saturday, you know. Aren't you taking the order?'

'I can't,' said Lumley.

'Can't?'

The traveller spread out his hands impotently. 'I'm sorry,' he repeated, 'I can't.'

Oscar halted before him and gazed down at the man accusingly. 'What's the matter?' he asked. 'Got the sack?'

'No. Not yet,' said Lumley.

'Well, open your book. This is a peculiar way of doing business!' he threw at him harshly.

'Peculiar or not,' the traveller answered, 'that's just how it is . . . I can't take your order, Mr Currie.'

Oscar was flabbergasted. If it were intended as a joke, it was a very poor one indeed, but a searching glance at Lumley's face revealed that the man was in deadly earnest. Oscar hardly knew what to think; coming so abruptly on top of the intense enthusiasm which he had generated in himself all morning to the exclusion of every other consideration, the startling announcement had thrown his mind completely out of focus.

'Why . . . I don't understand . . .' he protested feebly. 'If you didn't want my order, why did you come here?'

'Tell you the truth,' said Lumley, 'your orders haven't amounted to much lately; they've been falling off month by month. I was hoping you wouldn't have anything for me. That's why I didn't call last week and called today . . . I thought it might be easier . . .'

'I still don't understand,' Oscar snapped. The feeling of helpless bewilderment had given way to a violent, thwarted anger. 'Why, only two minutes ago you told me you were sane. Yet you come here for an order, and when I give you one you won't take it. In all the years I've been in business I've never heard anything like this before. What's the meaning of it, Lumley?'

The traveller sighed. 'It sounds paradoxical, Currie, I know. But I can explain. It's really very simple. My orders have been getting smaller and smaller – in fact, my commission lately hasn't been enough to run the car. A couple of dozen stockings from you, half a gross from someone else, all the little shops buying less instead of more. The position was getting desperate, so in a mad moment I went up to the head office of the House Traders.'

'The House Traders?' said Oscar suspiciously. '. . . Oh!' A sinking feeling clutched at his heart; he could sense now the impending catastrophe. 'When . . . when was this?' he asked in a more subdued tone.

'A couple of months ago,' the traveller replied. 'Since

then there's been letters and interviews, rushing back and forth every other day. My boss went to them, their head buyer came to us. Conferences, arguments, bargaining, and now it's all settled. The Empire House Traders take all the stockings the factory can produce.'

'. . . Oh! . . .' said Oscar, dully.

'I had to do something like that,' Lumley insisted, his high-pitched voice creaking beneath the burden of plaintive apology, 'otherwise the firm would have had to close down. It wasn't just a matter of getting a few dozen more from you or from someone else, we had to have orders, and now we've got them, not dozens but hundreds of grosses.'

'And you couldn't spare even a few dozen for me?'

'How can I?' Lumley asked. 'You're a competitor now. Ladex practically belongs to the Empire House Traders.'

'Well, what makes you so miserable about it still?' Oscar demanded bitterly. 'You'll get your commission – make a damn good thing out of it, too! *I* should be the one to cry. I'm practically ruined, and I see a chance of working up my stocking trade, and you come along with your boss and the House Traders and take my living right out of my hands.'

'Not me,' Lumley protested. 'Not even my boss. I don't see where *he* becomes so well off either. Before, he was independent, now he's sold to the House Traders. I saw the prices they offered him and got the shock of my life. It meant working full pressure just to meet bare overheads. To prevent that he's got to engage more girls – at lower wages, of course – and buy more up-to-date machines. They're advancing him the money, so actually it isn't his factory any more; he'll be a manager, a workman like anybody else, and the minute he doesn't do as he's told out he goes on his ear. As for me, what are *my* prospects? You're talking about yourself being ruined,' the small man argued spiritedly. 'How d'you think *I* stand? I may draw commission a while longer, but what'll happen after that? Of course, I'll get the air! What's the use of travellers any more when all the firm has to do is to send an office boy along to the buyer with a shade card?'

He tucked his order book carefully in his pocket, picked up his briefcase and rose to his feet, thrusting out his hand in farewell.

'No hard feelings, Currie, old chap?' he said.

For a moment Oscar half-reluctantly held back, then he gripped the traveller's skinny fist. It wasn't *his* fault, he saw that now; he, too, was being throttled by the same giant hand.

'No hard feelings,' he muttered, hardly above a whisper the words sticking in his throat. 'Good luck.'

'Thanks,' said Lumley. He shrugged his shoulders despondently, starting off towards the door. 'Thanks, Mr Currie. And how I need it!'

CHAPTER ELEVEN

Not until long after the bell rang was Oscar quite aware that Lumley had gone. He stood in the centre of the shop, exactly as the traveller had left him, like a man in a daze, until the full implications of the encounter sank in. He felt crushed and utterly forlorn, overwhelmed by the force of circumstances like an alpine climber marooned on a narrow, crumbling ledge, beyond earshot of rescuers, a wall of smooth rock rising perpendicularly above him, and below a sheer black drop to the ground. This little shop that he had pushed outwards with his grandiose words so that it became almost the equivalent of a departmental store had shrunk back into perspective, beyond that even, to the other extreme, as if he were seeing its puny limitations through the wrong end of a telescope.

It seemed that everything was finished now that his last chance had petered out in this tragic fashion; he had been too late again, as it appeared he had been too late for most things in his life. He had a shop but had nothing to sell, he was a businessman without a business, a spectacle that was probably more ridiculous than pathetic. He had the uncomfortable feeling that he was being mercilessly dissected, as if some higher creatures were having a fine joke at his expense. He could almost imagine himself picked up by a giant pair of tweezers and stuck like a microscopic specimen on a slide labelled 'genus businessman'. He wondered whether the celestial observers got any satisfaction from watching him squirm, whether it was really so funny to note in such careful detail the disintegration of a man and a business.

Slowly he walked to the door and shot the bolt on the inside. He no longer cared whether he would do any more trade today or not. Despairingly he echoed in his mind Lumley's ingrained pessimism. What's the use of it all anyway? He hung up his alpaca coat and, making his way towards the little parlour, stopped before the mirror and looked at himself. His shoulders were hunched as if he had suddenly aged in these past few moments, and even his moustache was bedraggled one end where he had unknowingly, in his agitation, pulled it to a disconsolate droop. 'This won't do at all, Oscar Currie,' he told his image. 'Buck up, man, put your chest out, square your shoulders. This isn't the end of the world after all!' Of course, he felt bad, that was only natural, but he'd have something to eat, and perhaps that would brighten him up a bit. Then he would go back in the shop, and, possibly, by the evening he would forget about Lumley or at least see the incident in a logical light, shorn of the artificial emphasis a whole morning's concentration had laid upon it.

There was a cold lunch set out for him on the table. He never sat down to a full dinner at midday; a snack and some tea usually lasted him till evening when, the worries of the shop behind him, he could sit down to a leisurely meal. And yet he hardly felt like eating or drinking or even sitting still. He didn't feel like anything at all excepting maybe sticking his head in the gas oven, like Jacob. That was a good way out, a quick way out, but it left more problems behind than it settled. Anyway, suicide was only for cowards, the Lumleys and the Rothsteins, and not for men of the Currie breed. He dismissed it from his mind and picked up the morning paper. Then, propping it before him against the water jug, he reached out for a sandwich and nibbled at it idly while he read. His reading and his eating were on the same plane, the sandwich grew no smaller, while the serried ranks of black print made no impression on him at all. It was the sporting page he was looking at, but, for everything it conveyed, it might have been the city column in French. Gradually his eyes worked down the page till they stopped at the list of runners for the two fifteen and could not get beyond a certain point as if a thick pencil mark beneath a horse had erected a physical barrier. Oscar was forced to take it in, the name seemed to stand out so boldly, as though it consisted of the only two coherent words in the whole paper. It was Last Chance, and Kim had underlined it that morning. Over breakfast he had told Oscar of Rusty's win and shamefacedly admitted that he was putting two shillings on the horse himself. Only for a lark, he had assured Oscar, but the older man, taking now a little more interest, saw how the fever had bitten his son by the pencil marks beneath the horse, against its previous form and beside the probable starting price. Second favourite now, at four to one, he noted; showed that the money was on Last Chance. Money . . . Money went to money . . . Vaguely he disliked the idea of Kim betting, but he couldn't very well protest because he enjoyed a little flutter himself, and the boy was like him, he knew, too level-headed to let it get a hold. He liked still less Kim's association with a gambler, and he determined to put his foot down if he saw it going too far. After all, staking hundreds of pounds on a horse was a bit thick for a youngster!

His thoughts drifted away from gambling, back to Lumley and the shop. To be logical, he had no cause to be so upset about it, for he had no guarantee that stockings would have solved his difficulties – but that wasn't really the point, it wouldn't have hurt so much to have tried and failed. To have his plans nipped in the bud like this was so galling, especially when it looked like his last chance. There! There it was again. Last Chance. It seemed to be cropping up in all his thoughts, and, now he looked back, a last chance had been the dominant idea in his mind all morning. Kim had two bob on it, the first bet of his life, and novices usually had a little luck, and then there was this cab-driver who had wagered a hundred and fifty pounds, or was it two hundred? . . . Last Chance . . . The association of words and ideas was goading him on.

It seemed like a gift from the gods, those same gods who, having had their fun, had unbent slightly and were handing him his salvation on a platter – probably chuckling the while as they derided his decision.

And they would laugh still more if he speculated a measly five shillings, or ten, on this divine information – and it won. 'What can you do with such a man?' they would think disgustedly, and they would be right. He had been too cautious all his life. He might have been in a much better position if he had taken a chance occasionally, a really worthwhile risk; at any rate, he couldn't possibly be worse off than he was now. The old canons of business as established since his grandfather's day no longer applied; wisdom and foresight and experience were valueless. Look at Kim's friend. He had turned a few shillings into pounds in a couple of hours, and today it would be hundreds. This was a clear challenge; it was his last chance, too. To the devil with caution! To neglect *this* Last Chance would be flying right in the face of Providence.

Revitalised, he sat up energetically and looked at his watch. It was nearly one. At half past Benny 'Tic-Tac', the bookie's runner, usually called to collect his bet, at least that was his ostensible purpose, but he only came on Saturdays when Pamela was home, and Oscar had an inkling that Benny was more interested in the girl than the bet. Oscar didn't mind if it gave Benny pleasure to look at her, for he knew very well that it could never go any further with the two than a one-sided admiration. Still, Benny was a useful fellow and very obliging, and he was honest as far as a gambler could be honest – within reason. But the problem was where to get that money. His immediate neighbours were nearly as badly off as he was. He doubted whether they could scratch up more than a fiver in cash between them, and five pounds was of no use to Oscar. He needed at least fifty . . . Fifty pounds at four to one . . . He ticked off all the succeeding shops until he came to Himey Golding, the cut-price grocer. That was his man, the only one of his neighbours who was likely to be able to spare fifty pounds in one lump sum. Himey always seemed to be busy, for Oscar never remembered passing his shop once – and he seemed to be open most hours of the day and night – without there being at least a couple of customers inside. He had known him fairly intimately for years, but he had never been overfond of him, especially of late, and it wasn't jealousy, he told himself – it was this unfair cut-price business that he detested on principle. He was sure he could get the cash from Himey, especially as he would promise to return it the same day, and on top of that he would offer the grocer a five-pound note as interest. That would clinch the loan. He knew Himey – a Jew would do almost anything for money.

Once he had reached this decision, Oscar decided to act. Glancing again at the clock, he put on his hat and hurried out, for Tic-Tac would be along in less than half an hour. As he approached Himey's stores, he found himself conceding the man a grudging admiration. Where all the other shopkeepers took care to smarten up their fronts, Himey liked to have his looking like the exterior of a junk shop, with labels and whitewashed slogans pasted and plastered all over the shop front. Where everybody else was putting in new windows, Himey took all of his out and replaced them by roller shutters, allowing the public free access to the shop the moment the shutters were lifted. His idea of display was to stack mountains of soap and condensed milk and packets of various teas all round the counter – the higher the better – and to ticket them with rough homemade cardboard signs. The shop looked like a market stall, and not a particularly tidy one either, but there was no getting away from it, Himey was the only one along this end of the road to draw the trade.

Oscar noted the well-filled shelves as he walked in, all of them bulging with proprietary lines, bread-and-butter stock, certain sellers, as safe as having securities in the bank. Himey was at the cash desk taking money, while his wife and Sam his son, a swarthy, blue-jowled Italian-looking youngster, served. Even during the luncheon-hour Himey had customers. He sat behind the cash desk, only his head and shoulders showing, looking like a very fat and complacent Punch. The moment he saw Oscar a wide smile spread across his face, he slipped agilely from his seat and bustled round the counter to welcome him effusively.

'Why, good afternoon, Oscar,' he said in a guttural voice that rose and fell in semitones like a muezzin, pumping Currie's hand and cocking his head to one side like a bald hen. 'This *is* a surprise . . . You want to see me?'

Oscar nodded. 'I do. Just for a moment. It's important.'

'Right,' said Himey. 'Come this way.'

He led Oscar behind the counter to the shop parlour, a dark, overfurnished little room bursting with a huge mahogany sideboard and a massive table of the same material, with two high-backed chairs and a three-piece leather upholstered suite hugging the walls impinging on the floor space like a crowded corner of a furniture warehouse.

'Well,' the grocer remarked, edging round the table and reaching for a whisky decanter on the sideboard, 'let's have a drink first anyway.'

'No thanks,' Oscar replied. 'Really, Himey, I haven't much time.'

'Takes no time at all,' Himey insisted, handing him the glass of whisky and lifting his own to his lips. '*Gesundheit!*'

'Good luck!' Oscar answered, tossing down the liquor.

'Another?'

'No. Really not.' There was an awkward pause while Oscar began to feel more and more uncomfortable beneath the scrutiny of those piercing black eyes. He began to have doubts whether the story he had concocted would hold water with Himey, and he was almost ashamed to start.

'How's business, Himey?' he brought out at last. That at least was a safe opening gambit.

The grocer shrugged his shoulders. 'Well . . . you know . . .' he replied non-committally. 'And how's by you?'

'Fiddling,' said Oscar. 'Fiddling.'

'At least you make a living?' Himey went on in his peculiar sing-song voice.

Oscar flushed. 'Of course!' he returned sharply. 'Nobody gives me anything.'

'Now, now, don't lose your temper,' Himey said soothingly. 'It's just my way of talking. I'm sorry. I shouldn't have spoken like that to a Currie.'

'That's all right,' Oscar answered, slightly mollified. 'But you *can* do me a big favour. I've got some goods coming in this afternoon, and I have to pay cash. I didn't expect the parcel till Monday, and it's too late now for the bank.' He watched Himey closely as the words slipped glibly out of his mouth, for the grocer's reactions would determine his method of approach. But Himey made no sign of evasion or disbelief, just those two dark eyes kept boring into him steadily without the slightest change of expression.

'Well,' said Himey impassively. 'How much do you want?'

'I'd like you to loan me fifty pounds till this evening.'

'This evening? Are you sure only till this evening?' Himey asked.

'Positive,' said Oscar. 'And I'll give you a fiver interest for yourself. I'll even give you a cheque for the whole amount as security if you like.'

A pained look of surprise crept over Himey's face. 'I'm surprised at you, Oscar,' he answered, 'talking to me like that. Security, cheques, interest – insulting me, absolutely! When I was a young man and I happened to be hard up, I always used to rush round to your father – *ovalashalom* – and I'd say, Mr Currie, let me have twenty pounds, thirty pounds – sixty pounds. And he'd give me whatever I wanted without a word, and he wouldn't even ask when I'd let him have it back. Could I refuse his son? Shall I ask security from a Currie?

Why, Oscar, your plain word's good enough for me – if you asked me to loan you the whole shop that's all the security I'd require, and I'd let you have it, without interest either!'

The grocer unbuttoned his white jacket and delved into his hip pocket, bringing out a packet of notes. Carefully he counted out fifty pounds and placed them on the table. 'There you are, Oscar,' he said.

'Are you sure you can spare it?' Oscar hesitated.

'Sure,' Himey replied. 'And if it's only till this evening, I've a hundred more here, and you can have the lot.'

'No, thank you,' said Oscar quickly. 'This will do fine.' Borrowing the money didn't seem such a simple matter after all. He was in two minds now whether to take it or not, for the ethics of the thing were beginning to trouble him. It had somehow seemed right before. The holding out of interest had appeared to justify his taking the loan, but this open-handed generosity had lifted the transaction from the plane of a business deal to the standard of a fine, friendly gesture, and only the worst kind of a cur, he reflected, would chance letting such a friend down. 'Are you positive you can spare it?' he repeated, picking up the notes and holding them towards Himey uncertainly in his hand.

'Of course,' said the grocer, pushing Oscar's hand away. 'And if I didn't have to pay it out tomorrow, you could have had it for as long as you liked. I've got about a hundred and fifty pounds now – with your fifty – and this evening it'll be around two hundred, yet by tomorrow morning there won't be a penny left. The wholesalers will come along and clear out every cent. Sounds funny, doesn't it – but it's true. Everybody envies me, everybody thinks I'm coining money hand over fist . . .' Himey sighed deeply. 'They ought to know!' he intoned. 'Between me and you, Oscar, the game isn't worth the candle, only I'm forced to keep on.'

'Forced?'

'Sure,' said Himey. 'That's how it is. I'm tied down hand

and foot. I owe so much money that when I went down that part of the city where most of my wholesalers are, I used to skip from one side of the road to the other to escape my creditors, like a sailing-ship scouting for the wind. But I've got over that now because I've found that they need me as much as I need them. They can't press me for money because I haven't got any, and if they close me down they'll be losing a damned good customer. They know they haven't much chance of getting paid what I owe them, so they put the pot on, threepence a dozen on this line, sixpence on that. I have to pay more for every single thing I buy.'

'That sounds strange,' Oscar remarked. 'You know you're being overcharged, yet you still buy at those places?'

Himey spread his palms outwards in a typical ghetto gesture. 'I can't help it,' he replied. 'To go elsewhere I must have cash, and these firms still give me credit, not for long, till the end of the week, it's true, but that's long enough. Everywhere else it's spot cash on delivery, so I've no option. I'm paying more and cutting prices to keep my trade, while the competition's growing all round. Why, the darned House Traders have even got a canned-goods counter now, and they're selling a line of tinned peas direct to the public for threepence that costs me threepence-farthing wholesale. That's what I'm up against, Oscar. I work, the missus works, my Sammy works, all of us slaving all the hours that God gave, and what have I got out of it? Enough to eat and the rent, and apart from that – Chuy-Kuk-Sirreh-Brom. A whole fat lot of nothing!'

Oscar nodded uncomfortably, feeling the money bulging in his pocket. A tradesman's cash. Not clean and crisp from the bank, but bedraggled, without shine, the gloss rubbed off by countless hands, money passed through reluctant fingers. It didn't seem right to take it somehow, creased and stained, weary as if in the struggle for possession and retention it had lost the sparkle of a remote symbol and become the receptacle of myriad hopes and fears. And he was going to put it all on a horse. No . . . No, it didn't seem right. Oscar hesitated. He ought to give it back. His fingers closed round the notes and tautened, pins and needles running up his forearm as though the contact liberated slight waves of electricity. He ought to give it back, but he couldn't. It meant more to him at this moment than to Himey, more to the individual Oscar Currie than to the welded mass of indistinct personalities whose brief ownership had lifted the printed slips beyond the realm of worthless, lifeless paper.

'Well,' he said at last, 'you don't know what this means to me, Himey . . . Thanks again.'

The grocer waved his arms deprecatorily. 'Don't mention it, Oscar. I told you, you're welcome.'

'All right,' said Oscar. Torn by conflicting emotions, he could hardly drag himself away. 'I'd best be leaving now . . . I'm expecting that parcel pretty soon.'

Himey nodded. 'Good luck. I gave you the cash with all my best wishes. It's the least I could do. I hope you double it – turn it into four times fifty.'

Four times fifty! . . . Again that heavenly prompting. The gods, surely, couldn't fail him now. The last remnant of indecision was banished as his heart gave a sudden leap. Shaking hands with the grocer, he preceded Himey to the door.

'I'll see you tonight without fail,' he assured him again. 'This evening, absolutely certain.'

Himey smiled at his solemn promise, half-embarrassed by the repetition. Oscar seemed so excessively grateful for such a small service. The older Currie had done as much for him and more, without in his gruff way expecting or receiving anything apart from a word or two of thanks. 'Don't worry, Oscar,' he said, his voice ranging over unfamiliar oriental notes. 'If I'm not worrying, you needn't. Don't hurry, any time will do before the morning. I know you won't run away. It's time, eh?' he chuckled. 'Time I *should* know the Curries!'

CHAPTER TWELVE

Outside, away from the grocer, things seemed muddled again, and in the short distance between Himey's shop and his own Oscar stopped several times, half-inclined to retrace his footsteps and hand back the money. That a reputed skinflint like Himey could so cheerfully give him fifty pounds without any bond other than his simple word was an eye-opener. It restored his confidence in the value of human relationships, a confidence that had been badly damaged in the disastrous events of the previous few days, and made him feel almost proud of his acquaintances. People in the main were really quite decent; he shouldn't hurt individuals so indiscriminately, even if the barb lay only in his thoughts. Why, possibly even Gunther might not be such a bad fellow when you got to know him well enough. A warm glow suffused his body. In those few moments Oscar felt it was good to be a man, good to be alive, but then, piercing the aura of serenity and well-being, came the harsh stab of conscience, pulling him up and urging him back.

He had read about such things in novels but had merely accepted them as conventions of fiction. Those still, small voices read glibly enough on the printed page, but divorced from books Oscar denied their authenticity. Yet now it was happening to him. Above the singing strings of self-congratulation, over the triumphant brassy paeans of the conqueror, a shrill woodwind clamoured singly for attention. It seemed to sound in words, echoing in his head, a phrase, one phrase, running horizontally from ear to ear. 'Give it back,' said the voice, each word clearly enunciated. 'Give it back,' a statement so authoritative that at its thrusting crescendo everything else was muffled and the whole symphony stilled. It was so real, so insistent, that at those peaks Oscar had to stop, but the feel of the money brought the joy of success rising so strongly again after each brief hiatus, that he was relentlessly impelled forward in spite of himself.

Near his shop he halted for the last time, overwhelmed by a sudden emptiness that replaced the strident pattern of warp and weft in his head, but before he could refocus his thoughts and reach independently a firm decision one way or another, Benny's slouching figure appeared down the road moving in his direction. Immediately all his previous vacillations were resolved, and one idea emerged dominant in his brain. Like a sensitised photographic plate exposed to the sun, his mind instantaneously became uniformly discoloured, the negative revealing no light and shade, no chiaroscuro, merely a blaze of shining blackness with but one imprint: Last Chance.

Benny's hands were thrust deep in his pockets but were restless even there, the knuckles of his slender, bony fists showing through the cloth of his trousers as he came closer, his fingers ever moving, twiddling with a key ring, a jack knife or some loose silver. His hands were the young man's living. Although he was not more than twenty-two, Benny, a racing prodigy, had been a familiar figure for years on every course in England, but the young Jew held the right end of the stick: he worked with the bookmakers, not as a punter. Everybody on the turf knew him as Benny Tic-Tac from his profession as a signaller of odds. He had graduated to that status from being, first, errand boy, then bookie's clerk and, later, hanger-on to a mob of racecourse thieves and cut-throats. There was nothing cheap about Tic-Tac now. He wore a Savile Row suit, and his shoes and shirts were made to measure. His reputation as a 'wide boy' was such that he was always in demand by professional backers to spread round large wagers discreetly amongst different bookies in order to avoid bringing down the price of a horse too precipitately when a big job was afoot. But Oscar didn't know all that. All he knew about Benny was that he was a local boy connected with a large commission agent, a tout like his drunken father, but very obliging and servile, which seemed without question the correct attitude for people of Tic-Tac's breed to adopt before respected citizens like Oscar.

Usually Benny wore a pair of leather-encased binoculars slung over one shoulder and suspended by a long, thin strap; he had never been seen without them, even at the 'dogs', but today they were missing, and Tic-Tac seemed almost naked without the dangling badge of his profession. He wore a light hat and a smart tweed suit with a subdued check design that, below his pale features, his long nose, thin lips and watery blue eyes, appeared almost blatantly loud. Benny had that face and that figure. On his stooping shoulders a garment that would not have disgraced the most dapper man about town seemed nothing other than a cheap reach-me-down, and with his shambling walk he looked like someone who never went anywhere other than a misfit store for his clothes.

'Afternoon, Mr Currie,' said Tic-Tac pleasantly. 'Want to see me?'

Oscar nodded vigorously, pursing his lips to emphasise the momentousness of this meeting and, opening the door of his shop, beckoned the young man to follow him inside. Benny, half-amused by his solemnity and urgency, strolled in behind him and, casually hoisting himself on the counter, swung his long legs before him, detaching at the same time one hand from his pocket and coiling a long platinum snake-chain round his fingers.

'Well?' he said.

'My boy,' Oscar announced pontifically, 'I've had a tip.'

'No!' said Benny, uncoiling the chain, throwing the key ring at the end of it into the air and catching it expertly with the same adroit movement. 'No! Not another one?'

'But this is different. It's something big,' Oscar assured him. 'It will win. I can feel it in my bones.'

The young man nodded, apparently engrossed in a study of his chain. 'OK, Mr Currie, I get you. You're going to plunge. Well, shoot! A shilling each way, what?'

Oscar smiled. 'A shilling? I told you it was something big.'

Benny looked up. 'And you're going to speculate more than a deuce of deeners? I don't believe it!' He grinned disarmingly. 'Why, if old Gabriel was to come down himself and tip you his white nag was coming in first, you still wouldn't put on more than a bob each way!'

'That's all you know,' Oscar grunted impatiently. Currie, burning with this tremendous excitement, didn't understand how Benny could stay so calm. It seemed to him that everyone about him must be quickened to a like response. 'This is the sort of thing that happens once in a lifetime!' he barked.

'All right,' said Benny, remaining quite unimpressed. 'I hope it's good. It must be if you're going the limit . . . Two bob each way?'

Tremulously, Oscar drew out the bundle of notes and placed it without a word beside Tic-Tac on the counter, watching eagerly for the effect it would have on him.

The young man whistled, sitting bolt upright as though he had been stung. 'Phew! All this?'

Oscar nodded. 'Fifty pounds,' he said, his voice wavering slightly, although he tried hard to control his excitement. 'Count it to make sure it's all there.'

Benny's chain dangled comically between his thighs as he leaned over and picked up the cash, holding the notes as if weighing them in his hand.

'Go on. Count them,' Oscar insisted.

Tic-Tac shrugged his shoulders, recovering his habitual calm. 'Tain't necessary,' he said quietly. 'I believe you, Mr Currie. What you been robbing, a bank or something?'

Oscar winced. 'Never mind about that!' he answered tartly

to cover his confusion, for the young man's raillery, resurrecting the voice of conscience, had found his weak spot, like a morsel of food crunched on the exposed nerve of a forgotten tooth inexpertly filled. 'Take the money and place the bet. Can you manage it for the two fifteen?'

'Sure!' said Benny placidly. 'There's tons of time. But you're not actually putting all that money on a horse?'

'Why not?' Oscar demanded harshly. 'I can take a chance once in a while on good information. After all, that's how most of your bookies get rich.'

Benny raised his eyebrows. 'Is it?' he replied. Carefully he laid the money down on the counter and groped with the other hand for his chain. 'I hope you won't mind me talking to you like this, Mr Currie,' he apologised in advance. 'You're an old man, and I'm a youngster, but I was born in the race racket and brought up in it. There's no such thing as good information any more than there's a system for breaking the bank at Monte Carlo. You can't win. You can't beat the book. Take your own case. Never mind about pounds, I've taken from you even in shillings ten times more than I've ever brought back. You can't deny it, Mr Currie . . . Look at it this way. Bookies ain't gamblers any more – if they are, they don't stay bookies long. They're businessmen, they got to be, it's just a matter of arithmetic, being quick at figures. Before every race they balance their accounts laying off money with other bookies or on the tote, so that they must break at least ten per cent to the good. Whatever wins, they can't lose – but you can, Mr Currie. Now I'll give you a *real* tip. Do what the smart chaps do – keep your money in your pocket!'

Oscar shook his head irritably. This heaping up of obstacles merely made him more determined than ever to follow what seemed to him the clearly marked guidance of Providence.

'It's no use your arguing,' he said peremptorily. 'Nothing will put me off. Nothing and nobody. I appreciate your consideration, Benny, but it's no use your trying, my lad.'

'OK,' said Tic-Tac, thrusting the chain back in his pocket with an air of finality. 'OK, Mr Currie. I hope you know what you're doing. Well, what's it to be – twenty-five pounds each way?'

'No. Fifty pounds to win – Last Chance.'

'Last Chance?' Benny looked at him incredulously. 'Did you say Last Chance, Mr Currie?'

'Yes. That's precisely what I said. Last Chance,' Oscar repeated.

'Well, that settles it!' Benny slipped down from the counter and pushed the money aside. 'I won't put it on!'

Oscar was thunderstruck. 'What do you mean, won't?'

'Look here, Mr Currie,' the young man pleaded, as though this meant a great deal to him. 'Keep your shirt on for God's sake – I'm a friend of yours. I don't know who gave you that stumer, but I wouldn't like to see you throw your money up the spout. Last Chance won't win the Torrington Stakes, he won't even get a look-in. Why, he couldn't win another race no more'n Tishy!'

'But he's well fancied,' Oscar retorted obstinately. 'The odds came down from six to one yesterday to four to one today. That surely proves he's carrying the money, doesn't it?'

Benny sniffed. 'Sucker money. Believe me, Mr Currie, that don't mean a thing. People think that if they back a horse long enough it's bound to win – but not Last Chance. Take it from someone who knows, he won't get near enough to catch the leader's dust. Why, I seen him at Brighton, at Epsom, at Ascot and even Northolt Park – and on that form he'd be too slow even for a United Dairies' milk-cart. For God's sake, Mr Currie,' he concluded earnestly, 'tell me what gave you the idea he could win?'

'It's not just an idea,' said Oscar. 'Yesterday a friend of Kim's turned ten shillings into two hundred pounds – and he's put the whole lot on Last Chance – to win.'

'It's crazy,' Benny replied, 'even if it's true.'

'Of course it's true,' Oscar answered. 'Why should I lie to you? And if that boy can speculate two hundred pounds, why shouldn't I wager fifty?'

'No reason at all,' Benny returned. 'Except I don't believe it.'

'Believe what?'

'That Kim's pal won two hundred pounds. Now don't get excited, Mr Currie,' he quickly forestalled the expected protest. 'I been in the game long enough to know that these "wise guys" keep mum when they lose but make such a song and dance when they win that if you hear two hundred you can bet your boots it wasn't more than twenty.'

'But I tell you it *was* two hundred pounds,' Oscar almost shouted.

'Hmmmmm!' Benny extracted a jack knife from his pocket and corkscrewed it in flashing silver streaks through the air. 'Did you see it – with your own eyes?'

'No.'

'Then I don't believe it,' said Benny.

Oscar tossed his head like a bull infuriated by a picador's dart. 'Ugh!' he ejaculated, words failing him for a moment. 'But whether you believe it or not is immaterial,' he brought out at last. Exasperated, Oscar gathered up the money and forced it into Tic-Tac's unwilling fist. 'There. You've got the cash. Put it on Last Chance.'

For a second Benny's whole body stiffened, even his hands remaining quite still, then very firmly he replaced the money on the counter and shook his head regretfully. 'I'm sorry,' he said, avoiding Oscar's intent gaze and concentrating his attention on the spinning knife. 'I couldn't do it. I won't put it on. It would be worse than highway robbery.' He lifted his head, and his innocent, moist blue eyes looked squarely into Oscar's face. 'I won't do it,' he repeated.

'Won't? You've got to do it!' Oscar snapped heatedly. 'You've taken enough money from me – now, when there's the chance to get some of my own back, I won't let you cry off. What's the matter? Are you afraid that "stumer" is going to win?'

'Afraid?' Benny laughed. The whole thing was so preposterous. 'It ain't that, Mr Currie. Cross my heart, it ain't.'

'What then?'

'I'm sure it's going to lose.' Benny spoke slowly and very deliberately. 'I'm sure. Absolutely certain. Now look here, if you can afford to throw away fifty quid, you'd get as much fun and a lot more profit using it to light your pipe.'

Oscar flared up anew, his nostrils distended with fury. 'That's no concern of yours,' he croaked angrily.

Oscar was furious. This whippersnapper was taunting him as though he were another guttersnipe ten years his junior. It was time he knew his own mind. He wasn't answerable to Benny or anyone else for his actions. The cheek of the fellow! Who the Devil did he think he was talking to? For two pins he would bundle him out neck and crop, except that he needed him. Just for this occasion and then no more. In his agitation Oscar glanced at the clock. Precious minutes were slipping by. Enraged, he grabbed the money and stuffed it into Benny's pocket, starting to push the young man towards the door. Tic-Tac only offered a feeble show of resistance, but at the door he made a stand. With surprising strength for a man of his slim build, he planted his feet firmly on the floor and, catching on to a window rail, remained stationary, in spite of Oscar's efforts.

'One minute, Mr Currie,' he protested. 'I'm going now.'

'Well go,' Oscar panted, dropping his hands. 'Hurry!'

'But the bet isn't on,' Tic-Tac said.

Oscar opened the door. 'Oh yes it is,' he replied warmly. 'And heaven help you if you keep that money!'

Benny straightened his tie and bent down to dust his trousers. 'All right,' he said softly, quite collected again, buttoning his jacket and giving the brim of his hat an unnecessary downward twist. 'OK, Mr Currie, but remember, it's your own funeral.'

CHAPTER THIRTEEN

The last harsh reverberations of the bell had ceased to disturb the air, the door was closed and Oscar was alone, but he remained staring out towards the street as if at any moment he expected Benny Tic-Tac to reappear. He felt physically exhausted, his hands were clammy and his knees trembled as though they might buckle beneath him at any moment. An air of lassitude swept over him, permeating his body almost exactly as it had affected him not so long ago when he had descended for the first time from an invalid's bed after a sharp attack of flu. Strange that such a commonplace incident should have so extraordinary an effect on him, but probably it was because he was overwrought. His nerves were on edge. He had not slept half the night, and his morning had ended pregnant with disappointments.

Slowly he turned and moved away from the door. He would have no patience with customers until the race ended. Not until that was over would he know where he stood. Soon he would be two hundred pounds richer, but what could he do with that? Pay his creditors back? Then there would be nothing left for the reorganisation that his shop so badly needed – a scheme that still left sympathetic echoes in his mind. Creditors would have to wait, he decided. A man must live, and Oscar's shop was his life. Without his shop he wasn't even half a man, he was nothing, and that nothing hung on a horse . . . Stockings, of course, were out of the question now, he would have to think of something else. The idea would come, it would have to come when he set his whole mind on it, but it wasn't yet time. First things first. First the horse must win. Must! Must! Last Chance must win, then there would be a time for cabbages and kings and hose and vests and countless other things.

He left the parlour door open and drew his adjustable chair towards it, ensconcing himself comfortably and gaining an uninterrupted view of the entrance to the shop. From where he sat he could see, beyond the thick plate glass, people passing in the street, unknown individuals fussing about their little business; buying and selling, off to appointments, running to lecheries and calling for children, searching for meals, begging or on their way to bed. And Oscar Currie, a sober citizen in his right mind, was seated here like a paralytic glued to his cushion, watching the door, waiting for good news. Waiting, not praying, repeating the 'musts' over and over till he was arched with a semi-circle of unuttered words, an almost tangible barrier that confined him, entranced, to his chair shut off from, and oblivious to, the rest of the world. His body seemed all eyes, all ears, tensed to a superhuman pitch, and every eye and every ear was focused on a centre of activity fifty miles away. At a quarter past two, seventeen horses would touch the tape on a course fifty miles distant, fifty miles as normal men measured miles, but to Oscar Currie, self-hypnotised into this heightened sensibility, all that was happening just outside the window. Away from the bricks and mortar, the smelly drains, the rumbling lorries and belching buses, in a green, clean world of top hats and floral dresses, the shiny, sleek thoroughbreds would come close gingerly and shy off from the starting post like frightened deer. All that would happen very soon, and Oscar, sitting here, was part of it, part of the hoof-beats thundering down the turf, egged on by whips and spurs and frenzied voices.

Automatically he looked at the clock and subconsciously passed the message on to his mind. Not quite two. In twenty minutes or so the race would start, and in a fraction of that time it would be over; a period of destiny peeled at a flash from the unending book of hours, erased and forgotten.

Fifty miles away people would be shouting with excitement, yet before their strident echoes died away, the achievement of an undeveloped boy on a straining horse would crackle through the air, ringing the world. In five minutes the ethereal message would be solidified into printers' ink and pressed on paper, and in ten the news would be on the streets; a race run before a comparative handful of people a long way off, the intimate experience of a few become almost instantaneously the common knowledge of millions.

He looked away from the door for the first time as Kim came in through the side entrance, yet his whole attention was still outside. He seemed to have suddenly developed a dual personality, the real Oscar Currie being entirely concerned with a horse race while his shadow talked for him and answered Kim's questions. His inner self was on tenterhooks, bursting with a feverish expectation, yet words issued coherently from an insubstantial double, and his harsh, wheezy voice croaked on without the slightest tremor.

'Tired?' said Kim.

'Yes. I'm having a rest. And I see you're having a change.'

'Change?' Kim seemed puzzled.

'Certainly,' Oscar elaborated with acerbity. 'Of course, it's a change having you in the house this time of day for a meal. I don't understand what's come over you lately. It's lucky you still come home to sleep, otherwise we wouldn't know you lived here.'

'Sorry, Dad.' Kim flung his hat on the shabby settee. 'Didn't even suspect you missed me.'

'Don't flatter yourself,' said Oscar sarcastically. 'I don't. But all the same you're not a lodger. I'm still entitled to know what you're up to all day.'

'Nothing, Dad,' Kim replied, pulling a chair up to the table. 'Nothing questionable, I assure you. I've been at the garage the whole morning, practising on a cab."

'Hmmmm!' Oscar grunted. 'I'm sorry for the cab.'

Kim grinned and reached over for a large sandwich, wolfing it hungrily as though he were famished. Oscar leaned back and closed his eyes, quivering with wakefulness in the semblance of sleep, at one not only with the roaring life beyond his doors but so aware of Kim's presence that he could sense the sandwich in his hand and almost feel every bite. He had hardly meant to attack his son like this. Weeks ago he had thought vaguely of bringing up the matter. Yet now, of all times, this triviality had emerged as an item of importance, as though he had nothing of greater moment on his mind. The clock ticked loudly on the mantelpiece, and he felt a subdued echoing from his own watch throbbing in the waistcoat pocket below his heart. As the minutes slid past he envied Kim eating so heartily, tasting the food with such audible relish. Man's first concern after all was his stomach. Everything – philosophy, art, even God – waited on that. There could be nothing serious worrying Kim if his appetite remained undiminished . . . Now, apparently sated, he had gone into the kitchen. Oscar heard the kettle being lifted from the stove, the water rolling thickly from the tap and, a little later, the harsh grating of the gas-match as Kim rubbed it into flame . . . And now, suddenly, the newsboy's voice rose shrilly in the distance. Even before it had crystallised into sound his whole body had apprehended its nascent approach. WINNAH! 2.15 WINNAH! ALL THE RUNNERS. WINNAH! WINNAH! . . . Oscar stiffened and sat up as a hot thrill ran through him; every nerve of his system seemed taut and vibrating. He opened his eyes, wide but unseeing . . . WINNAH! 2.15 WINNAH! WINNAH! ALL THE RUNNERS . . .

Kim's voice broke in strangely. 'Can I get you a paper, Dad, or something?'

'No,' said Oscar. 'What for?'

'Well . . . you know,' Kim answered uneasily. 'I've had a couple of bob on Last Chance . . . I'm itching to know what's happened.'

'There's no need to itch. You'll know soon enough.'

'That's right, Dad,' Kim said. 'Believe me, I want it to win, and yet . . .' he hesitated, 'and yet I'd prefer Last Chance to lose. More than prefer, I *hope* so, for my own sake. Damn foolish of me, I know,' he continued ruminatively. 'Not that it makes any difference, but I'm convinced betting is nothing more than cupidity allied with stupidity, and if Last Chance loses, that'll prove it.'

Oscar drew a deep breath. Lose! . . . That was the first time he had allowed the thought to enter his mind. 'And supposing it wins?' he asked quietly. 'What will it prove then?'

'I don't know,' said Kim. 'Possibly that I'm a bigger fool than I imagine. Anyway, I'll soon find out.' He turned towards the door, retrieving his hat first from the settee. 'So long, Dad, I'm off.'

'Aren't you coming back?'

'Not right away. I've got to see Rusty.'

'Then turn the light off before you go,' Oscar reproved him. 'My gas bills are heavy enough as it is.'

'All right,' said Kim. He darted impatiently into the kitchen and turned off the stove. 'Anything else, Dad?' he asked flippantly as he returned, expecting no answer.

'Yes,' said Oscar slowly. 'If you're buying a paper, you may as well drop it here before you leave.'

Oscar hadn't expected it to happen like this. At the first sound of the newsboy's voice he had felt an impulse to jump from the chair and buy a paper immediately, not waiting for the boy to come but rushing towards him in the street. Yet he had restrained himself in those few moments, determined not to budge. Big wins never seemed to come off like that. The last time he had won money on a horse he had quite forgotten about the bet, but, off-handedly picking up an evening paper, he had discovered that his two shillings had brought in more than four pounds. That was how it should happen, and he wanted this to occur the same way, unexpectedly; now the race was run, to banish all thoughts of it from his mind and bring them back later in pleasurable abundance with the added thrill of victory. While he was occupied with other matters, someone would mention it casually, in passing . . . But it was no use deluding himself. He had just now no other matters, the urge for knowledge was too strong and the hazard too high to be lightly forgotten. It was something more than a bet; his whole life was at stake, and he knew that if Kim had not forestalled him he would have intercepted the newsboy himself before he could pass the door.

In a few minutes the voice grew louder, intimate as though it were here in the room with him, then it receded, and after a tantalising pause Kim reappeared.

Oscar could contain himself in patience no longer. 'Well . . . what's happened?' he asked.

Kim smiled sheepishly. 'You were right,' he said. 'I could have waited. And I'm right, too. I've proved it. Betting *is* stupid.'

'Has . . . has it lost?' Oscar whispered, reluctant even to utter the words.

'It's lost right enough,' Kim replied. 'Not in the first three.' He tossed the newspaper on the table. 'Well, Dad,' the young man announced, 'that ends my career as a gambler.' He half-turned and moved towards the door then halted, as though he had suddenly recalled his friend's predicament. 'Gosh!' he muttered, shaking his head commiseratingly. 'I wonder how poor old Rusty must feel!'

Momentarily, Oscar was too numbed by the shock to answer, but fortunately a reply was unnecessary, for Kim, having delivered his piece, had dismissed the whole incident with a shrug of his shoulders and, leaving the house immediately, had failed to notice anything wrong. Currie tried to pull himself together, the blank amazement of his first distress replaced by a bewildering host of conflicting impressions, as though, his entire being shattered by this explosion, all those scattered thoughts that somehow belonged to him had pierced his mind with the sting and velocity of shrapnel splinters. He closed his eyes and leaned back again in his chair, breathing deeply and with effort, a tired, worn man. It was impossible that this thing had happened to him – impossible. And yet the most impossible things were happening these days all over the place to all sorts of people. He tried to mark time while the violent clamour continued unabated in his head, until with intense concentration he sat up, managing to dispel for a brief period the cerebral hubbub. He reached over to the table and with a trembling hand picked up the paper. Somehow he still didn't believe it. He would start again from the beginning, quietly, rationally. He had put money on a horse, and the result was in the paper. Kim could have made a mistake; he was going to see for himself.

The two fifteen was there all right, solid black numerals that only an imbecile could take for something else. One . . . Two . . . Three. All strange names. Last Chance not second, not third, not even fourth but somewhere in that dark cluster of thirteen failures. Seventeen ran, Last Chance, too; the name stood out plainly enough, Last Chance with a capital L and a capital C. He read the words again and again, convincing himself that it was no misprint, assured that there was no longer the slightest possible shadow of doubt.

Gosh! Poor old Rusty! Kim wondered how he felt. Well, Oscar could tell him, Oscar knew, but Kim didn't. Kim didn't know, he couldn't even imagine how utterly crushed a man could feel at such a moment, how low and despicable and worthless in his own estimation. Now he understood how Jacob must have felt when he had taken his life; just like this, beaten and forsaken, with all hope gone, the last standard taken and the poor vestige of self-respect lost. God! It was worse than the most hideous nightmare . . . How the other traders would talk about him, point him out. Why, he wouldn't be able to show his face in the street, the street that the name of Currie had dominated for a hundred years. Peculiar that this should be his first reaction, for it was nothing but blind selfishness, the whole debacle envisaged primarily as a blow at the unsullied reputation of Mr Currie – Oscar Currie, the great I AM. It didn't strike him immediately that Himey would be waiting for his money, he didn't think of his wife and his son straining like pack-mules for the money he had stolen – stolen, a hard word but the right one – money that was compound of their bitter sweat. No, his primary regret seemed to be that a Currie would lose caste . . . Himey's wholesalers would come in the morning, and he would tell them he had loaned the money to a respectable businessman, a friend, and, of course, they wouldn't believe him – Oscar wouldn't either under like circumstances. They would probably close him down or sue him, and it was all Oscar's fault. He had been given the money with such a good heart, with such touching humility and deference. 'It's time I knew the Curries.' . . . 'You won't run away!' How could he face the man? Unless he could raise the money he would have to run away, obliterate himself and his crime. God alone knew where he would go, what he could do, and yet he would have to do something in expiation. Racked with shame and remorse, he began to heap reproaches on himself. He was a confidence trickster, a blackmailer; worse, an assassin, a slimy sneak-thief who battened on struggling tradespeople worse off than himself. Oscar groaned aloud, tortured by this mental anguish; he hadn't been replete with his own misfortunes but had to drag three innocent people down with him. God! . . . God! . . . He would give almost anything in the world to undo this latest, this vilest piece of mischief.

The bell rang, causing Oscar to start violently as Benny came into the shop. No longer was Oscar split in two; he was one entity again, but physically weakened and ultrasensitive like a victim of rheumatic fever burdened by every wrinkle on the counterpane, every breath compressing his ribs with excruciating agony, oppressed even by the shadow of a fly crawling across the wall, its every movement another pain. Slowly, like a monstrous inquisitor, Tic-Tac shuffled towards him, flicking his knife in coruscating cartwheels through the air. Oscar watched him, repelled yet fascinated, mute, but inwardly whimpering like a tortured dog. What did Benny want with him? Why couldn't he leave him alone?

At last the young man halted at the threshold and looked down at the pallid draper, grinning smugly the while. 'Well?' he said.

Oscar nodded, tightening his grip on the arms of his chair. It was unnecessary for him to speak, for he knew that his face adequately conveyed his discomfiture. But Tic-Tac apparently wasn't satisfied. He wanted to have aural confirmation. It wasn't enough for him to see the creature squirm, he wanted, Oscar thought bitterly, to hear it squeal as well.

'Well,' Benny repeated, 'the race is over.'

'I know,' said Oscar.

'Have you seen the paper?'

For reply, Currie waved his arm towards the table, remaining silent.

Tic-Tac stepped down into the parlour and looked at the crestfallen man in the chair. 'Well, what did I tell you?' he brought out triumphantly, emphasising his words with painful jabs of the sheathed silver knife. 'Didn't I say he was a stumer? . . . Didn't I?'

'Wait a minute,' Oscar raised his hand wearily, cutting him short. 'I know,' he muttered. 'I know. I can repeat everything you said, and it's come true, every word of it . . . Please, Benny,' he continued plaintively, talking just the way he felt, like a sick, old man, 'please go away. It's my own funeral exactly as you put it. Now be satisfied and leave me alone . . . I can't stand any more.'

'But . . . Mr Currie,' Benny protested.

Oscar shook his head determinedly. If that was the only thing left, at least he could be firm about it. 'Don't!' said Oscar. 'Don't talk about it any more. Don't say anything. Think what you like, only go away.'

'OK, Mr Currie,' Benny answered cheerfully. 'But first, I got to tell you something . . .' Up spun the knife on its endless circle through the air. 'You know,' he said, catching it automatically and propelling it with two strong fingers on a further pointless journey, 'one day I'm going to be rich. I'll be a bookie. Not a tuppenny-ha'penny one but a big shot like Duggie Stuart or David Cope. You know why? 'Cause I've got my head screwed on the right way, I've got a *yiddishe kopf*. Plenty of people give me bets to place, but, whatever happens, I always make money. If the horse is a long shot in a big field, the gelt stays in my pocket; if it's a good one, I go careful, but I still make money. Sometimes I lay it with a bookie, sometimes on the tote, and whichever pays the smallest odds is the way I've done it for the sucker. The balance is mine. Get me?'

Oscar nodded. 'I understand. But honestly, son, I'm not in the listening mood right now.' He waved his hand despairingly, not quite knowing what he intended to imply by the gesture. His wager was no longer of vital importance, yet he felt impelled to get it off his mind, as if imparting its true significance to a second party would somewhat ease his conscience . . . 'I'm in trouble, Benny,' he said dully, 'and your yarns won't help . . . I'm finished. Nothing will help me any more – excepting, perhaps, a miracle.'

'But that's where you're wrong, Mr Currie,' the young man broke in, bending over him. 'I can help you without a miracle. You got to listen!' He straightened himself importantly, assured of Oscar's attention. 'When you give me that money,' he continued, 'what d'you think I do with it? Stick it on that cripple? Not on your life! I know too much about gee-gees. You shoved it into my pocket, and that's where it stayed!'

Like a green shoot suddenly appearing in a waste of brown stubble, a ray of hope flickered up in Oscar. 'So . . . so you didn't . . .' he whispered.

'Sure I didn't!' Benny returned. 'I told you I wouldn't all along.' He thrust his hand into his pocket and drew out the wad of notes. 'Here's the gelt,' he said, tossing the cash on the table. 'Count it, Mr Currie,' he added mischievously. 'Count it to make sure it's all there.'

Oscar reached over for the money and clutched it in his hand. Still warm from Tic-Tac's pocket, it seemed to have an animate, pulsating existence of its own. He felt he had to say something, yet he was too befuddled to find the opposite remarks.

'But . . . but supposing it would have won?' he said at last.

'Aw!' Benny uttered contemptuously. 'It couldn't have won – not Last Chance. I seen some queer things happen on the turf, but nothing so impossible as that. The only way it could have come off was to buy all the other sixteen jockeys, and the Torrington Stakes ain't worth that much to anyone. Anyway, I could have raised a couple of hundred quid. I ain't exactly broke myself, though I'd be worth a hell of a lot more dough if the old man wasn't so fond of the bottle, and I got a few pals would stand by me . . . I tell you, Mr Currie,' he concluded emphatically, 'when I stuck to that bet, I wasn't more sure of anything in my life.'

'Thank God for that!' Oscar ejaculated. 'You don't know what you've done for me, my boy.'

'Aw, forget it,' said Benny. 'There's nothing in the world I wouldn't do for Pamela's old man.'

Pamela . . . So that was the snag; he might have known it. The rising warmth of his regard was suddenly chilled.

'Pamela . . .' he brought out lamely, 'was it because of Pamela?'

'Sure!' said Benny. 'I known her since she was so high. Even when we was kids I was daffy about her. She's a real lady, and one day I mean to have a wife just like her, a lady. I tell you, Mr Currie, I got a future. I'll be rich. I won't always be tic-tacking or running other people's bets. I'll have runners working for me . . .' He paused, slightly embarrassed. 'Of course,' he continued after a moment in a more subdued tone, 'I know I ain't your class, or Pamela's, but . . . but . . .' He looked at Currie appealingly as the words dried up.

'I'm sorry,' Oscar answered coldly, 'there's nothing I can do about that. Pamela is old enough to handle those matters for herself.'

'I know,' said Benny. 'I just wanted to make sure you wouldn't mind if I took her out one night. I promise you,' he assured Oscar earnestly, 'I'd treat her like she was my own sister. 'Course, I been out with dozens of girls, but Pamela – well, she's different.'

Oscar shook his head, still unwilling to commit himself. 'It's nothing to do with me, Benny. If you want to take her out I'm afraid you've got to ask her yourself.'

'Sure I'll ask,' said Benny, 'so long as you don't mind.'

'No,' said Oscar, 'I don't mind.'

'Thanks!' Benny leaned over and pumped his hand with delight. 'Thanks, Mr Currie. I'll be round tonight, about seven thirty.'

'Tonight?' said Oscar. 'Saturday? Aren't you supposed to be working at the dogs?'

'Sure,' Benny returned. 'But for one night they can chase the hare without me.'

He watched the young man pass down the lane between the counters to the door, his slouching walk brightened almost to something jaunty. He was sorry now he had given his consent. It would have been better to rebuff him immediately rather than to leave him wide open to the humiliation he could expect from Pamela. He should have spared him that nastiness, and yet he could have expressed his gratitude no other way in face of Benny's joy, which had blistered up so expectantly like bubbles of pitch on a tarmac road beneath the heat of the midsummer sun.

The ring of the bell, following on the young man's departure, brought him sharply back to reality. The money was still in his hand. He had to give it back quickly, for the longer it remained in his house the more dangerous it became. The Lord only knew what demon would spring up at his elbow, prompting him to some further foolishness and charming the money irrevocably from his possession. He had to give it back – and right now. Oscar rose determinedly from his chair, dismissing every other thought from his mind. He wouldn't wait till evening. In ten minutes the cash would be back where it belonged. 'Here it is, Himey,' he would say, feeling like a Currie again when he said it, an honest tradesman who kept his word. 'Here. I'm very much obliged to you, but I didn't need the money after all.'

CHAPTER FOURTEEN

Pamela looked at herself in the mirror of her wardrobe. In her attractive new grey pin-head costume, with the flimsy hand-embroidered Hungarian blouse, she was a neat enough companion for any man, but she had decided not to leave the house at all, not even for a walk. It was nearly half past seven, and Dai had promised to call at the hour. He was usually punctual, so that meant he wouldn't come. She hadn't intended to go out with him anyway; she had a biting speech ready instead, rehearsed to dismiss him with a proper sense of his ignominy, but first she wanted to demonstrate tantalisingly how physically superior she was to his other lady love and how independent of his attentions. But he wasn't coming; maybe he had an inkling of the reception he could expect, and all that pent-up fury within her had to work its way back into her system again.

She felt doubly deceived. She had known what Dai had intended when he took her out the day before into the country. He was a man, and she a woman, and all his manoeuvres she had recognised clearly as part of the sex game. That was all right, she understood the rules, but she had held him off until they returned to the flat. She hadn't wanted to let herself go too quickly, make herself appear too cheap. Even the thought of that passionate scene afterwards at the flat made a flush of anger rise to her cheeks. She hadn't asked for those protestations of undying love; she hadn't expected them; he shouldn't have been so adoring unless he meant it. He attracted her as a man, that was sufficient for her, and she only demanded that he be equally attracted without unnecessarily romanticising their relationship. It was ridiculous to expect her to marry every man with whom she had had sexual relationships or even to desire such a thing – why, she would have to become as polyandrous as the women of those tropical sects she had read about somewhere or other. No. Dai hadn't played the game. If he had been prepared to take it as she had done, like a normal affair between adults, his betrayal the same night would not have seemed so shocking. She hadn't told him she loved him, she hadn't sworn she was crazy about him, as he had done, only to find him deceiving her so soon afterwards with a woman ten years his senior.

Dai had attracted her in the first place because he had seemed so completely masculine, even his blob of a nose and bullet head were features that impressed her by reason of their rugged maleness. Then she had taken to the Party because of its policy. 'Hate the Jews' was easy to understand; it boiled down pretty much to that, and it was as easy to carry into practice as putting two and two together, especially when she had an object lesson in the person of her father, Dai's tutelage constantly emphasising that the Jews had driven him to his present precarious position. And there were so many nice people in the True Britons, aristocratic youngsters she had met through Dai, although at close quarters most of them had acted rather like corner-boys. But it was Dai she was really interested in, and it intrigued her to think that her bodily attraction had completely captivated one so high up in the Party hierarchy. He was the District Leader, the golden orator of the True Britons.

She had been thinking of that when she left him the previous evening – rather suddenly because he had remembered a Party conference he was due to attend. She had been in a delighted frame of mind, mentally patting herself on the back, pleased with the picture of Pamela Currie as a modern du Barry, the power behind the throne, when, on the stairs, she had passed Lady Enid going up. The supercilious 'Good evening, Comrade' still rang in her ears, and she had noted how the older woman had reddened rather guiltily. Like a pair of cats, they had sized each other up, both of them immediately sensing that they enjoyed the same man's favours. The office door was open, and she had caught some whispered remarks from a couple of cheery young men before she passed into the street. They had confirmed her suspicions. So Lady Enid was the Party conference he was so anxious not to miss, a woman nearly old enough to be her mother . . . She picked up her skirt, and, bending her knee, hitched up her stocking more firmly beneath her corselet suspender. Catching her image in the mirror, she looked like the girl in the lingerie advertisements, displaying shapely limbs in just such a pose. It infuriated her that Dai could even pretend to prefer, before what she saw, the sagging breasts and spindle shanks of that crusty old dowager. It was sheer blasphemy to bemean himself with that so soon after her youthful body had been in his arms . . . She began to invent a little dialogue to make him think that she had returned last night. She would tax Dai about his visitor, and she could imagine him saying, 'But she's the Leader's wife. I've got to be nice to her. It doesn't mean a thing.' And she would answer back, 'But the things you were doing weren't so nice.' Then he would flush and say, 'What do you mean?' and she would cryptically answer, 'Never mind.' Then he would fall on the defensive if it were true and protest it was nothing. He would try to wheedle his way back into her graces. He would beg humbly to be allowed to take her out, but she would stand quite still before him, and while his hungry eyes were piercing the almost transparent blouse in the way he had of looking at her – a sexual overture in itself – she would say very coldly, 'Don't bother.' She had dwelt with increasing relish on those two words, 'Don't bother,' but all her ingenuity was wasted. He wasn't coming, and she was denied even that satisfaction.

She walked slowly downstairs, her resentment still smouldering, and wandered into the shop. Empty as usual, even on Saturday night, and there was her father pottering about futilely, like a squat old ghost amongst ghostly wares.

'Hello, Dad,' she said. 'Busy?'

'Fair,' Oscar replied, 'fair.' He seemed very jovial for some unaccountable reason, and suddenly he laughed. 'Funny thing happened this afternoon,' he said.

'Really?'

'Yes . . . I had a proposal of marriage.'

'No!' said Pamela. 'I had the idea you were married.'

'So I am,' he answered. 'At least, I hope so, but the proposal was for you.' He watched with amusement the puzzled expression on her features and burst into another chuckle. 'You'll never guess the suitor,' he wheezed.

'Do I know him?'

'You do.'

'Well, don't keep me in this suspense, Dad. Who was it?' she demanded.

'Benny.'

'Who? I thought you said I knew him.'

'So you do. Benny Tic-Tac. That young Jew chap who works for the bookie.'

'Oh!' Pamela muttered, the disappointment showing on her face. She had half-expected some septuagenarian crony of her father's, but this was beyond a joke, it was an insult.

'Did he really mean it? Seriously?' she asked.

'Seriously, he meant it. Honest and truly.'

'Well, what happened?' she snapped. 'Did you throw him out?'

'No, I didn't,' said Oscar. He tried to excuse himself. 'Benny was really very nice about it. He wants to take you out.'

'Well? . . .'

Oscar shrugged his shoulders. 'I told him to ask you himself. He'll be round this evening – but, of course, you won't be in.'

'I don't know,' Pamela answered thoughtfully. 'As a matter of fact, I don't think I'll be going out after all.'

'No?' said Oscar. 'Well, do me a favour. If he asks you, don't insult him. He did me a great service today, much greater than you can realise . . . Please be gentle,' he pleaded, 'for my sake, Pamela.'

She tossed her head with an annoyed, defiant gesture. 'Why, what is it? Am I to be his pound of flesh?' she asked pointedly.

Oscar flushed. 'No. It's nothing like that, and you know it, child. I'm really under no obligation, but . . .'

'All right,' Pamela answered after a moment. 'You don't have to worry so much about it. I won't insult your little pet.'

'Thanks,' said Oscar, relieved. 'You're a dear.'

'In fact,' she said slowly, 'perhaps I will let him take me out.'

'You mean it?' Oscar could hardly disguise the incredulity in his voice. 'You'll go?'

Pamela nodded acquiescently. She had nothing to lose. Better than staying in the house all night alone. Maybe she could shake off this vicious mood or, better still, she reflected, work it out on Benny's thick hide. 'I don't see why not,' she said. 'If he's done you such a service, I don't mind in the least. After all, he's not a savage, and I'm old enough to take care of myself. Anyway, it will be an experience going out with a Jew for a change.'

Before Oscar could reply, the bell rang, and Benny barged clumsily into the shop. All smiles at his entrance, he suddenly became the picture of confusion as he saw Pamela standing before him.

'G . . . good evening,' he stammered, addressing Oscar first. 'Evening, Pamela – I mean, Miss Currie,' he hastily corrected himself.

'Good evening,' said Pamela as Oscar muttered a reply.

For a while there was an awkward silence, then Benny licked his thin lips nervously and turned to Pamela like some gawky schoolboy confronted unexpectedly by a distantly worshipped goddess. 'I'm early, Miss Currie,' he apologised. 'I couldn't wait. You see . . . I thought . . . well, perhaps . . .' His speech stumbled off into silence again.

Pamela nodded, coming to his rescue, although she was secretly enjoying his embarrassment. 'I know,' she said in a matter-of-fact tone. 'Dad told me you were calling. If you want to go out, I'm ready.'

Without another word she took his arm and, smiling mischievously at her father, led Benny into the street. They found themselves walking towards a bus stop before Tic-Tac could quite grasp what had happened, and at last they halted at the High Road where Benny seemed to recover his powers of speech.

'Well, Miss Currie,' he said, 'where's . . . ?'

'Wait a minute, Benny,' she interrupted him. 'Don't be so boiled shirt. My name's Pamela.'

'Thanks, Pamela.' He brightened as though she had conferred some distinction upon him. 'Well, where's it to be?' he asked. 'A show? Pictures? Anywhere you like. Expense is no object. Sky's the limit with Tic-Tac tonight.'

'Up to about three-and-six?' she murmured maliciously.

Benny looked hurt. 'No. I really mean it. You got to understand me, Pamela, I ain't one of these East End schnorrers.' He dipped into his hip pocket and drew out some notes. 'Five pounds here,' he said. 'If you want to go somewhere special and that ain't enough, I'll nip back home. Won't take me a tick, and I'll get some more.'

'That's quite all right,' she answered with a restraining movement of her hand. 'Couldn't you see I was only joking?'

'Sure?' he asked.

She smiled reassuringly. The earlier antagonism was dispelled. She no longer desired to hurt him. On the contrary, she was touched and immediately placated by the genuineness of feeling apparent behind the gaucheries of his speech and behaviour. 'Absolutely! I'll tell you what. Let's go for a ride. It's much too fine to be bottled up in the pictures or a theatre.'

'OK,' Benny agreed readily. 'Anything you say goes, lady. Well, where?'

'Anywhere,' said Pamela, 'but let's get to the West End first.'

By some devious route they reached Hampstead, Benny obviously relishing every moment of the journey. It was quite dark when they got to the Heath, and having crossed over Spaniards Row they walked slowly down the Vale of Health until they stumbled on two chairs drawn up, invitingly shadowed, by a clump of trees a little way from the path, stage-management for a romantic interlude that could scarcely be bettered.

'Let's sit,' she suggested.

For a while Benny was silent, and she could feel him trembling at her nearness. He had been like that on the bus but had seemed to recover his composure, bandying odd small talk while they were walking; now he was dumb again, shy, and quivering like an adolescent in the first throes of calf love, hoarding secret fires that would leap tremulously at a touch.

'I'm glad we came here,' he said at last.

'Really . . . ? Why, Benny?'

'Because it's Hampstead Heath,' he said. 'I feel as if I know every bit of grass, yet I've only been here once before, on a bank holiday. That was with a couple of kids from our street about ten years ago.' The young man chuckled heartily at the remembrance. 'We walked all the way here and spent our coppers on the sideshows, and all we won was a coconut between the lot of us. That's all we had to eat that day, and we had to walk back home. And yet . . .' he became serious again, 'that was the most enjoyable day of my life . . . and this is the most enjoyable night.'

'Is it?' she asked, 'Tell me why?'

'Well . . .' Benny seemed embarrassed for a moment, then

he turned his face away from her and gave his tongue full rein. 'Because I'm sitting here with you,' he said simply. 'I'd be happy just sitting here and looking at you for ever. Sounds silly, don't it? Maybe it ain't happened to you, so you can't understand. You've got an ideal, a woman say, if you're a man, and when you get neck and neck with it, it seems like the sky's opened up and sort of yanked you right alongside the stars.'

'And . . . and I'm your ideal?'

He nodded without speaking, his face like a grey clay mask in the dim light. Pamela clasped her hands in her lap, staring straight in front of her. Funny how she couldn't look squarely at him either. This was the last situation in the world she had envisaged. She had been prepared to repel his crude advances, but this adoration was entirely unexpected, and she hardly knew how to cope with it.

'I'm sorry, Benny,' she said, 'you'd best get that idea out of your head. I know myself. I'm scarcely anyone's ideal.'

'You are,' he insisted obstinately. 'I seen you grow up. You are to me.'

'But I've been out with other men.'

'Well, I've known lots of women,' he countered.

'That's different,' she said. 'I'm not demanding anything of you or expecting you to be something other than you are. You're putting me on an impossibly high pedestal . . . I'm just an ordinary girl, Benny – please believe me – and I've done all the things modern girls do. Don't have any illusions about that, it isn't fair on either of us. Why, I've even run around with married men, too.'

'I know,' he replied obdurately, 'but it still don't make any difference. I seen you chasing about with Dai Phillips, but –'

'You know Dai?' she interrupted sharply.

'Sure I know Dai,' he said. 'He used to work races with the boys, dipping sponges in buckets for the bookies.'

'But Dai isn't married,' she protested.

'Ain't he just!' Benny returned. 'He's got a wife and a couple of kids knocking about somewhere in Wales.'

'No . . . Are you sure?'

'Sure as this is my right hand,' he said.

She looked at him curiously for a moment, then burst into a fit of tears. Somehow, this seemed an added betrayal of Dai's, yet it really made no difference to what had gone before or what had happened since. Benny was distressed at this unaccountable paroxysm, until it sank into him that Dai must have seduced her under the promise of marriage. It couldn't be anything else from the way she was crying. Now he understood, and it was as if a light had gone out within him. His face hardened as she leaned against his chest, her body glowing with a moist softness, and he put his hand across her shoulders, patting her gently like an ailing child. Pamela was glad she had given way to tears, for they seemed to have broken down Benny's reserve. His arm was resting on her shoulder, and she lifted her elbow slightly, expecting that the hand would slip down naturally over her breasts. She wanted him to do that; his hard, dry masculinity attracted her irresistibly. She had forgotten about Dai, all she wanted now was to feel Benny's bony fingers closing tightly round her breasts. Instead, he sat up stiffly and, with an abrupt movement, shifted his hand. He groped at his pocket and drew out his knife as if he had become oblivious of her presence. Suddenly, he pressed the spring, and the blade shot out naked from the sheath. With a click, he shut it back into position and almost immediately swung it open once more. His complete attention seemed focused now on the knife, and, as the blade shot out time and again, Benny shook his head slightly with a rhythm that followed the path of the glinting steel.

'Oh!' he muttered as if talking to himself. 'Oh . . . oh . . .'

Pamela sat up. 'I'm sorry,' she apologised, wiping her eyes. 'I didn't mean to cry . . . And what's the matter with you?' she asked.

'Nothing,' he said. 'I was thinking of Dai.'

The girl moved closer to him, pressing the rounded flesh of her thigh against his trousers as a hot flame ran through her groin. 'Don't let's think of Dai now,' she whispered. 'That's all over.'

Benny shook his head. 'Not for me,' he answered gloomily. 'No . . .' His voice changed. 'How about making for home?' he said briskly.

'Home? But it's still quite early.'

'Don't matter,' he said, clinching the argument by rising determinedly to his feet. 'I told your father I'd look after you. It's getting on for eleven, and I promised Mr Currie I'd bring you back soon.'

The shop was in darkness when they reached Pamela's house. She knew from the preoccupied expression that had isolated Benny on the bus, and still kept him apart from her, that he wouldn't come in. He might linger for a moment on the doorstep of the side entrance, but she couldn't expect even the slight satisfaction of a goodnight caress. The most she could get out of him would be merely a clumsy handshake. The pity of it was that she wanted Benny. The tendons of her thighs seemed knotted together, and she ached for at least the prelude of a fierce, possessive kiss on the lips or the feel of his hard fingers holding her breast. She wouldn't resist; she felt she could even put her arms round him and draw the young man to her body. A tentative plan fluttered through her mind for smuggling Benny to her bedroom if he showed the slightest desire to stay; but he remained aloof and icily detached, and a sudden anger stirred in her so that she could hardly prevent herself from slapping him in the face for his unresponsiveness. Any intelligent man who had been out with women could recognise the signs of surrender, the glazing eyes, the quickly indrawn breath, the thousand tiny twitchings of the body, but Benny apparently was a fool or didn't want to recognise them. He looked at her sharply, and hurriedly withdrew his eyes as though he were afraid of seeing too much, then, with a delicate gesture that seemed completely foreign to him, he bent down and lightly kissed her hand.

'Goodnight, Pamela,' he said and was gone.

She watched him until he disappeared round the corner, then she walked slowly up to her room. She was aching with her body's frustration. Nothing seemed to have gone right with her today – she hadn't even the energy left just now to undress. Pulling aside the sheets, she flung off her jacket and threw herself face downwards on the bed. Clasping the uncovered mattress against her, she pressed the hard buttons of the springs to her breasts, as if she were delivering up the swelling softness of her flesh to be bruised. She lay like that, biting her lips, until the mattress clung limply to her, uselessly infused with her warmth. Then she sat up, shaken and unsatisfied, her head throbbing violently. She despised Dai and hated Benny: she was angry with the whole world.

CHAPTER FIFTEEN

Tic-Tac walked slowly down the street, the same, preoccupied expression on his face, absentmindedly twisting the keychain round his fingers. He had no conscious idea of where he was going; but, after a while, he found himself in Paxton Street, and a little later he stopped outside the district headquarters of the True Britons. There was a light in the ground-floor window, reflected from the inner office. A display of brightly coloured literature fastened on to a black painted sheet of plywood was set out facing the street as an attractive backcloth to the picture of Lord Harkness perched on a little platform in the foreground, a head-and-shoulders portrait, the upward tilt of the bald head and the heavy, scowling, out-thrust jaw posed in a passable imitation of Mussolini. On the side of the door were several oxidised copper name plates, and there Benny noted beside a bell push 'Dai Phillips – Third Floor'. He stepped back a pace on the pavement and, looking up, saw a light in the top window that he judged must come from Dai's flat and, returning to the door, his fingers rested for a fraction of a second on the bell. Suddenly, he changed his mind and, pushing open the door, walked into the passage. Through a second glass door on his right he saw a burly, red-haired young man leaning over a pile of pamphlets on the counter. He was immersed in one of them, and near him was a woman copying addresses. Quietly, Tic-Tac slipped past them unobserved and walked carefully up the stairs. Passing down a long, carpeted corridor, he came to a thin bar of light that shone beneath the entrance to Dai's flat. He knocked softly, and after a short interval Dai himself opened the door.

'Hello!' said Dai in a very surprised voice. 'What are *you* doing here?'

'Nothing,' Benny answered, unobtrusively pushing his shoe against the door post. 'Just a friendly call.'

Dai peered suspiciously down the passage. 'Are you alone?'

'Sure!'

'Anyone see you come up?'

'No,' said Benny. 'I just happened to be passing this way. The door was open, and I didn't meet a soul on the stairs.'

'Good!' Dai whispered. 'Come in.' He locked the door swiftly behind his visitor and put the key in the pocket of his gaudy dressing gown. It struck Benny as vividly as an American boxer's robe, and he half-expected to see Dai's full name emblazoned in coloured silk across his back when he turned.

'You'll have to go out the back way,' Dai informed him.

'The back way?' said Benny.

'Be your age, Tic-Tac,' the other replied. 'You know our policy. It would look darned funny if I were always hammering at the Jews from the platform and was caught entertaining one in my own rooms – above the Party office of all places. You know, officially, I shouldn't have anything to do with Yids.'

'I know,' said Benny. 'I understand. As a matter of fact, there's plenty of Yids I don't like myself.'

Dai nodded, looking very spruce in his purple silk gown and blue leather slippers. His black hair, shiny with brilliantine, was neatly brushed back, and he smelt freshly barbered, as though he had just had a shave and a bath. Shorter than Benny, his voice was very deep and resonant, and there was a grace about his movements that, combined with his pugnacious flat nose, tiny deep-set dark eyes and red ears pressed close against his bullet head, gave him the appearance of a professional boxer about to step into the ring for an important bout. He led the way through a small lounge into a sumptuously furnished living room like a section of a modernistic show-flat.

Benny was astounded. He had hardly expected such a setting from what he knew of Dai.

'Yours?' he asked.

'Sure,' said Dai with a gratified smile. 'All mine. And there's two more rooms like it. And a bathroom and a posh kitchen.'

'Phew!' Tic-Tac whistled. 'Doing pretty well for yourself, eh?'

'Not too bad,' said Dai nonchalantly. He motioned him to a seat and sat down opposite him in an easy chair. 'And you?'

'I'm OK,' Benny answered.

'Still at the ponies?'

Tic-Tac nodded. 'Sure. I keep in circulation.'

Dai pushed a small cocktail table towards him. 'Cigarettes in that box. Drinks on the shelf below. Help yourself.'

'Thanks,' said Benny. 'I don't smoke, and I don't feel like drinking.'

Dai picked out a cigarette from the inlaid mother-of-pearl cabinet and, lighting it, blew a cloud of smoke appreciatively into the air. 'Turkish. Handmade,' he said. 'Class, eh, Tic-Tac?' He leaned forward without waiting for a reply. 'You know,' he observed smugly, 'it's a shame you're a Yid. I could do with a couple more strong-arm boys like you in our organisation.'

'Maybe you could,' Benny answered drily, 'but I ain't doing so bad as that.'

'Rubbish!' said Dai emphatically. 'What can you get out of that cheap racecourse riff-raff? There are plenty of suckers on the turf, but they're not a patch to the suckers you meet in politics – it's a racket that knocks racing into a cocked hat. You've got the whole public to work on. You don't sell them anything, you don't give them duff tips, yet, just the same, you ride them all for a load of mugs.'

'Why you telling me this?' Benny interjected. 'Ain't you afraid I'll split?'

Dai grinned. 'I'm not afraid of you, Tic-Tac. I've known you a long time. No. We've too many secrets in common. Anyway,' he chuckled, 'who'll take your word against mine?'

'That's right,' Benny reflected. 'That's right.'

'Of course it's right!' said Dai. 'I'm respectable, and you're still a hoodlum. But look what I've got out of it. This flat, a regular screw and a snorter of a car with garage free and all expenses paid. Round here I'm a little tin god; I even mix with society, with lords and ladies on level terms. I've got a following now, and if you ever heard me on the platform you'd know why. Nobody else in the Party can hold a crowd like me – I always could, even in the old days when all the spiel was about a horse, but these people I talk to now believe in me; why, some of them would even die for me, like that red-haired Danny Lynn below. And the Party won't stop at talking. We're getting stronger and stronger. We'll take power one day, and when we do I'll be right next to old Harkness.' He paused, drawing deeply at his cigarette. 'Or, more likely,' he continued, thoughtfully exhaling the aromatic smoke, 'Harkness will be next to me.'

'You seem pretty sure about it,' Benny remarked.

'I have reason to be,' Dai answered confidently. 'It's coming all right.'

Benny stretched his legs. 'I ain't worrying yet,' he said. 'You got a long time still to go.'

'Don't be too sure about that,' Dai retorted. 'There's much more going on behind the scenes than you imagine. They laughed at Mussolini and they laughed at Hitler just as they're laughing at us now, but it's no joke, Tic-Tac, we're on the road to power. We've got influential friends on our side. They're not the lousy schnorrers who march about waving flags; they don't make a noise, but they're the people with the dough, the ones that count.'

'So soon I'll be all lined up for a concentration camp?' Benny murmured sarcastically.

Dai smiled. 'No. Not you. I won't have you sent to a camp. Just for old times' sake I'll be easy with you. I'll have you stuck against a wall, with my compliments, and shot.'

'Fine, pal!' Tic-Tac replied in the same tone of badinage. 'But I ain't so sure your lot will be the ones to do the shooting.'

Although he seemed to be entering into the inconsequential spirit of the conversation, these inanities were galling to him, for he had to curb the mounting violence of his feelings, like a jockey pulling at a straining horse, until it was time to give anger its head. As soon as he received confirmation of his suspicions, he would proceed to make a mess of this 'patent-leather kid' with his smarmed hair, ingratiating voice, shiny slippers and music-hall robe.

'Do you know Pamela Currie?' he threw in irrelevantly.

'Pamela?' said Dai. 'Why? What makes you ask?'

'Well . . . I was out with her this evening.'

'You know,' said Dai with mock severity, 'that's another thing will be *verboten* when we take over. Can't have you Orientals polluting our good Nordic maidens.' He grinned. 'At the moment, Pamela's an exception, of course. Anyway, she's easy.'

'What you mean, easy?' Benny demanded.

'Now don't play Little Lord Fauntleroy, Tic-Tac. I know you're not in the habit of taking girls out for nothing. Pamela's game for any man, and if there wasn't a man handy when she felt like it, she'd take anything that looked like one. I'm sure that's why she joined the Party. She's working her way through it, from the bottom up.'

'I don't believe you!' said Benny heatedly.

'Please yourself,' Dai answered. 'I know most men like to think that nobody's been there before, but it's not like you to make a fool of yourself over a woman. Why, there are at least half a dozen chaps she's slept with that come into this very building.'

Benny set his teeth, controlling himself with difficulty. 'And you?' he asked.

Dai gave a tiny chuckle. 'Why should I be an exception?' he returned. 'She's a lovely built girl, and my feelings aren't watermelons. Anyway, she practically throws herself at trousers. She'd even sleep with Lord Harkness, except that the old pansy doesn't sleep with his own wife.'

Benny took out his knife and turned it over thoughtfully in his palm before he spoke again.

'You remember Cherry Carstairs's girl and Nat?'

'Cherry Carstairs?' said Dai suspiciously. 'Well . . . I remember.'

'So you know what happened to Nat . . . you remember how we carved him up?' Benny continued softly without looking directly at Phillips.

Dai dropped his cigarette and sat bolt upright, a note of alarm creeping into his voice. 'What are you getting at, Tic-Tac?' he demanded.

'Nothing,' said Benny, 'except Pamela's my girl.'

Dai looked at him sharply. 'That's news,' he said. Benny sat like a stone, no sign of emotion on his face, his only movement the expressive fingers caressing his knife. 'I'm sorry, Tic-Tac,' he added apprehensively, 'I didn't know.'

'Don't make any difference,' Benny returned implacably. 'You know now.' He flicked open the blade, and his mild blue eyes crept coldly up to Dai's face as he tensed himself on the chair, like an animal about to spring.

'Wait a minute,' said Dai, anxiously watching the knife. 'You don't mean . . . ?'

'That's just what I do mean,' said Benny.

Dai rose shakily to his feet 'But why . . . ?'

Opposite him, his visitor rose, too, the knife thrust threateningly before him, the blade straight and true in line with Dai's chest, held without the slightest trace of faltering indecision. 'You only got her here because you told her you were single.'

Dai flushed. 'That's a lie!' he returned indignantly.

'I'd sooner believe Pamela,' Benny said.

Dai edged round to the back of the chair, but the other moved sideways, still remaining within easy striking distance. Beads of sweat began to gather on Dai's wide forehead as a queasy emptiness grew in his stomach. 'It's a lie,' he said hoarsely. 'It's a lie, I tell you. She knew I was married.' His voice rose hysterically. 'Anyway, nothing happened. I swear I didn't touch her.'

'And those other boys in the building?'

A ghastly smile forced its way painfully over Dai's face. 'Aw, Tic-Tac . . . I was only joking.'

'Well, I'm joking, too,' said Benny grimly. 'I'm going to have a little game with you like you had with Pamela. But you won't be able to play any more games like that with other girls when I've done with you – you won't be much use at that lark any more. And you won't have that lovely voice for long. When I'm done, you'll be lucky if you can squeak like a eunuch!'

'Don't!' Phillips whined appealingly, panic-stricken before Benny's menacing approach. 'Don't, Tic-Tac – for God's sake!'

He made in the direction of his bedroom. If he could get to his jacket, the knuckle-duster he always carried would help him to defend himself. Otherwise, he would have no chance against the knife and the lithe strength that he knew lay behind the apparent inertness of Benny's slothful carriage. Tic-Tac, however, seemed to anticipate his move and closed in on him, forcing him into the alcove against the window. Now there was no escape, only a thirty-foot drop to the ground. If only he could get word to Danny, he would be up in a couple of minutes, but Tic-Tac was moving inexorably towards him, stalking him like a cool, ruthless, predatory beast. Suddenly Dai dug his elbow through the window and, as the glass shattered on the pavement below, he shrieked with all his might, 'Danny! Danny! Help! Help!'

★ ★ ★

The crash of the glass was the last thing Dai remembered when he opened his eyes. He tried to move his head, but a sharp pain constricted his muscles, and his limbs seemed stiff and unresponsive as though the whole of his body was tightly swathed in bandages like a mummy. He was in a cool, cream room on an iron bed banked by masses of flowers, and Danny was standing over him, looking anxiously into his eyes.

'Where's this?' he said weakly.

'Dai!' Danny answered joyfully. 'You recognise me?'

'Of course I recognise you,' Dai whispered. 'Where am I?'

'This is the West End Clinic – the best in London,' said Danny proudly. 'We in the Party think that nothing's too good for one of our heroes.'

'Hmmmm!' Dai didn't seem very impressed. 'How long have I been here?'

'Today's the fifth day. You've had your eyes open before, but this is the first time you've recognised anyone . . . Don't talk if you don't feel up to it. The doctor says you've got to be kept quiet . . . Can you understand me?' he asked solicitously, bending over him.

'Of course I can,' said Dai. 'What are all these flowers here for? Who sent them?'

'They're from members of the Party. And loads of letters and telegrams,' he added, pathetically eager to please.

'I'll see them later,' Dai replied. 'And get those flowers out of here. I'm not a corpse – yet.'

Danny nodded. 'I'll get the nurse to shift them . . . Oh . . . Dai, I . . .' his voice faltered, and he suddenly broke down. Kneeling beside the bed, he buried his red head in his huge, freckled hands, the tears trickling unashamedly through his fingers. 'Thank God you're with us again!' he muttered fervently.

If there had been the slightest streak of sentimentality in his make-up, Dai would have been deeply touched by the spectacle of this mountain of a man blubbering like an infant at his bedside. He knew the tears were the genuine expression of Danny's feeling, and a hard pride grew in him that he could affect a grown man in this manner. He waited calmly until the paroxysm ceased.

'Now, tell me what happened,' he demanded.

'You know about as much as I do,' Danny said, wiping his eyes with a generous handkerchief edged with the Party colours of red and black. He rose to his feet. 'God knows how he got into your flat – I could kill myself, Dai, if I thought it was my fault,' he assured him earnestly. 'But as soon as the window smashed I was upstairs in a jiffy and busted down the door when I heard what was going on inside. Only just in time, too. He was rolling all over you, and you were bleeding like a stuck bullock. Then I got him on the floor, under my feet. He was a pretty sight, I can tell you, and I'd have made a proper job of it if the cops hadn't arrived.'

'What's that?' Dai was alarmed. His association with Benny, if it became public, could ruin all his plans. 'Police?'

'Sure,' Danny answered.

'No.' Dai tried to shake his head, but a burning pain immobilised the gesture. 'No. Keep the police out of it,' he insisted. 'I'll deal with him in my own way later.'

'Too late,' said Danny. 'The cops have got him. It's a criminal charge. But he won't say a word – why he did it or who sent him.' Danny scowled, clenching an enormous fist belligerently. 'He doesn't have to say anything,' he continued. 'We know who sent him. You're getting too dangerous for the Red gang, Dai, and he's one of them right enough.'

Dai was silent. He had been worried for an instant, but he knew now that his fears were groundless. On maturer consideration he knew Benny wouldn't talk – of course, he wouldn't dare implicate Pamela. He winced as a sudden jab of fire shot through him. Hell! It was painful, but he was beginning to see that it might turn out a good thing for him after all. Quickly, he changed the subject.

'How's the Party?' he asked. 'How are things at the district office? Who's in charge?'

Danny smiled. It was just like Dai to put his own plight second and the affairs of the Party first. Always the Party without thought of self. That was the breed they wanted to lift England out of the rut. Men of steel, sacrificing even life for an ideal. 'Don't worry, Dai,' he consoled him. 'Everything's under control, and I'm carrying on exactly as if you were there. We're running two or three meetings every night, and since this happened they've been the biggest ever.'

'Good,' said Dai. 'Anything else happening?'

'Only you,' Danny replied. 'You're the most important thing at the moment. There's even an article about you in next week's *New Briton*, a front-page leader. Lady Enid wrote it herself . . . I've got a proof copy with me. Would you like to hear it?'

'All right,' said Dai, a trifle wearily. 'Shoot.'

Danny whipped out some galleys from his jacket pocket and perched himself gently on the edge of the bed. 'Here goes, Dai,' he said. '"At this moment the hearts of all our members go out to our comrade Dai Phillips, lying on a bed of pain, hovering between life and death, a victim of a murderous assault. Let our enemies take notice now that all their slanders will not intimidate us nor all their brutality frighten us. We are a constitutional party, strongly disciplined, and we will do nothing contrary to the law of our country, rather we are defenders of the Faith and upholders of our traditional freedom as Christians and Englishmen. But let it be clearly understood that we forgive nothing and forget nothing. When we attain power by legitimate means, as we will do before long, then woe betide the gangsters and assassins! All our British blood that has been shed for the Cause will be heaped on their heads. Everything will be reckoned; for every drop of our blood that has been spilled, we will take a bucketful of theirs.

'"While our Dai is lying mutilated, and unconscious, his

precious blood draining away, a creature with the good old Anglo-Saxon name of Benjamin Jacobowitcz is being held in custody. Such scum have brought into English politics the methods of the Oriental bazaar, and where they are unable to sway free Britons to their machinations with Eastern cunning, they resort to roguery and violence, using the weapons of the ghetto sweepings – the knife, the blackjack and the razor – against their unarmed opponents.

'"With a proud spirit and an eager heart, we await news of Dai's recovery, but even if he passes into the Valley of the Shadow we know his work will not have been in vain. Rest assured, Dai Phillips, we will not forget you. Whatever happens, your memory will always be green in every English heart, and we solemnly swear as True Britons to avenge you. With the English salute, the English greeting: HEIL HARKNESS! HEIL PHILLIPS! HEIL VICTORY! BRITAIN FIRST!"'

Danny's voice grew husky as he finished. He was obviously moved. Fresh tears were gathering in his eyes as he commented, 'Good, eh?'

'Fine,' said Dai. 'Only I don't deserve it.'

'You do,' Danny answered jealously. 'Every word and more.'

'Anyway, we can't print that. The case is *sub judice*. We'll be held for contempt.'

'That's all right,' said Danny. 'We're prepared to chance it. They won't get anything out of us just the same.'

'But they can suppress the paper,' Dai protested.

'Let 'em suppress,' Danny chuckled. 'Be damned good propaganda if they do. We'll make the most of it and come out next week as the *New Englishman* or something like that.'

Dai closed his eyes, breathing deeply as though exhausted. Danny was learning fast. Dai felt assured that the Party would hold its ground while he was abed, making capital of his injuries. He had gleaned all he desired to know from Danny; he wanted now to think it over in peace.

'Dai . . . Dai,' Danny whispered bending close to him.

Phillips made no reply, although he heard his henchman very well. For a moment Danny was perturbed. Had he been injudicious in disclosing to Dai the gravity of his illness? Still, he was breathing regularly, and there seemed to be a trace of colour in what little he could see of his face, so it couldn't have done him much harm. The truth wouldn't hurt Dai; he would face it like a True Briton with an iron will and an unshakeable determination; and even if he knew he was dying, he would have liked to hear that tribute from his comrades. Yes, he decided, news of the Party would be a better tonic than any medicine.

Silently, Danny moved from the bed and, glancing tenderly in Dai's direction, tip-toed from the room. Dai opened his eyes again. So they thought he was going to die. Be very convenient for a lot of people if he did. The Party needed a martyr badly, but he didn't fancy Dai Phillips in the role of a Horst Wessel. Sooner be alive and unsung than dead and have a marching song made of his bones. Harkness would like to see that, no doubt. He wasn't a fool; he could sense Dai's growing influence in the Party, and more than once, Dai suspected, would have kicked him out if he had dared. Now, of course, that was out of the question. Dai had become an heroic symbol, and when he returned to activity he was sure it would be to find his prestige vastly enhanced and his power correspondingly increased. Already he was boss of his district. The members were True Britons only incidentally: primarily, they were Dai's men. His real triumph was coming, and this was a steep rung up the ladder of success. After all, they wanted to create a mass movement. They had the money, but it was time the millionaires and industrialists behind it understood that they would never accomplish that through an effete old aristocrat like Harkness. They needed a man of the people – like Dai. Hitler was a painter; Mussolini, the son of a blacksmith. Lloyd George, England's man of destiny during the war, the child of an ordinary lay preacher – and, to complete the juxtaposition, a Welshman, again like Dai. He wouldn't die now. Destiny was ahead of him. From his sick bed he would accelerate the spinning of the web of intrigue. Soon it wouldn't be Heil Harkness but for him the conqueror's triple salute; already he could hear that glorious chorus from ten thousand lusty throats: Heil Dai! Heil Phillips! Heil Victory! Britain First!

CHAPTER SIXTEEN

'Where's Mother?' said Oscar.

'I really can't say,' Kim replied. 'Maybe she's shopping. She had her coat on when she left.'

'And you? Off, too, so early in the morning? I know' – Oscar good-humouredly supplied the inevitable rejoinder himself – 'I know, you're going to the garage.'

'Right first time,' said Kim. 'You needn't laugh. I'm serious about this, Dad. Look at these hands.' He stretched out his palms, already calloused and ingrained with lines of grease, the fingernails cut short but indelibly begrimed. 'From tinkering about with different engines,' he remarked, proudly.

'I thought you'd done with that sort of thing?'

Kim shook his head. 'You've never done with any sort of job if you're out to do it properly,' he said. 'I don't have to know all about taxis, but they're going to be my livelihood, and that's at least one thing I'm going to study thoroughly . . . Anyway, I've passed the doctor. Next week, some time, I should have my cab.'

'Congratulations, Kim,' Oscar tried to infuse some warmth into his voice, but his tone could hardly avoid hinting at the disappointment he really felt. 'So you're all set for your new job. Plenty of changes around here now. Pamela's left her job, too, and taken up a position in that crazy Party of hers . . . I suppose that I ought to be looking for a job as well to make a new deal all round.'

'Job? You're not serious, Dad?'

'Why not?' said Oscar. 'I could do with a job, and anybody would gladly employ me for the wages I'm earning at present – that is, minus a few pounds a week.' He smiled rather forlornly. 'But that isn't good enough. If I'm to lose money, I might as well stay in the shop. I can't see what else I'm good for. For ages you've been saying I'm sunk. It's time I faced up to the truth. You were right. Men like me are no use any more . . . They ought to take us old crocks – the over fifties,' he added bitterly, 'line us all up in a churchyard and shoot us!'

'Don't talk like that, Dad,' Kim protested. 'Things are bound to improve,' he added awkwardly, without thinking.

Oscar looked at him quizzically. Now that he knew he was as good as ruined and was prepared to accept the inevitable, the positions had changed. He had become the fatalist, and the iconoclastic Kim was trying to bolster up his shattered hopes.

'Things *are* topsy-turvy, aren't they,' he remarked. 'Peculiar finding you taking such an optimistic view, especially just now. I'd like to know how you can justify it.'

'Well . . .' said Kim. 'I'll be working soon. All I need are cigarettes and a few bob to spend. You can have the rest – I owe it to you. A couple of pounds a week will probably make things a lot easier . . . About time I did something like that, too, you're no doubt thinking,' he concluded shamefacedly.

'I'm not,' Oscar replied. 'Quite the contrary. I'd rather you didn't worry about helping me. If you can only manage to earn enough from now on to keep yourself, your mother and I will both be more than satisfied.'

'But it can't do any harm if I do contribute to the communal exchequer,' he insisted.

'Thanks, son,' said Oscar. 'I appreciate it, but don't imagine there'll be any profit for us out of that. Your board and lodging would cost money anywhere.' He sighed . . . 'I've always managed to support my family by myself, and it does go against the grain to accept any sort of assistance from children. That's all right for an infirm old dodderer of ninety, but I'm still strong and healthy, and I can do a day's work with anyone –

if I had the work. For all that your wages will be welcome, I could have done without your money – it doesn't make all that much difference. The shop's slipped too far. I'd have managed to support you a while longer. Losing so much, I could afford to lose a bit more every week – it isn't my money, anyhow; it belongs to my creditors,' he forced himself to admit grimly. 'But all that scheming would have been worth the trouble if at the end I saw you in a job more suitable to your education.'

'Sorry, Dad,' Kim answered. 'I don't agree with you. I've got the most suitable sort of job right now. As a matter of fact, it's only since I've mixed with the boys at the garage that I've discovered I haven't had any education at all.'

Oscar gestured resignedly with his hands. 'I can't stick my head on your shoulders,' he mumbled regretfully, 'but I'm afraid you'll be sorry later.'

'I don't think so,' Kim said. 'Anyway, Dad, keep your pecker up.'

Currie nodded. 'I'll try, son . . . But it's hard with a fresh batch of bills stuck in my face every other day. And I've got to get some money from somewhere . . . Well,' he brought out reluctantly, 'I suppose the only thing left is to have another shot at the bank.'

'I wish you luck, Dad,' Kim returned sceptically, 'if you think it's going to do you any good.'

'Oh, I'm pretty sure I'll get some money out of them. The manager is an old friend of mine.'

'Friend!' Kim ejaculated sarcastically, forgetting himself for an instant. He had intended to humour his father, to agree with him about everything in order to make things easier, but this sudden attachment to banks got up his nostrils, 'Friend . . . like hell he is! He doesn't do you any favours!'

'Indeed he does,' said Oscar. 'I don't know what I'd have done without him.'

'Without him you'd still own your own shop and your

house and your stock,' Kim replied in the same acrimonious tone. 'You can be certain that he sees he has damned good security before he lets a farthing go the wrong side of his grille. Now *there's* a career. Banking, the goal of small men with single-track minds, obsessed with how to make money and how to keep it – and in reality the whole thing's a gigantic confidence trick. People beg the banks to look after their money for them, and if they're lucky they get back one and a half per cent interest, but if they have to come to the banks for cash they are loaned someone else's and charged five per cent for the accommodation. And all the time the banks are financing oil wells and insurance companies and real-estate deals and moving pictures – with their clients' money. If those speculations are remunerative the banks profit, and if they're not the customers suffer. They're not philanthropists, they're hard businessmen. They know you're on the rocks and that they hold every scrap of collateral you can put up, so if you expect to get another penny out of them, you're mistaken.'

Oscar shrugged his shoulders. 'From the way you spoke before I thought you'd reformed. Now I see that you're still suffering from the same disease – knowing all there is about everything and talking too much about it.'

'Well,' said Kim, 'I hope I'm wrong. Anyway, I wish you success. I mean it, sincerely.' He moved to the door. 'Don't keep any food for me. I don't know when I'll be back.'

Oscar looked at his watch. It was nine thirty. The bank had been open since nine, and, although the manager was not obliged to turn up until an hour later, being a conscientious servant he was probably there already. The difficulty lay in approaching him, but as he walked out of the shop Oscar hit on a scheme that would bring him some money immediately or else lead him straight to the manager's private office. The bank was at the bottom of the street, in the High Road. Oscar remembered when its whole business was transacted in the two tiny ground-floor rooms of a cottage, the former manager living above the premises. Now, instead of one assistant the manager had ten, including a couple of lady clerks and an adding machine. It testified to the business development of the neighbourhood, and Oscar felt a glow of pride in the knowledge that the Curries had played no insignificant role in that rapid growth. They were part of this city, part of these streets, as he was. Even dead, they were still alive in the century-old shop that stood as a monument to their industry and perspicacity, while he was their chosen representative carrying on the same mercantile tradition.

As he pushed open the heavy glass door, the reception from the clerks did nothing to dispel the feeling of gratification that had sustained him on the short journey. Those that noticed his entrance beamed on him obsequiously, murmuring politely 'Good morning, Mr Currie', or merely smiling if they were some distance away. Oscar was prepared by now to dismiss the incident of the returned cheque. It was probably a mistake after all, for everybody was so conspicuously courteous, as befitted the acknowledgment of a client in good standing. He walked unhesitatingly up to the cashier's grille.

'Good morning,' he said.

The cashier smiled as he recognised him. 'Oh, good morning, Mr Currie.'

Unhurriedly, Oscar drew out his cheque-book and wrote a cheque for fifteen pounds, made payable to himself in cash. He slipped it under the grille and waited to see what would happen. They had never before queried a cheque that he had drawn on himself, and he had changed hundreds in this manner; but if it came to that, he had never, until that solitary occasion a fortnight back, had a cheque returned RD either. Anyway, he would know in a minute whether that was really an error or if he would have to start pleading with the manager again for a further accommodation.

'Pound notes?' asked the cashier, turning the cheque over casually to see if it was properly endorsed.

'Please,' said Oscar.

He smiled. It looked very much as though the scheme would work without the necessity of a painful interview in the manager's sanctum, but, as the cashier bent down to open his drawer, the head clerk, Stannard, came over and, after saluting Oscar respectfully, whispered something in his colleague's ear. The cashier straightened himself and, flashing a sharp glance at Oscar, handed the cheque to the chief clerk.

'Just a moment, Mr Currie,' said Stannard. 'Won't keep you a jiffy.'

He hurried off to the manager's room, bearing the strip of paper in his out-thrust hand like a banner, while the cashier, avoiding Oscar's eyes, busied himself about his desk. A few minutes later Stannard returned, still smiling ingratiatingly, but without the cheque.

'Would you please come through to Mr Lyon's office?'

'Certainly,' said Oscar. 'Thank you very much.'

Although he had expected the summons, he felt a chill of nervousness shoot through him. He knew that the moment he entered the office he would be reduced to a quivering state almost bordering on apprehension, but he knew equally well that after the first few minutes he would collect himself and be at ease again. He was a businessman, a Currie, and the manager by comparison a traditionless upstart. He recalled the fact that his father had been the very first customer this branch had had and, nodding to Stannard, he walked calmly enough towards the office and opened the door.

It was a small room, the only furniture a large table littered with important-looking documents, a filing cabinet and three chairs, the only decoration a framed certificate on the wall testifying, in bold copperplate, that Charles Peter Lyon was the accredited representative of the XYZ Assurance Society. The manager greeted him with a smile. He was a tall, spare man with soft white hair and handsome aquiline features, too youthful looking for the years his snowy hair betokened.

Rising to his feet, he leaned across the table and shook Oscar's hand.

'Good morning, Currie,' he said.

'Good morning.'

'Take a seat.' The manager waved him to a seat and sat down himself. First rapping thoughtfully on the table, he picked up the cheque and held it towards Oscar. 'Now what's the idea?' he said in a severe yet friendly tone. 'You didn't expect to get away with this, did you?'

'The cheque?' Oscar pretended not to understand. 'What do you mean?'

'Now come, Currie.' The manager frowned. 'You know as well as I do that you're hopelessly overdrawn already. You didn't really think this would go through, did you? . . . Anyway,' he continued, without waiting for a reply, 'I'm glad you've come. I'd have sent for you in any case either today or tomorrow.'

'Well, I'm here,' said Oscar, quite unperturbed now the initial nervousness had worn away. His interviews with the bank manager always commenced in this atmosphere of chilly discomfiture and usually ended with warm handshakes and a substantial addition to his overdraft. 'What's the trouble, Mr Lyon?'

'I'll get to the point at once,' Lyon answered briskly. 'Your account is in a very bad state – so bad that our inspector gave me hell about it. The trouble is that your obligations are way ahead of the security we hold.'

'I can't be so terribly behind, surely?'

'You are. Look at your passbook. As a matter of fact, I've allowed you too much latitude in the past. I had the Devil of a job convincing the inspector that you were an old and valued customer, but I'm afraid that won't hold water any more.'

'There's my house and shop – freehold,' Oscar protested. 'Those deeds are worth much more than you originally loaned me against them.'

Lyon shook his head. 'On the contrary, Currie, they're

worth a lot less. Property doesn't fetch a tinker's cuss these days, and you know it. Who's going to buy property when there's a war expected every weekend? Anyhow, your premises are donkey's years old – if a decent-sized bomb fell half a mile away the concussion would blow them down like a pack of cards.'

'Possibly,' Oscar admitted. 'But there's no war yet – and it's still a business.'

'You mean it *was*,' the manager interjected. Oscar winced. 'I can't help being blunt,' Lyon apologised, 'but you've got to understand the position. In any case, it's at the wrong end of the road to be of value even as a building site.'

'But the goodwill . . . ?'

'Tch!' The manager clicked his tongue with a little gesture of annoyance. 'Goodwill! You know as well as I do that your goodwill isn't worth tuppence!'

'Not even if we've been there for a hundred years?'

'A hundred years!' Lyon laughed derisively. 'What does that mean, sentiment aside? . . . I'll tell you. Precisely nothing! Your shop could have been established five hundred years, if that were possible, and if someone opened up right next door to you and was a ha'penny cheaper on anything, they'd get all your trade, five hundred years' reputation notwithstanding, even if the customers liked you and hated your rival like poison.' He sat up, thoughtfully fingering the cheque, while Oscar, opposite him, seemed to be wilting away, battered by this ruthless attack that made his shop appear as nought, reduced his family to the stature of nonentities and made him feel like a bedraggled charwoman before a board of directors. 'This is the point, Currie,' he continued forcefully. 'You've got to get your overdraft down. You must reduce it within a month or I'll get it in the neck, too.' The manager unbent slightly. 'Not a lot, old chap – something, anything – even a few pounds just to show you're trying to pay . . . I hate talking like this to you, Currie, but it's for your own benefit.

Otherwise, we'll give you ample notice, but we shall have to foreclose.'

'. . . Foreclose . . .' Oscar muttered. 'Oh!'

There was a painful silence before the manager spoke again. 'There is a way out, of course,' he suggested. 'How about your brother . . . couldn't you approach him?'

'I suppose I could,' Oscar admitted grudgingly.

'Well, why don't you, man?' Lyon demanded. 'All we need is Spencer Currie's signature, and you can have all the money in the bank.'

'You haven't enough here to make me do that,' Oscar returned harshly. 'There are some things even a desperate man won't do for money.'

'And asking your brother a favour is one . . . even if your very livelihood depends on it?'

Oscar rose to his feet. 'Even so.'

'Well,' said Lyon. 'I suppose you know best.' He glanced again at the cheque, and with a brisk, decisive movement tore it across and, screwing it in his fist, flung it into the waste-paper basket. 'Useless,' he remarked. 'Another tuppence wasted.' He rose from behind the table and approached Oscar. 'One thing more,' the manager said gently. 'I'll give you a tip, Currie. I shouldn't distribute any more cheques for a while, if I were you, or bank any money to meet them, because we can hold the cash you deposit against your overdraft, a procedure to which we are legally entitled . . . Mind you,' he smiled, 'I don't say we will take that action, but if the inspector happens to drop in, he might insist that we do.'

Going out, Oscar was hardly aware of the clerks watching his departure. He was no longer interested in their reactions. For all he knew they might still be smiling, but he knew of the bank's official attitude from the most authoritative source. In other words, he had been told very diplomatically that his account was worthless and had best remain dormant. Several people brushed past him at the door, tradesmen deferentially acknowledging him, but he passed into the street quite oblivious of these encounters.

Begirt by the bustle of traffic and the murmur of pedestrians, his mind was still confined to the cold cubicle he had so recently vacated, and only when he bumped into a stout lady carrying a shopping basket did he come to his senses and readjust himself to his new surroundings. Things seemed to be going on in the same old way; his troubles hadn't the slightest effect on the outside world. Shops were open and people were buying; buses and trams were rolling along as usual. In this world of live people he seemed to be the only dead man . . . A car drew up to the gutter and delivered a bundle of papers to the newsboy. Glancing at the chassis, Oscar saw a placard affixed to the polished side: 'DAI PHILLIPS – LATEST . . .' Perhaps he was dead, too, cut off from all this tremendous activity. That was a queer business altogether, Pamela and Phillips and Benny. It had happened on Saturday, the same night, but Oscar couldn't quite connect it up. It was as if a tiny link were missing somewhere within reach but just eluding the grasp of his mind. Until he stumbled on that clue, the whole affair would remain incomprehensible. Anyway, he would worry about that some other time. The facts were that Phillips was dying, or dead, and Benny held in custody. It occurred to him that he might even have stooped so low as to ask for financial assistance from Benny. He knew from last week's experience how easy that would have been, but he was in jail now, and that was impossible. For that small mercy he was truly thankful; it showed the full extent of his moral degeneration for him merely to think of such questionable devices . . . Now he had received his quietus from the bank. He was finished. Nothing could save him now, excepting, perhaps, a war. The thought stirred uneasily in him, even hopefully. Everybody knew that a war was imminent; it might break out today, tomorrow. If it was only a matter of time why didn't they get it over now and done with? Start off the cannons and fight, stop fraying each other's nerves with continual threats and mobilisations. Then the government would have to enforce a moratorium, wipe out all business debts. He would join up again, and gladly. That was a business he understood and was proficient at, he thought bitterly, killing men. But at least he would be fighting for *something* and would have weapons to defend himself . . . As the wife of an officer Matilda would receive a good allowance, and she could carry on in the shop herself . . . He shuddered. His mind was being warped; this was but one step removed from madness and bestiality. He was prepared to face that senseless carnage and slaughter again, to see young brains splattered over barbed wire, and young bodies disembowelled and blown sky high, women mutilated and helpless children torn limb from limb – all that rather than quietly admit the reality that Currie & Son was doomed.

Pulling down the blinds, he opened the shop and automatically changed into his alpaca jacket. Then he walked wearily into the parlour, where he found Matilda seated before the table drinking a cup of tea. The familiar, homely spectacle momentarily soothed his nerves, but her first utterance set him on edge again.

'You've opened rather late this morning,' she remarked, setting down the cup.

'Late!' said Oscar bitterly. 'For all the trade I'm doing I might just as well not open at all.' He sat down heavily on his adjustable chair. 'I've just come from the bank,' he told her.

'Well?'

Oscar threw up his hands. 'Nothing doing. In fact, I was given to understand that if I closed my account they wouldn't raise too many objections about it . . . Well, I half-expected it anyway.' He tried to change the subject; he felt he had had enough of it for one morning. 'And where have you been? . . . Shopping?'

'No. I've been at the accountant's.'

'Holmgren's?'

'Yes. He's had the books there for over a week.'

'Well,' said Oscar, 'what did he say?'

'First, tell me how much your stock is worth.'

'Say eight hundred or a thousand pounds,' Oscar answered unconvincingly.

'I asked how much it's worth,' Matilda returned sharply, 'not what it costs.'

'Worth?' Oscar shrugged his shoulders. 'Depends on who wants it. Maybe a hundred pounds, maybe fifty . . . maybe nothing at all.'

'I thought so,' said Matilda. 'If your stock is valueless, you're insolvent.'

Oscar lit a cigarette. He knew he shouldn't smoke so much because it brought on recurrent spasms of his old war complaint, but he couldn't help himself. Lately he had been neglecting his pipe and smoking far too many cigarettes. He felt the tightness gathering in his chest, the mucus choking his weakened larynx and his hoarseness becoming more pronounced, but he continued mechanically to drug himself with tobacco although its soothing effect was negligible, the indulgence bringing him merely a headache, a bitter taste in his mouth and a correspondingly significant hole in his pocket.

'Did you hear what I said?' Matilda repeated. 'You're insolvent, Oscar.'

'I know,' he answered calmly. 'I've known for a long time.'

'Well, why didn't you tell me?' she demanded.

'Why should I?' he croaked. 'It's not news. I've been insolvent for years. But so are most of the traders in this street, yet they still carry on.'

'That's the trouble,' Matilda broke in. 'Holmgren says you can't carry on any longer.'

'Yes,' said Oscar, 'I know that, too.'

'For God's sake stop puffing like a chimney!' she interrupted testily as his face reddened and he started to cough. 'It's serious, Oscar. What are you going to do?'

He waited till the bout subsided and, spitting the phlegm into his handkerchief, calmly replaced the cigarette in his mouth. 'I . . . well, I don't really know,' he admitted, at last.

Matilda laid her broad, capable hand on the table and leaned slightly towards him. 'Listen, dear,' she said, 'it's no use attempting to carry on like this. I know what you're going through, and I won't let you do it any longer. You've never been a coward, Oscar; you've got to face up to the situation like a man. Explain the position to your creditors. After all, they can't hang you for owing people money.'

He shook his head. 'That's true, they can't hang me, but they can despise me – and they will.' Involuntarily, tears sprang to his eyes. Matilda couldn't understand this; it was beyond all reason, a matter of feeling. To her it was just a problem of cash, but to Oscar it was more even than the dishonouring of a name; it was an affair that seemed to strike deep down into the secret sources of his blood. 'I'm a Currie,' he said morosely, 'and I've let them down, the people who trusted me. To me that's worse than dangling at the end of a rope. It unnerves me even to think of telling them. Why, Matilda, I'd sooner die a dozen times than have to show up at a bankruptcy court once.'

She stretched her warm hand across the table and laid it on his trembling fist. His head was bowed, as though the spectre of Carey Street rising before him made him ashamed to face even his own wife. 'It may not come to that, Oscar,' she said, soothingly. 'It all depends on your creditors. Perhaps you can come to some arrangement with them.'

'What arrangement?' he asked hopelessly. 'I can't pay – and that's all there is to it!'

'Not quite. They may offer to help you in some way.' Matilda tried to speak brightly, although her thoughts belied her words. 'That's been known to happen before,' she said, 'and your past record is certainly in your favour.'

'When a tradesman can't pay, nothing's in his favour.'

'But still,' Matilda insisted, 'you owe the money, and if you can't pay you've got to tell your creditors so. You can act like a businessman even if you are insolvent.'

'All right,' Oscar agreed with a sigh. According to the ethics of commercial conduct she was correct. That was the one thing that reconciled him to this decision; if a Currie went down, at least he would sink with flying colours. 'All right,' he repeated firmly. 'It's no use putting it off any longer, I suppose. What did Holmgren recommend?'

'Call a private meeting of creditors.'

'Very well,' said Oscar. It didn't matter now. 'You can arrange that with Holmgren.'

Matilda straightened herself and picked up her tea with an air of relief. 'I've already done so,' she said quietly. 'The letters have gone out. They'll all be here on Wednesday evening.'

CHAPTER SEVENTEEN

'And that, gentlemen, is the position,' Forsythe Holmgren concluded. He placed his typewritten sheet of notes between the pages of the ledger and closed it perfunctorily. 'If there are any questions, Mr Currie or I will be glad to answer them.'

He sat down with a bored expression on his rubicund lace. He was a small, stout man in the early forties, who looked more like a prosperous pork butcher than a shrewd and successful accountant. Mr Holmgren presided at the head of the table; on his right was Martin Berg, a Houndsditch warehouseman, and on his left Josiah Rayling of Rayling's Interlock. Opposite were two more creditors, Houghton and Gunther, while Oscar himself leaned uneasily against the mantelpiece, drawing nervously at cigarette after cigarette and throwing them half-smoked into the empty grate. They were gathered in the top front room, in the slightly musty odour of a chamber not often used and infrequently aired that affected them as though they themselves were just such old-fashioned pieces as the spired and mirrored furniture that stood around firmly implanted with all the dull and heavy solidity of pre-war middle-class pretentiousness.

Matilda had had some qualms about allowing the meeting to take place there, but, as Oscar insisted that it must be absolutely private and refused even to allow her to be present, she had been forced to give way. All the time they were upstairs, Matilda, seated in the little shop parlour below, had them constantly in mind. She wondered what was happening, worried not so much now about Oscar, for she was confident that he had everything to gain from this meeting, but more concerned with the danger of having half a dozen untidy men loose in her best – her only respectable – room, free to scatter tobacco ash all over the place and littering cigarette butts on, maybe even burning, her cherished Axminster carpet. It was by no means new – in fact, it was very nearly twenty years old – but Matilda had nursed it with such unscrupulous attention that from a cursory glance it might have been bought just a few months ago. Even Oscar seemed impregnated with the room's significance as the cherished symbol of impeccable respectability, for as he watched Holmgren light a cigarette and flick the spent match carelessly on the carpet, he had an impulse to bend down and pick it up in order to deposit it in the proper place. He controlled himself, however, and lit another cigarette himself. At the beginning of the meeting he had fussed around unobtrusively picking up matches and scraps of paper but had quickly given up the unequal combat which he soon felt was making him appear ridiculous, although nobody had actually noticed his preoccupation. He knew he should be ashamed of himself for worrying about such trifles at a time when he was on trial for his commercial life, but so many years of restraint were associated with this room that he found it difficult, almost impossible, to adjust his mind to a proper perspective, to realise that the carpet didn't matter so much, that the important thing now was no longer the room, but these five solemn men.

Holmgren waited patiently for questions. He didn't really expect many, for the brief statement of affairs he had presented was a very convincing document. In any case, this didn't seem like a creditors' meeting; it had more the appearance of a family conference. He had sent out fourteen letters to creditors; some hadn't even bothered to answer, and only these four had come to the meeting – without a single solicitor between the lot of them! He was sorry about that, for he enjoyed nothing better than a tussle with the law. Holmgren's chief clerk was a former solicitor, and, having learned most of the tricks from him, Holmgren had become an adept at punching artistic holes in the loosely woven fabric of the bankruptcy Acts. It gave him extreme pleasure, when he had hidden assets, to fight like a hawk to keep them concealed from his professional enemies – the solicitors. They couldn't catch him out in any legal niceties, for even his own clerk had to admit that his mastery of those abounding intricacies was superb. Confident of his ability, he enjoyed the flash and fury of battle, the loud voices, thrusting words and veiled innuendoes. Nothing like this would happen here, he could see that, for it was as quiet and sedate as a funeral. Everything would be settled amicably, he could wager his professional reputation on that, not forgetting sincere condolences all round.

What really annoyed him slightly was that Currie had missed such a golden opportunity. If he had called him in six months or a year earlier, he could have gone bankrupt like a gentleman with a few thousand pounds safely lifted from the wreck. Holmgren would have seen to everything for him. He didn't need six months' notice to produce a fake set of books; provided he had the relevant receipts he could do that in a weekend, aided by his stock of realistically begrimed and faded ledgers, seasoned by long exposure to sun and dirt. Currie had such a mint of untapped credit that he had thrown away. A year ago it would have been the easiest thing in the world for him to obtain almost an unlimited amount of goods. Holmgren knew where to dispose of them, below the market price, of course, and without receipts – and even, if necessary, he could backdate legal documents. Then going broke would have been worth while; there would have been good pickings for him, too. As it was, he would probably be fortunate to get all his fees. The bank owned the premises, the stock was worthless and this furniture, Holmgren computed rapidly with a contemptuous glance round, would be lucky to fetch a fiver for the lot. Pretty expensive in its day no doubt, but nobody used that stuff any more, and it wasn't quite old enough for museum period pieces . . . Where were Currie's brains? It was hard to believe that his family had been in business for close on a century, for he hadn't provided himself with the most elementary safeguard of a businessman. Why, even the wireless set was his own property and hadn't been prudently signed over to his wife. If his creditors wanted to be nasty, they could sell him up lock, stock and barrel, leaving him simply with a bed and a couple of sheets. Just that to call his own, when, with a little foresight, or rather Forsythe – he chuckled mentally at the pun – Currie could have had so much. It was truly fortunate for him that his creditors had nothing to gain by being nasty; they would be fools to take this matter further – unless they failed to realise that they had lost sufficient money already and wanted to give fat fees to solicitors without the slightest hope of any return.

Holmgren prided himself on being a judge of character. As he looked at the four people who represented most of Oscar's unsecured deficiency, he felt certain that he had them all pretty accurately taped. Old Josiah Rayling now, that queer-looking bird, with his peculiar clothes and timid bearing, his flat chest and the stomach that swelled out suddenly at the waist in a tight egg-shaped protuberance like a pregnant woman. His suit was of that coarse, hard-wearing grey Derby tweed usually associated with convicts and charitable institutions, made in the style of Edward VII with high lapels, long jacket and narrow trousers, the pile flattened to a shiny smoothness through constant wear. Looked as if he were a superannuated Water-Board clerk from pre-Metropolitan days, yet was probably as rich as Croesus, a member also of one of those queer Nonconformist sects that met in tumble-down chapels, and a good family man with a couple of dozen grandchildren. He would live quietly in a suburban villa when he could afford a mansion in Kensington Palace Gardens. Went to church twice every Sunday and to his business punctually at eight thirty every morning, travelling by bus or the Underground, and when he died he would surprise all his friends by leaving a cool couple of million. Samuel Houghton, though, puffing stolidly at his pipe, looked exactly what he was, a silent, bluff Yorkshireman . . . 'Ee, Sam – that's summed thee up a treat, lad! . . . Gunther next to him seemed a starchy old gent, mingy, too, the only one who wasn't smoking. Instead, he looked as though he were incessantly chewing gum, but in reality he was clicking his ill-fitting rather prominent false teeth in position; a cadaverous blighter in his sombre clothes, with his wide drooping moustache, craggy eyebrows and long upper lip, resembling a cross between a caricature of Mr Chamberlain and a second-class undertaker. Sour, Holmgren decided, but harmless . . . Martin Berg, again, was a different proposition. This chap from Houndsditch was the fellow he had to watch. He was cute like most Jews, but Holmgren had tricks worth a dozen of his. It was the hell of a job slipping something over that type, but in this case there was nothing to slip over – it was a perfectly straightforward, honest failure.

He looked at the plump, bald-headed little Jew again. Martin Berg. The Martin just didn't belong. Holmgren felt a sudden urge to lean over and pluck his neighbour's sleeve and ask him if his name wasn't really Solomon. That would have been just right, Solomon Berg, and nothing like so ridiculous as two of the clients he had on his books, Madame Priscilla Goldfarb and Clive Edward Levinsky. Changing your name on business grounds was permissible and even desirous. Why, he had actually heard of Britishers adopting Jewish surnames in New York, and it was quite possible that Forsythe Holmgren, like John Brown, would sound ludicrous to a Russian or a Turk. Still, that didn't alter the fact that fine old English Christian names didn't go with these Oriental tongue-twisters. Berg should have done the job properly; he should have avoided that monstrous hybrid and become completely Martin Sinclair or something like that, although his execrable accent would always stamp him unmistakably as one of the Houndsditch-Odessa Bergs.

The uneasy silence was punctuated at last by a burst of coughing from Oscar, and, when this had subsided, Josiah Rayling rose self-consciously to his feet. First, he twiddled with the massive gold chain that seemed to weigh down his skinny chest; then, grasping the pince-nez that dangled from a length of black braid almost to his knees, he stuck them diffidently on his nose. Holmgren glanced at his wristwatch. It would soon be over, and he might be in time for a couple of rubbers of bridge at home. He looked up expectantly at the old man, and he was ready to swear that Josiah was more perturbed by this business than Currie. He could even imagine Rayling apologising for causing Oscar all this trouble . . .

'Hmmmmm!' Josiah cleared his throat nervously. 'Well,' he began in a thin, high-pitched voice, 'as the largest creditor present, perhaps it will not be out of place for me to say a few words first. I have known Mr Currie for a long, long time. He has been a customer of mine ever since he began business. His father, God rest his soul, was a customer before him, and I do believe that we have records in our firm showing that his grandfather purchased goods from Rayling's as well. It is true that he owes me nearly four hundred pounds, but these are troubled times, bad for everybody, and I prefer to think not of the money he owes but of the thousands of pounds he has paid me in the course of our long and honourable association . . .' Rayling paused and removed his glasses. His words, although kind, had seemed lifeless, as if he were merely reciting them by rote; now he dropped the pretence of impersonality and addressed himself directly to Oscar. 'Why didn't you come to me before, Currie?' he said gently. 'You know I would never have allowed it to come to this. I would have given you every possible support.'

Oscar reddened and hung his head, twisting a cigarette nervously in his fingers without replying.

The old man replaced his pince-nez and continued in the same fatherly tone. 'As it is, I am prepared to waive the debt for the time being, until things improve, and then I shall continue trading with Mr Currie as heretofore, if he is willing. My suggestion is that he starts a fresh account, while I am prepared to extend him credit again up to any reasonable amount.' He stopped and opened his mouth as if he had something more to add, then, sweeping off his glasses with a graceful movement, he sat down abruptly.

Holmgren shot a quick glance at Houghton, and even in that brief instant the Yorkshireman intercepted the questioning look and, interpreting it aright, nodded emphatically without removing his pipe from his tightly clenched teeth. As the accountant was congratulating himself, Berg bounced like an agitated ball to his feet.

'I second that,' he uttered, surprisingly. 'Everything what Mr Rayling says goes for Martin Berg also.' Like Josiah he turned to Oscar with a personal appeal. 'Why didn't you come to me, Currie?' he asked, spreading out his hands in a voluble gesture and pressing them beseechingly against his bosom. 'Am I a rogue or a cut-throat that you should be frightened of me? After all, we've done a lot of business together. It's true you owe me money . . .' he dropped his hands and glanced at a slip of paper before him . . . 'a hundred and forty-five pounds, sixteen and ninepence, to be exact, but am I asking for it all at once? Did I ever press you to pay? . . . I know I've been hard with people who owed me less, but there's a big difference between swindlers and old-established businessmen. When someone starts out with the intention to do me down, he finds he don't get much change from Martin Berg, but if *you* had the money, I know you'd pay. You haven't got it now, so we may as well start fresh. That's my offer, Currie,' he concluded. 'And all my lifetime, people should deal with me fair and square like I've been treating you.'

Holmgren breathed a sigh of relief. He didn't expect much trouble from Gunther, whose debt was insignificant compared with the others, but he sat there inscrutably, his heavy jaws munching like a melancholy cow. It had worked out exactly as he had expected – well, more or less so, except for Berg – and Gunther would probably follow the lead of the larger creditors. Possibly he was holding back his words to give the maximum effect when he staked his claim in this magnanimous gesture, but Holmgren felt it was all over, bar shouting. He looked at Oscar and again felt a twinge of disappointment at the chance he had missed, although that simpleton probably imagined that he was the luckiest man in the world. Oscar's heart was really too full for words. These people were so unspeakably good to him that he felt he could hug them all with gratitude. Matilda, with her shrewd common sense, had been right as usual. His creditors had propped him up again, and how easy they had made it for him. This ordeal that he had so much dreaded was shaping as though it might eventually prove his salvation.

Still no word from Gunther one way or the other, so Holmgren, thinking impatiently of those rubbers, decided to expedite matters by taking the bull by the horns. He rested his podgy fists on the table and spoke, judiciously summing up the feeling of the meeting.

'Well,' he said, 'everybody here seems pretty unanimous that Mr Currie should continue trading. That being the case I –'

'One moment,' Gunther interrupted, baring his large, yellowy dentures. 'There are one or two questions I should like to ask your client.'

'All right,' said Holmgren jovially, thinking that the man sounded like an undertaker even more than he resembled one. 'That's what we're here for.'

Gunther swivelled his chair round to face Oscar. 'Is what we've got before us a true statement of affairs?' he asked in his even, oleaginous voice.

Oscar nodded. 'Absolutely.'

'And you have no assets other than you have divulged?'

'Quite right.'

'Tell me,' said Gunther, 'have you tried every possible means of raising money?'

'I have,' Oscar replied.

'Have you tried to obtain any loans?'

'Yes, but I no longer have any security on effects upon which I can realise.'

'Hmmmm!' A greasy, disquieting smile broke across Gunther's face. 'I understand that you have a brother who is an extremely rich man . . . Is that correct?' he said slowly.

Oscar flushed, biting his lips with vexation. He could sense what was coming. First the bank manager and now Gunther. Well, nobody would drive him to wear horns for Spencer, since accepting his help would condone that infidelity and make him a party to it. Vividly, that single, shameful embrace shot across his mind – the night before the wedding, too! He had seen it with his own eyes, but what had happened before he could only guess at and had preferred, for his peace of mind all those years, to forget. What he had seen was enough, more than enough to prevent him from humbling himself before that robber of tills, that swindler and adulterer, that Cain of a brother . . . No! He wouldn't even think of it, not for a million Gunthers!

'Well?' Gunther repeated. 'Is that correct?'

'Yes,' said Oscar, grimly.

'Have you approached Spencer Currie for assistance?' Gunther watched him keenly, hanging on his reply. 'Come now,' he demanded impatiently, 'have you?'

'No . . .'

'Is there any reason to believe that he would not have advanced you sufficient money to meet your obligations? . . . Well?'

'I . . . I don't know,' Oscar said at last.

'Would it be possible to expect such assistance if you did?' Gunther pressed.

'I suppose it might be possible,' Oscar admitted.

'Very well,' Gunther brought out triumphantly. 'Why didn't you approach him?' He leaned forward argumentatively, determined to force an answer from those unwilling lips. 'Well, why not?'

Oscar's eyes blazed, and he felt his whole body twitching with an uncontrollable resentment. 'Mind your own business!' he retorted angrily. 'That's a purely personal matter!'

'Indeed!' Gunther returned, his voice remaining irritatingly at the same, even pitch. 'You owe me eighty pounds, and that is a very personal matter to me.'

'Come . . . come . . .' Josiah Rayling interrupted gently. 'That's hardly fair, Mr Gunther. I am certain Currie has some excellent reasons for adopting this attitude. You must consider his pride, which is a very real thing to a man like Currie, who is not accustomed to begging for assistance, especially where that assistance is problematical, in spite of his admissions. Personally, I like him even better for his refusal. I must say, I do admire independence in a man.'

'So do I,' said Gunther drily, 'but not when it's got to cost me eighty pounds.' He sat up stiffly again. 'I want that money, Currie – and within twenty-four hours!' he announced abruptly.

'For God's sake, man!' Martin Berg interjected agitatedly. 'Be reasonable. You don't expect in one lump sum the whole lot? . . . Do you?'

'I do,' said Gunther. He turned his long face solemnly in Berg's direction. 'That is precisely what I expect. Otherwise I shall make him bankrupt!'

Martin Berg was shocked. 'You wouldn't do that, surely!' he protested. 'Not for a measly eighty pounds?'

'I want you to understand me,' Gunther replied suavely. 'I haven't done thousands of pounds' worth of business with Currie over a long period like Rayling, or even yourself, or Houghton, and eighty pounds means as much to me as twice eight hundred to Josiah Rayling. Currie has only been dealing with me for a couple of years, and most of this debt was contracted comparatively recently when he must have known that he was already insolvent. Why, I didn't earn eighty pounds out of him the whole time I was supplying him with goods, and I refuse to be sidetracked by cheap, unbusinesslike sentimentality . . . Pride! Pride! . . .' he spat out maliciously. 'Pride for what? . . . The Currie name? Then why didn't that prevent him from taking in my goods when he knew he couldn't pay for them? . . . I repeat, I want that money within twenty-four hours, otherwise,' he threatened with menacing deliberation, 'I shall get a receiving order immediately.'

'But you can't do that,' said Martin Berg. 'You've got to take him first to the county court. Then he can make an offer to pay off the debt by instalments, so even if the judge says five bob a month, you've got to accept.'

'I don't have to do anything of the sort,' Gunther answered incisively. 'I have had experiences of this kind before. Once a debtor has called a meeting of creditors, his action comes within the seven acts of bankruptcy, and any creditor, provided his debt is above fifty pounds, can apply for a receiving order forthwith.' He turned to the accountant. 'Am I right, Mr Holmgren?' he enquired sarcastically. 'Is it the law? You should know, and if it is, perhaps you will inform Mr Berg that I am perfectly within my rights.'

Holmgren shook his head. 'That's quite correct,' he admitted smoothly, 'but I don't see what you have to gain by such action. If you know that much, you must also know that making a man bankrupt costs a tidy sum, and as all Mr Currie's assets are absorbed by a preferential creditor, the bank, you're simply throwing good money after bad.'

Gunther rose sardonically to his feet, revealing himself as far and away the tallest man present. 'I am prepared to chance that speculation,' he said. 'But somehow I don't think Mr Spencer Currie will relish seeing his family name in the *London Gazette* . . . I have an idea I'll get my eighty pounds.' He grasped his umbrella that was hooked to the table beside him and tucked it firmly under his arm. Remember, Currie,' he smiled malevolently, 'this is my last word. You've got twenty-four hours.'

As Gunther descended the stairs, the other creditors rose and gathered sympathetically round Oscar, who was half-stupefied by this sudden turn of events. They saw that obviously the best thing just now was to leave him.

Mr Rayling was the first to shake his hand. 'I'm sorry, Currie,' he said earnestly, 'but you know that whatever happens you can rely on me.'

'Me, too,' Martin Berg broke in. 'So long as I am in business, you always know where to go.'

'Thanks,' said Oscar, 'thanks . . . Thank you,' he muttered to Houghton, who, having remained silent the whole evening, was signalling his departure with a nod and the gentle pressure of his warm hand on Oscar's back. He waited until the footsteps faded down the stairs, and he heard the faraway thud of the street door; then, recovering his composure, he turned to Holmgren, who was just replacing the last of his papers in his briefcase.

'Well?' he said. 'What happens now?'

'It all depends,' the accountant answered. 'That old boy Gunther was very melodramatic with his twenty-four hours – but was he really serious?'

'Serious?' Oscar nodded gravely. 'I know Gunther. He meant every word he said.'

'Well then, there's nothing to do – except wait.' Holmgren closed his briefcase with a snap. 'And don't worry,' he said, 'as soon as you receive the court order just get in touch with me.'

CHAPTER EIGHTEEN

Only in bed that night did the events of the meeting stir Oscar again. He had mentioned Gunther's attitude casually to Matilda when she had asked how the meeting had gone off, but he hadn't stressed the ultimatum overmuch or seemed to be unduly distressed by it; in fact, as soon as Holmgren left, he himself had begun to wonder why it had affected him so badly. Bankruptcy was no longer the terror it had once been. He was quite hopelessly insolvent, but what he had dreaded was meeting his creditors face to face, and now that that had been amicably disposed of, and he knew that his reputation was still untarnished with the people he respected, he felt strangely at ease and even quietly defiant. If Rayling and Houghton and Martin Berg were sympathetic, that was all that really mattered – as for Gunther, he could do his worst!

He dropped off to sleep like a baby, but soon doubts began to invade his dreams, the old problems that he thought were settled parading before him in fantastic forms. He was busy writing cheques, scribbling feverishly as he tore the slips from an enormous book, but as fast as he gave out the cheques, they were returned to him with the legend RD stamped not in a corner but right over his signature. He wrote Oscar Currie larger, with more elaborate flourishes, and no sooner did he tear the cheque out than it was beneath his hands again, disfigured by those grotesque purple capitals RD . . . RD . . . RD . . .

His figure faded into the background, still writing cheques desperately, and he was in Mr Lyon's office. 'I'll give you a hundred pounds,' he was saying, 'I'll give you two hundred pounds.' But Mr Lyon kept shaking his head replying, 'No,

I must foreclose . . . I've got to foreclose . . . I'm sorry, Currie, I've got to foreclose. Now he had left the bank, although he could still see his image arguing with the manager, and he found himself standing outside his shop. For a moment he was unable to recognise it, since a huge TO LET sign was fixed to its front. Oscar was furious. The bank manager had said he would give him ample notice; in fact, he was still saying it, and here, behind his back, he had erected this shameful structure. 'What do you mean by it? What's the idea?' he demanded, and Mr Lyon shook his head and answered, 'I'm sorry, old man. That's the law, Currie. That's the seven acts of bankruptcy.'

Dwarfed by the gigantic sign, Oscar rushed inside his shop and found the shelves bulging with goods as they had never appeared for years. It was monstrous! Lyon couldn't do this to him. He had no right to disfigure his premises with that vulgarity – not so long as they remained his . . . TO LET! . . . Such a thing had not happened to a Currie in a hundred years. Grasping an axe in his hand he ran up to the top front room, past Holmgren and his creditors, who were still frozen there, and began to hack viciously at the signboard. Astride the window ledge, one foot resting on the floor and the other dangling in space, he laboured futilely to the accompaniment of Holmgren's droning voice, while the accountant kept tossing matches on to the carpet that by now was littered with a thick layer of rubbish, at the same time reading interminable statements of affairs to his creditors, propped owlishly in identical positions round the table. Oscar wanted to scream 'Stop it! For God's sake, stop it!' at the top of his voice, but he had become too involved in what was now developing into almost a personal tussle, and, just when he was about to give it up despairingly, one felicitous stroke, delivered with Herculean strength, shattered the wooden framework, and the whole structure toppled to the ground.

Miraculously it had fallen into the centre of the shop, and

Oscar stood beside it, surveying the debris triumphantly. So they thought he was finished . . . They wanted to take over his shop . . . Well, nobody else would have it; it had always belonged to a Currie, and it would stay that way, a Currie's, or nobody's. His grandfather had built it when the High Street was nothing but sodden fields. Dust it had been then, and to dust it would return. It had to be Currie & Son or nothing; sooner than let it go out of the family, he would raze it to the ground with his own hands.

He began to hack down the shelves, piling them on the splintered sign. Effortlessly they fell beneath the blows of his axe that next demolished the heavy counters as though they were made of plywood, and, when nothing but the four walls remained standing, he took out a box of matches and set the whole heap ablaze. Only just in time, for outside the windows watching were Gunther and the bank manager. They were dressed as he had seen them last but wore steel helmets of a German design. Ah! Oscar understood. They were the enemy. He wished he could lay his hands on his old gun, and immediately a service revolver was clutched in his fist. At this moment Oscar was half-aware that he was dreaming, for only in a dream were events so fluid, only in a dream were thought and action so admirably interwoven, translated with such immediacy from one to the other. He wanted an axe, and forthwith an axe was in his hand; he needed a revolver, and here he had one ready to repel his foes. Through the crackling flames that scorched the walls, burning fiercely without raising any smoke, he saw Gunther and the manager come closer as though they intended to break in and frustrate him. Raising his revolver, Oscar took aim, and, pressing the trigger, saw with satisfaction that the shot had clipped a round hole through the top of Gunther's helmet. The incident was almost a replica of something that had happened to him during the war, when, emerging from a shell hole, he had found himself faced by an enemy soldier and had shot him just like this, except that the bullet had gone clean through his forehead. This wasn't so different; it was war, too. His terrain was the shop, and he would fight for it, tooth and nail, with every weapon that came to his hand. Germans . . . Englishmen . . . They weren't so different. They wanted his life or his shop, but obtaining either meant destroying him first.

Quickly Gunther and the manager withdrew, Oscar on guard in the midst of the flames watching with gloating approval as the fire ate slowly into the walls. No phoenix would arise here, but this spot would henceforth be hallowed; whatever else grew, this earth would belong to Currie & Son till the end of the world. Suddenly the whole building crumbled at his feet, and he stood alone in the street surrounded by smouldering flaky grey dust. That was as it should be, ashes to ashes, and – 'I'll give you a hundred pounds,' he was saying to the manager, and Mr Lyon was shaking his head while, superimposed above it all, his vast, brooding shadow ceaselessly wrote enormous cheques. 'No . . . I've got to foreclose.' – 'I'll give you two hundred pounds!' – and having them back one by one, RD . . . RD . . . RD . . .

When he opened his eyes it was daylight, and he became acutely conscious of a suffocated whistle that struggled from the top of his chest with every laboured breath. Turning, he saw that Matilda had her eyes open, too, and was looking at him curiously.

He smiled wanly. 'Good morning.'

'Good morning,' she said. 'How do you feel, Oscar?'

'All right,' he answered.

Something in her eyes betrayed her anxiety. Oscar had been half-conscious that he had uttered inarticulate cries during the night; in the disturbed borderland of sleep he had sensed that some jumbled words had slipped across the frontier. He wondered what she had heard and what she had understood, or whether what was troubling her was merely this strangled long-drawn-out gasp – like the expiring wheeze of a locomotive dipping into a distant tunnel – which was really nothing more alarming than a symptom of excessive smoking. He stretched his hand across to the table and then lit a cigarette. Just a few puffs, a cough or two to shift the rubbish down below, and now, his throat fairly clear, he could talk.

'I tell you, I'm all right,' he repeated, as though to silence the unuttered doubts that were still evident in Matilda's eyes. 'Why did you ask?'

'It's nothing . . . Only you don't look too well.' That was an understatement, for he looked quite ill, with two vertical folds in his skin stressed overnight on each side of his mouth and his face waxen and pinched and somehow completely shrunken like that of a corpse drained of blood. He appeared pathetically old and weak, with his piebald moustache drooping loosely and the few hairs on his head tousled into a sparse tuft as though some mischievous child had attempted to twist them into plaits . . . 'I think you'd best stay in bed a while longer,' she said. 'Can't do you any harm to have an extra lay-in.'

'Lay-in?' He glanced at the clock and, surprised, propped himself up on his elbow. 'Why, it's half past eight!'

'Well . . . and what if it is?'

'You're right,' he admitted, lowering himself reluctantly on the pillow. 'There's nothing particular to get up for anyhow.'

Matilda threw aside the coverlet and stepped briskly from the bed. 'Just relax, Oscar,' she said. 'I'll fetch you up some breakfast in a jiffy.'

'Don't bother, dear,' he answered wearily. 'I'll be down in half an hour or so myself.'

'No . . . stay in bed for a bit,' she urged him. 'You look awfully tired.'

Oscar shook his head obstinately. 'I'm coming down.'

'Don't be too long then,' she said, slipping on her dress with the rapid preciseness that characterised her every movement. 'I'm going shopping . . . and I have one or two calls to make as well.'

'Don't worry about me, dear,' he insisted. 'Do just whatever you've got to do. I don't feel particularly hungry, and if I want something I'm quite capable of frying myself an egg.'

'All right.' Matilda moved towards the door; then she appeared to change her mind and, returning to the bed, bent over him and kissed his face gently, smoothing his straggly hair tenderly to the side of his head. 'You'll find eggs in the pantry and a fresh jar of marmalade on the top shelf with the butter.'

'Go on . . . go on with you.' Playfully he pushed her away. 'Stop fussing about me and see to the children. I'm old enough to look after myself.'

Her firm tread descended the stairs, each unhesitant step stamping her as a completely business-like person, as if every decision she made were unequivocal and her every action planned. Her house was run like that. Everything was always in its place, scrupulously clean and tidy, and she controlled her domestic budget to a farthing. If he had been anything like her it would never have come to this – waiting for receiving orders. She had wanted to bring him up breakfast, but he knew that he didn't deserve a cup of tea or even a crust of bread. He didn't work, so he wasn't entitled to eat. That came from the scriptures somewhere, and it applied to him, right enough; he had been caught out, shown up in his true colours as a sponger and a parasite. He stretched his legs beneath the counterpane and closed his eyes, exhausted as though his night-long tussle with those terrible phantoms had taxed his physical resources to the utmost. He felt like that pyjama-clad man in the Bovril advertisements, except that there would be no smile on his face and no succour within reach, only an angry sea and his feet getting wet . . . Well, the next move was up to Gunther . . . What would happen now? Where did Oscar Currie go from here?

That morning Kim was down punctually, arriving at the breakfast table before Matilda had even uttered the first of that rising crescendo of 'Kims' that usually preceded his descent. There was an ebullient air about him that his mother, despite her engrossment in Oscar's troubles, could scarcely fail to glimpse. When Matilda came in from the kitchen she found him very upright in his place, and, before she got over her surprise at finding him down so early, he greeted her brightly with a formal bow.

'Good morning, Mrs Currie.'

'Morning, Kim,' she answered.

'And it is a good morning, Ma,' he said. 'Don't you notice anything different about your son?'

She gave him a perfunctory glance as she moved towards the kitchen. 'Not unless he's washed behind his ears!'

Matilda disappeared from the room, and he heard the bacon sizzle appetisingly in the pan.

'Joking apart, Ma, did you see anything special?' he called.

'Can't say I did,' she replied. 'I've put your bacon on.'

'Do come in, Ma,' he urged. 'I want you.'

'You'll have to wait – unless you prefer your breakfast burned.'

'Never mind,' he said. 'Come in. I won't keep you.'

'All right . . . One moment.'

Kim waited impatiently for her to return, bubbling like an infant with a secret, but he felt he had an excellent excuse this morning for his childishness. He rose to his feet as she appeared at the threshold.

'Well, what is it?' she asked irritably.

'I'm starting work today,' he announced with a grin. 'Out on the road for the first time.' He pointed proudly at the oval green enamel badge that hung conspicuously from his lapel. 'Do you like my badge?'

'Oh, that? . . . To tell you the truth, I didn't even notice it.'

Unabashed, he moved towards her and held out his badge banteringly. 'Here, Ma, spit on it for luck!'

She pushed him away with a little gesture of annoyance. 'Don't be silly, Kim! Of course you know I wish you all the luck in the world,' she added hurriedly as she observed the hurt expression on his face. 'But I'm in no mood for such horseplay this morning.'

'Oh!' he muttered. She went back into the kitchen, and Kim returned to his chair. Obsessed with his own good fortune, he had been slow to realise that something was troubling his mother; but, as he sat down, toying with his knife and fork while he waited for his breakfast, he began to understand that this unusual brusqueness was the outward sign of some deep-seated uneasiness.

Apparently, Matilda had repented of her behaviour, for when she came in with his food she twisted her face into a bright but mechanical smile. 'Here, Kim,' she said, placing the meal before him. Her broad hand fluttered lightly over his unruly hair. 'I'm sorry, son,' she apologised.

'Thanks . . . That's all right, Ma.' He bent over the plate and suddenly looked up. 'Tell me, what's the matter?' he asked.

'Matter? . . . There's nothing the matter.'

'Yes there is,' he insisted. 'What's wrong, Ma?'

She sat down at the table opposite him, fumbling nervously with the cruet. 'It's your father,' she brought out at last.

'Dad? . . . What's the matter? . . . Is he ill?'

Matilda nodded. 'I'm afraid so. This business is preying on his mind . . . He was writing cheques all night . . . and quarrelling with his bank manager and shooting Germans in the war.'

'Oh . . .'

'He looks shocking . . . really queer. He frightened me when he opened his eyes first thing without a word, half-staring at me as if I were a stranger before I got a "good morning" out of him. His mind seems touched . . . I'm afraid he'll have a nervous breakdown, Kim – if that'll be the worst.'

Kim carefully cut off a slice of bacon and, impaling it on his fork, dipped it into the mustard, but before he brought it to his mouth he set it down on the plate again. 'That's bad,' he said. 'I didn't realise it was as serious as that.' He looked up at Matilda. 'We'll have to do something about it, Ma.'

She nodded acquiescently. 'That's right. I've already decided to do something. And I shall do it this morning,' she added firmly.

Kim looked at her questioningly. He had a vague idea that he was about to hear some disquieting news.

'Well, what is it?' he asked. 'It will have to be pretty drastic to have any effect now.'

'It is drastic. And it's the only thing that can help.'

Kim chewed his bacon thoughtfully. It tasted suddenly like straw, and he swallowed it without relish. 'Is it a secret, Ma?'

Matilda shook her head. 'It's no secret . . . You can guess.'

'Oh . . . Uncle Spencer?'

'Yes,' she admitted calmly, 'Uncle Spencer.'

Kim put down his knife and fork. 'Must you go to him again?' he demanded. 'Must you do it?'

'I'm afraid I must,' she said.

'But isn't there some other way?'

'I wish there were . . . What else do you suggest?'

'Well . . . I can't think of anything at the moment,' he said at last. 'But all the same, I'd sooner almost anything than that.'

'I see,' she said grimly. 'You'd prefer to see your father driven out of his mind with shame and worry rather than do the only thing possible to save him.'

'No, Ma!' Kim protested. 'You know that isn't true.'

'Of course it is!' she answered brusquely. 'You're just as pig-headed as Oscar to keep hugging all those stupid pre-judices that have kept two brothers apart all these years. I'm going to bring Spencer back here. Your father's got to see reason, and I want you to be at home to help me.'

'No . . . I'm sorry . . . I couldn't do that.'

'Why not?' she asked testily.

Kim squirmed. 'Well, for one thing, I'll have the cab out this morning . . . I've got to start work.'

'When have you got to start?'

'Around eleven, I suppose.'

'Then you can start an hour or so later,' she said in a tone that admitted of no denial. 'Your father comes first.'

'All right,' he brought out grudgingly. 'I'll be here. What time do you want me around?'

'About midday,' said Matilda. 'I may have some difficulty getting hold of Spencer. He's a busy man . . . We'll say about half past twelve.'

'Right,' Kim answered reluctantly, 'I'll be here at half past twelve.'

CHAPTER NINETEEN

When Oscar came down the house seemed deserted. It was not quite ten o'clock, but the breakfast table had already been cleared of dirty dishes and was covered by a spotlessly clean tablecloth. A neat pile of sliced bread on the breadboard, a glass dish filled with creamy butter, an empty plate and some sparkling crockery were neatly set before his chair as a dumb invitation for him to eat at leisure. He went into the kitchen where the smell of fried bacon still lingered, the only clue that this tidy, cool little room had so recently been the scene of such warm, bustling activity. It seemed a pity to spoil the artistic arrangement of the pots and pans again, to sully the glistening polish of the gas stove, merely for a cup of tea. It was strange how the respect for domestic orderliness had grown upon him. Originally the untidiest of men – outside his shop, of course, where his movements were simply automatic – he had been unconsciously conditioned over a period of years never to leave dirty utensils about the living room and even to find such slovenliness irksome when he came across it elsewhere. Matilda, in spite of all her other household duties, seemed to be constantly washing up. After every meal the dishes were immediately whisked to the kitchen, cleaned, drained and replaced on the shelves. Oscar had never got over his own dislike of washing up, so, sooner than leave evidence of a meal on the table, he decided to eat nothing at all, contenting himself at the last moment with extracting a couple of biscuits from the tin and nibbling at them half-heartedly.

He passed into the shop, still chewing the last brittle crumbs, apparently deep in thought, and, before he had any idea of his intentions, had walked behind the counter and donned his alpaca coat. With the blinds drawn the shop had a gloomy aspect, almost a cloistral air, although the sounds of the street penetrated without difficulty through the walls . . . People must understand by now that something was wrong, for Currie & Son was usually one of the first shops to open. Now, however, that it was shut, it would stay shut, Oscar decided. The decision was painful and had only just come to him, like a flash. Nobody was forcing him to close, he had done that of his own volition, but it was really the obvious thing to do. It was useless prolonging the agony, making a farce of the honourable civic function that he and his family had always respected above every other, that of the shopkeeper. But what was there to make such a fuss about? What was so important? What *was* a shopkeeper anyway? Did he create something out of nothing? Did he twist shapeless lumps and make of them a marketable commodity? Did he dig in the bowels of the earth and bring up warmth and light? Did he fly or stoke trains or sail the seven seas? No. All he did was buy other people's finished labour for as little as he could and sell it for as much more as possible – something that required not brains but a low animal cunning, something a child ought to be able to do and which Oscar Currie, with a hundred years of experience behind him, no longer found a paying proposition. It wasn't really a job for an adult man; all those things he had been doing for so many years, dusting shelves, opening boxes and closing them again and waiting for customers, that was all it amounted to, and he wouldn't be doing it any longer. He didn't know what else he would be doing, but in spite of this false, almost masochistic belittlement, the thought of not doing all these things seemed unbearable.

Last night everything had been settled. Before then, during all the preceding weeks and months, there had been merely a vague uncertainty that had allowed an occasional glimmer of hope, but that faint flame had been effectively snuffed by

Gunther. At least he knew exactly where he stood, for the certainty of failure admitted of no more hopeful mirages, and he had even felt the better for that knowledge. That had completely satisfied him last night, for it had seemed merely a matter of waiting for a receiving order and the long drag of litigation leading inexorably to the end of Currie & Son, but that satisfaction had given place to a hundred other doubts. He became dimly aware that that end, so desirous now, was not so clear cut in view but bodged around with a nebulous host of frightening barriers until it seemed as far away a goal and as unattainable as solvency . . . What was going to happen? Not next week or next month, but right away? . . . While the shop was open he had always had money in his pockets; true, it wasn't his own, but when Matilda had wanted money for food he had given it her, when she wanted money for the pictures it was there and when he needed cigarettes all he had to do was dip in the till. Now that the shop was closed, never mind about the luxuries, about pictures or cigarettes, where was the money coming from to live? He would no longer be able to juggle easily with pounds, he would have to look twice at every penny . . . All his life he had worked for this, to be reduced, at practically a moment's notice, to the level of a jobless labourer. Level? That wouldn't be so bad! Below it even! A hundred years a trader, and now he wasn't even eligible for the dole!

The rattle of the handle being turned startled him for an instant, and immediately he moved towards the door. Then he remembered – he wasn't open – and halted in his tracks. Currie & Son was closed. Closed for the first time in nearly a hundred years. Peevishly the handle turned again, and the door shook, then an impatient tattoo on the glass and silence . . . It's no use, madam, he thought, you've got to go away. Go somewhere else. Try the Empire House Traders; you can't miss them, twenty yards down on the left. No use coming here any more. If it's stockings you want, I haven't got them;

if it's the latest brassiere, I'm right out of those, too – or, to be truthful (I can afford that now), I've never had them in stock. Go to the Empire House Traders. Whatever you want, you'll find it twenty yards down. Even if I were open, you'd most probably have had to go there in any case . . .

Turning his back deliberately on the door, he walked to the corner furthest away and sat down on the high stool, resting his elbows on the counter so that he commanded a full view of his shop. Out of this dark little oblong box three generations of Curries had made a living. It seemed that for a century there had been the Midas touch about it; there was always gold on those shelves. Now the spell had failed, the magic had worn off in his generation, the shop was no longer a munificent influence but like Pandora's box prised open, releasing the evils of mankind, all of which had seemed to descend on him at the same time. The first falling-off of his business had been hardly noticeable. Like an enormous boulder falling down a hill, it had moved ponderously, dropping a few inches, halting, bouncing, slipping sideways, then imperceptibly gathering momentum and suddenly crashing headlong to the bottom. He had reached rock bottom now, although he was still shaken by that violent descent.

Where his elbows rested, there was a light patch on the counter. Just there, the cash register had stood for years. It had cost eighty-four pounds when Oscar had bought it, but a few weeks ago he had been fortunate to sell it for less than a quarter of the original price. Compared with other mechanical gadgets it had kept its value fairly well; compared with his stock it had turned out even a gilt-edged security. He had realised twenty pounds, and the money had run through his fingers in a few days like water dripping on to sand, absorbed without trace. He had had the money but didn't even remember what he had used it for. All he knew was that every penny of it was gone without making the slightest appreciable difference to his position.

He began to brood on the injustice of it all. He felt as though he were baulked of his birthright, as though he wanted to protest and was being forcibly prevented from voicing his feelings. He didn't deserve this diabolical punishment. He had never exploited people; he had never wanted to make a fortune. All he had worked for in his shop was to make an honest living, and every man, whatever his occupation, was entitled at least to that. The workers were always crying, always demanding more wages, shorter hours. It wasn't all honey for them, he knew, but they had *something*. He couldn't remember the last time *he* had earned the equivalent of a week's wages. How would *they* like to work fifty, sixty, seventy hours a week for nothing – for less than nothing? They didn't really know how well off they were compared with people like him, with shopkeepers. If the humanists, the novelists, poets and reformers were actually looking for a tortured, martyred class to succour, they need search no further than the one represented by the Curries – and the Rothsteins . . . Take Jacob, now. Hadn't it been precisely like this with him? He realised that he had done his memory an injustice. Smothered by writs and left without a penny in the world, what else could he have done but take his life? Funny how thoughts of Rothstein kept recurring more and more frequently in his mind of late and how Oscar kept finding parallels with his own case. There was a tradesman who had died, a man with a family like himself, and no sooner was he dead than the whole family disintegrated. The vengeance of society had pursued him beyond the grave. If he had been a workman, his widow would have had a pension. As it was, her troubles had driven her into a lunatic asylum or, rather, a hospital for mental disorders, for there weren't asylums any more; they sounded too grim. Leah had had to give up her art school and was working down the road; ironically enough, behind a counter at the Empire House Traders, working for the same sort of people that had killed her father – yes – and the people that were slowly killing him, too. The kids had come off best; they were young and would soon forget. The two boys were well cared for at the big Jewish orphanage in Norwood. He knew this from Matilda, who had even gone there once to see them. One thing about the Jews he had to admit: they looked after their own. But *he* would hate having to leave babies behind to the tender care of the parish. Fortunately his children were grown-up, and Matilda was far too rational to be driven off her mental balance, whatever happened to him. Kim was working, earning his own living at last, and Pamela was the type that would always fall like a cat on her feet. His family was all right – in fact, so far from suffering, they would be better off without him. He was no longer the breadwinner; the truth – he had to face it now, however unwelcome – was that he was simply a liability and likely to remain so for the rest of his life.

Now last night's dream became comprehensible and so merged with reality that this morning seemed merely an extension of his struggles in that shadowy half-world. He felt again as he had felt in his dream, like demolishing every stick and stone that was associated with his name so that nobody else could have the satisfaction of lording it over his ruin. First Gunther would come and then the bank, and there would be another sign above the shop. Whoever came next would have no use for these antiquated fittings either. Those shelves that his father had erected with such deliberation and painstaking care when Oscar was a boy would be pulled down and chopped up for firewood. A bitter surge of resentment tore through him, canalised into a personal hatred of the interlopers. If he had had an axe at hand, he would have cut down the shelves himself to prevent that dishonour as he had done in his dream, but he had no axe, any more than the service revolver was a cold reality . . . And yet – there *was* a service revolver somewhere in the house. He had brought it home from France as a souvenir of the war, that last war to end war, he thought bitterly. He hadn't imagined then that there would come a time when he might have to use it again for the grim business of killing. He no longer considered the imminent threat of another conflagration or how it would affect him and his business; all he knew was that he had fought his own war and lost. Although he had not set eyes on it for twenty years, he suddenly remembered where it was. It would be wrapped in greased oil-silk in the bottom drawer of his bureau in the top front room. The last time he had gone near it the drawer had been jammed, and that was years ago, but Oscar knew that the revolver was there, and, even more, he knew that there were three live cartridges still in the magazine.

He rose resolutely from the stool and, as an afterthought, bent down and picked up from beneath the counter the pronged steel jemmy which he had used to open cases of merchandise. At last he had a legitimate use for it once more. Clasping the cold bar firmly in his fist, he made for the stairs, feeling a joy in his activity as though he were doing something really worth while again, something big and important, consistent with his training and ability and the Currie reputation. Unhesitatingly he went straight up to the bureau in the top front room and tried the drawer. It was stuck fast, so without any further preamble he pushed the tapered end of the jemmy above the lock and levered it downwards with a fierce pressure. The polished mahogany creaked and strained in protest, but soon there came a sharp crack, and splinters of wood sprouted suddenly beneath the steel. He twisted the jemmy round and pressed again until the lock came off entirely, carrying with it a strip of veneered wood. Oscar sank to his knees. Matilda would probably have something to say about the mess he had left on the carpet and even more about his violation of a treasured piece, but he couldn't be bothered by such trifles now. He pulled out the drawer and emptied it on the floor. Some faded photographs, an old insurance policy, addresses of war comrades, a ball of grey wool, a length of lead piping, nuts, bolts and a box of rusty pen nibs, and, beneath all the bric-à-brac, a bundle wrapped in yellow oil-silk. Triumphantly he took out the revolver. It was still in good condition, thanks to the prodigality with which he had applied the coating of grease so long ago, and, pushing open the magazine, he found the three bullets that he had known must be there.

For a moment, regarding the heap on the carpet, he felt a twinge of compunction and was almost tempted to tidy things up as best as he could. He dismissed the thought; another time, not now, and somebody else, not him – he had far more urgent matters on hand. He was even confirmed in his resolution by that very disorderliness so much in spirit with the sense of magnificent devastation evoked by his dream. Everything was part of a pattern. Hitherto he had been a loose scrap; now he fitted snugly into a groove; he knew precisely where he had to go, exactly what it was necessary for him to do.

Passing down the stairs, he heard a movement from Pamela's room. The knowledge that there might be another person in the house disturbed him, for he had thought that he was alone. Putting the revolver in his pocket, he rapped gently at the door and, receiving a reply, entered. He found Pamela standing before the wardrobe. Two suitcases were open on the floor, while a heap of dresses and lingerie lay scattered over the bed.

'What's the matter?' he asked. 'Going away?'

The girl nodded, casually flinging a pair of befeathered slippers on the bed. 'I only heard last night,' she said. 'Didn't have a chance to tell you before. I shall be off tomorrow for a week or so – to Venice.'

Oscar closed the door behind him and perched himself on the edge of the bed.

'Why Venice?' he asked quietly.

'Oh . . . we're having a conference there.'

'Who's the "we"?'

Pamela dropped the slip she was holding critically against her body to the ground. 'The "we",' she said, 'are the progressive national movements of the world. Lord Harkness is going along to represent the True Britons, and I'm his private secretary.'

Oscar looked at her. She wasn't a child any longer, she was a woman, and her body, developed beyond the awkward lines of maidenhood, had all the mature fullness and repose of a woman's flesh. A lot of things he hadn't understood became clear to him. Even the connection between Pamela, Benny and Phillips was no longer a mystery . . . So she was going away with Lord Harkness, but Oscar knew why she was going. He began to see things with a terrifying clarity but impersonally, not like one intimately concerned with them but with the sober detachment of a bewigged, sombre-gowned judge.

'So . . . you're Harkness's private secretary . . .' He spoke with deliberation. 'Is that what they call it now?'

Pamela flushed. 'That's what it's always been called!' she retorted.

'And what sort of qualifications have you got for a private secretary? Apart from being pretty?'

'I'm proficient at shorthand and typing,' she said tartly, 'and that's more than a lot of private secretaries can claim.'

'That still doesn't make you one,' he said, 'not for this trip . . . Anyway, you're not going.'

She bristled antagonistically. 'What do you mean?'

'You know what I mean,' he replied slowly. 'When a rich old man takes a pretty young girl abroad, what should it mean?'

For a split second Pamela hovered on the verge of an angry outburst, but the funny side of the accusation overwhelmed her, and she chuckled instead. 'Don't worry, Dad,' she laughed. 'If you knew Lord Harkness you wouldn't talk like that.'

'I don't know Harkness, and I don't want to know him,' he said. 'But I still say you're not going.'

The girl tilted her chin obstinately at this unexpected

opposition. Oscar had never interfered in her affairs before. It had even appeared for long periods that he had hardly been conscious of her presence in the house. There was a strange look about him as he confronted her – probably due to the strain of his business troubles, but that still didn't entitle him to take over the role of the heavy father. She was of age and could do as she pleased, and even if this trip abroad were not in reality so innocent of sexual motives, he had no right to dictate to her. All these years she had been hanging about the house regarded as a sort of vegetable, and now he had suddenly woken up to the fact that she was a woman. Well, it was too late in the day for him to assert his parental authority and much too late to attempt to initiate her into the mysteries of life; she knew all about pollen and pistils and seed boxes and fertilisations, but she hadn't learned it from him. She had skipped botany and gone directly to the authentic source, and by now was probably qualified to teach her father several things *he* didn't know. Another time, she decided, if their wills clashed, she would have a stand-up battle, but now, since he looked so old and haggard in spite of the queer brightness of his eyes, she wouldn't burden him with a fresh irritation. She would simply make it clear that nothing would deflect her from her purpose and leave it at that.

'I'm sorry, Dad,' she said firmly. 'I've made all arrangements. I've got to go.'

'You won't go,' he repeated. 'You're not going, I tell you.'

She shrugged her shoulders resignedly, refusing to argue any more, but, to make her intentions perfectly clear, she resumed her packing. Oscar made no attempt to stop her, but watched the girl as she kneeled before the suitcase straightening the garments she had carelessly tossed inside.

'Do you know Dai Phillips?' he asked.

A red flush spread again over her face as she straightened herself. 'Why?'

'Do you know him?' he said.

'Yes . . .' Pamela answered reluctantly, 'I know Dai Phillips.'

'I thought so,' said Oscar. 'What happened between you and Benny that night?'

She remained silent but dropped what she was doing and rose shamefacedly to her feet.

'Well? . . . Answer me!' Oscar insisted. 'What happened to make Benny act like that?'

She shook her head. 'Nothing.'

'I don't believe you!' Oscar returned harshly.

'Honestly, Dad,' she repeated, 'nothing at all.'

'You're lying, Pamela,' he said. 'I can see it in your eyes. Benny was a good boy. He helped me, and I know he would kill himself for you. Now he's in prison – and it's all your fault!'

He suddenly saw her eyes dilate with terror and, looking down, noticed that he had unconsciously taken out the revolver and was caressing it in his lap.

'Dad! What's that you've got there?' she demanded.

He picked up the gun and held it before his face, turning the barrel beneath his nose with the ease of long familiarity. 'That? What does it look like?' He nodded, although she had not replied. 'Yes . . . that's what it is, a revolver. I used it when I was a hero in France, the same revolver. I shot Germans with it – and a couple of Englishmen, too,' he added ironically, 'in the back when they ran away.'

Pamela seemed fascinated by the gun. 'What are you going to do?' she asked in a quick whisper without taking her eyes off it for a moment.

'Do? . . . I'm going to shoot myself,' he announced calmly.

A quiver shook Pamela's body as though an electric current had rippled through her from head to toe. Immobilised for an instant, she seemed to recover herself and moved towards her father, holding out her hand.

'Give me that, Dad,' she said urgently. 'Give that thing to me!'

Oscar slipped off the bed. 'Keep away!' he barked with icy determination.

The girl stopped, and her face twisted into a frightened grimace. 'But, Dad . . .' she protested weakly.

'Keep away!' he repeated hoarsely. 'Get out of the house, or I'll shoot you, too – I mean it . . . Quickly! Before I change my mind.' He watched her walk hesitantly to the door, following her dragging movements with the levelled revolver. 'You deserve to die, you little beast!' He flung at her as she turned, her mouth open with the obvious intention of pleading with him again. 'God knows I never expected to have to talk to a daughter of mine this way,' he added bitterly, 'but even shooting's too good for you!'

A little horrified gasp escaped from her, and, before he could say any more, she had vanished from the room. He heard the rapid clop of her high heels as she ran frantically down the stairs, and, before he could even emerge from the room himself, the street door slammed violently at her departure. Oscar walked unhurriedly down the stairs. Pamela would be searching now for a policeman, and he had ample time before she could return, but to make certain there would be no interruptions he would lock the side entrance. It was necessary for him to be alone in this old house for the final consummation, alone in the shop that no one else alive understood or fully appreciated. The side door locked, he moved into the shop with a light tread, feeling almost happy. He had come quite to the end of his tether. The trusts and combines wouldn't let him live, in his own house, in his own shop; the arrogant money bully was boss, driving the small man down. Well, Oscar Currie wasn't the only one; high-handed knavery and forceful intimidation were features of this age. With him it was the Empire House Traders, while with the rest of Europe an Austrian paperhanger was trying out the same trick on a world scale. Anyway, he had three bullets; if not the first, the second or the third would do the trick. He was not afraid of death, he had seen too much of it in France, but that was ugly and unpremeditated, while he would die like a dignified person in a manner of his own choosing on his own premises, like an Englishman, a shop-keeper and a Currie.

CHAPTER TWENTY

The boys at the garage gave Kim a right royal send-off. Yielding to the entreaties of Rusty and his friends, the proprietor had entrusted Kim with a new cab on his very first day, a most unusual concession to a novice, and the drivers, washers and mechanics lined up solemnly and shook his hand before he drove off, speeding him on his way with a hearty cheer.

Kim cruised aimlessly down the first major road. He was in no particular hurry, for he had informed the garage proprietor that he was going home first, a gesture which his employer naturally understood as a desire to show off before adoring parents. The proprietor didn't mind him going home so much. It was the cab he was worried about, but as Kim had established himself as a general favourite he had given way on that point, thereby tacitly admitting that even he held a sneaking regard for the lad.

Kim seemed to be seeing the familiar streets for the first time from his driving seat; even the people looked slightly different, breast high. The engine purred smoothly beneath his feet, a symbol of leashed energy waiting for a touch to release the strength of twelve horses, and Kim, his hand resting lightly on the wheel, revelled in the feeling of power and responsibility it gave him. Looking at his watch and checking it by the large clock on the tower, he saw that it was half past twelve, later than he had thought, for some minor adjustments had kept him in the garage till now. Immediately his joy dulled as he thought of his uncle. A sense of depression swooped over him, and not even the sweetly running engine was able to divorce him from the mood of savage bitterness that Spencer Currie aroused. He hated his uncle for the malevolent influence even his name seemed to exert over his father, but fortunately he could face him today with his head held high. He was no longer an unemployed college graduate; he had a job and was earning his own living. The thought consoled him a trifle. He was completely independent now, and maybe, to spite his rich uncle still more, he would one day have his own cab, if there wasn't a war . . . If there wasn't a war . . . There seemed to be that proviso in every conversation and every thought, the whole future seemed bounded and each horizon restricted by that damnable phrase, already so plugged that the words had almost lost their hideous connotation. A gigantic cata-strophe was taken as a matter of course, and Kim could even imagine those words becoming part of his native tongue in some varied form as a pious utterance like 'God willing' or 'Please God', being adapted and modified by the genius of the language that took and naturalised phrases necessary for its full expression from whatever source . . . If there won't be a war . . . Wherever one looked there were evidences of its oblique implications. Even in the sky he could see the ugly grey tethered blimps of the barrage nosing lazily with the wind like floating rhinoceroses, mute reminders of the heritage bequeathed to his generation, reminders that they need look no nearer heaven than those swollen gasbags. It was, possibly, all part of the war of nerves, yet these grim, unceasing pre-parations boded something far more serious than that. The boys at the garage were right, they should have throttled the beast last September, but it wasn't too late even now. Kim had never bothered much about politics previously, but in these tense, pregnant days it had become interwoven with the texture of his, of everybody's, life. He saw it all so clearly, although, like Rusty and the others, he could not say 'I told you so.' He had learned late but absorbed the lesson well. Poland was on the spot now, and the gangsters behind their honeyed words and protestations of peace were moving up machine-guns, tanks and bombers into position. What in heaven were the democracies waiting for? Couldn't they see these things that were so plain even to uneducated cab-drivers? That after Poland would come France, and after France, Britain? And if Britain were left to fight alone, what could save the last relics of twentieth-century civilisation being engulfed in the dark tide of barbarism?

He shrugged his shoulders as he glanced at his watch. If it was his funeral it would be everyone else's, too. It was time he drove home. If he made for home immediately he would still be about fifteen minutes late by the time he arrived. Kim could hardly imagine anything more distasteful than this interview, but he had given his word, and Matilda was expecting him to show up. Perhaps the most painful part was over by now, but it was no use postponing the meeting any longer, best to get it behind him, erase the inevitably bitter impression and forget about his uncle for another ten years.

Cutting through a side turning, he emerged a few yards from his home. At once a chill of horror pierced him, for outside the shop a small crowd had gathered, mostly women with shopping baskets, who paid very little attention to a genial middle-aged policeman who was gently trying to shoo them away. Kim drew up to the gutter and jumped out of the cab. It was his father, he knew it. Something had happened to him, something that possibly could have been avoided if he had arrived a little earlier. He elbowed his way towards the constable, regardless of the protests his roughness aroused. He couldn't stand on ceremony now. Something had happened to Oscar, and he felt that somehow he was to blame.

At the door the policeman stopped him. 'What do you want?' he said.

Kim was almost breathless, and at the strangeness of the question seemed at a loss for words. 'I . . . I want to go in,' he said at last.

'You can't,' replied the policeman sternly, smoothing his large moustache in a manner reminiscent of Oscar. 'Nobody's allowed inside!' He waved his arm peremptorily. 'Drive on, son.'

'But I've got to go in,' Kim insisted agitatedly. 'I live here.'

'Oh . . . all right,' said the constable. He opened the door and laid a paternal hand on his shoulder. 'But don't park the cab here too long,' he admonished him in friendly fashion.

Kim shook his head and passed down the shop, treading over a patch of sawdust that stuck in a thin layer to his soles and grated irritatingly between his shoes and the smooth linoleum all the way to the parlour. He was an accessory to a heinous crime. He had stayed away on purpose, dragging out the fatal minutes when he should have been here, toying with cynical mental sophistry while his father was suffering, while his father was dying, and now he had arrived when the agony was over. Oscar was dead. He wouldn't have to be told; he knew it. He knew it! . . . He knew it!

He found Pamela and his mother seated limply side by side on the settee, while Spencer Currie was standing solicitously over them. All three looked up as Kim came in, and Matilda and his sister immediately buried their faces in their handkerchiefs again and wept, as though his appearance were a signal for fresh tears.

'What's happened?' he demanded impatiently. 'Where's Dad?'

Matilda shook her head without replying as the questions evoked a new outburst of sobbing from his sister, and Spencer, brisk and efficient as usual, came across to Kim and laid his hand gently on the young man's arm. A shiver of distaste ran through Kim at the contact, but he repressed the urge to shake him off roughly and quietly allowed his uncle to lead him to a chair.

'He's dead . . . He's dead . . .' he muttered, looking up hopelessly at Spencer for confirmation.

Spencer Currie nodded. 'Take it easy, Kim,' he said softly, patting his shoulder.

The warm hand became irksome to him, as though its negligible pressure imposed an intolerable burden on his body. The intense physical revulsion had worn off, but he still felt uneasy at this vampire-like contact that had fastened on him so tenaciously.

He shifted his chair away. 'When did it happen?' he asked. 'Just now?'

'No,' said Spencer Currie. 'This morning, about half past ten.'

So it *wasn't* his fault – thank God for that! Irrationally he tried to shift the blame on to his uncle. Wherever Spencer Currie moved he brought tragedy with him. If he hadn't come here, Oscar would still have been alive. But Oscar didn't know, he hadn't had even an inkling of this visit . . . Oh, hell! He couldn't pretend to understand anything now. Of course Spencer could have had nothing to do with it, but the shock had rendered him incapable of viewing things objectively, and his uncle had always appeared to him in the light of a sinister omen . . . He would soon calm down, and everything would fit in. It wasn't *his* fault, it wasn't Spencer's, it wasn't – Oh, what the hell! What the hell! He felt like groaning aloud with the heaviness of his heart. He was dead . . . D-E-A-D . . . That embraced all there was to it, everything that could be said or thought.

Spencer moved up a chair and sat beside him, watching Kim intently. He wanted to stretch out his hands and comfort him, but he saw jealously his touch was repugnant, and yet the boy ought to understand that these were not strange hands, to feel instinctively, as he did, that they had more right to caress him than any other hands in the world . . .

'You know, Kim,' he remarked irreverently, 'you look a lot like me.'

'That's not so surprising,' Kim answered sharply. 'After all, you're my father's brother.'

Kim could sense quite a different emotion behind the

apparent kindness of his uncle's casual words. He knew, deep down, that Spencer hated him as he had hated his father. He reciprocated that feeling, and now that there was no reason to be diplomatic he wanted an opportunity to make it perfectly clear and felt thwarted because the conversation hadn't so far given him the slightest opening.

Spencer seemed disappointed. He nodded. 'That's right,' he said without warmth. His tone changed. 'Kim . . . your mother and Pamela are coming to stay with me – I want you to come, too.'

Kim shook his head. 'No.'

'But you can't stay in this house any longer!'

'Why not?' said Kim. 'I was born in this house – and I'm not afraid of ghosts . . . It will do till I get fixed up somewhere else.'

'Kim, don't do that, please . . .' Spencer Currie pleaded. 'Why must you go to strangers? I'm a rich man, and I'm lonely. I've got no family of my own. You Curries are all I have left in the world. If it will make you come, I'll be glad to adopt you . . . I've got so much to offer . . . I want you all round me, the last of the Curries.'

'You've got Mother,' said Kim, 'and Pamela. She's a Currie, too.'

'No,' Spencer answered. 'She'll be married one day, maybe pretty soon, and then she'll be something else. But you, you'll stay a Currie all your life.'

Kim rose determinedly to his feet. 'That's how I mean to stay all my life – Oscar Currie's son!' He saw his uncle's lips move as though framing a reply. Kim understood what it was. Spencer felt guilty, too, and was trying to salve his conscience with alms. Well, he could keep his money. Kim wanted to be free of him, completely separated, but Spencer's words pursued him, they clung to him like leeches, and he couldn't shake them off. Resolutely he moved to the door . . . 'Well . . . I've got to get to work,' he said.

'Wait!' Spencer Currie jumped to his feet and came up to him, his grey eyes shining with a peculiar, moist glint. 'Kim . . . there's something you've got to know . . .'

'Well?' Kim looked down on him contemptuously. He felt like a giant beside this little man. Why, he was simply a dwarf, and he wondered at the frightened awe in which he had held this mannikin for so long. Considered apart from his wealth, he was nothing, not even presentable flesh and bones, and this freak had had the power to subdue him even in his absence! He could almost laugh now at this foolishness, and he knew that the last link between them was irremediably cleft. 'Well?' he repeated brusquely. 'Hurry up.'

Spencer felt a tug at his sleeve. Matilda had moved to his side. Without a word she demanded his attention and looked steadily in his eyes. Just that, and he knew he couldn't say what he wanted to say. In that moment he acknowledged defeat and understood that the battle was lost for ever.

'You must come with us,' he said lamely. 'My car's waiting at the side door, please, Kim,' he begged.

The young man shook his head. 'No thanks,' he said. 'I'll be all right here.' He felt himself growing in power and confidence as his uncle diminished in stature before him. 'Besides,' he added more considerately in a friendlier tone, 'I've got my own car waiting outside.'

'Very well,' said Spencer resignedly. He pressed a white slip into his hand. 'Here's my card. Don't be afraid to come if you change your mind . . . And we'll keep in touch with you all the time.'

Kim nodded and, bending down, kissed his mother lightly on the forehead, then turning his back abruptly he passed once more down that familiar lane between the counters, gingerly avoiding the tell-tale sawdust patch.

When he opened the door, a murmur of excitement greeted him, and, as he made his way to the cab, a man had the temerity to approach him, his head cocked interrogatively. Angrily Kim brushed him aside before he could utter more than a querulous monosyllable and, climbing to his seat, started up the engine. What were all these ghouls waiting for? No need for big drums. A death meant 'Roll up. The greatest show on earth.' But it was all over. There was nothing else to see. Mr Oscar Currie, the man who had shot himself, was now a discoloured lump of flesh on a cold slab in the morgue. They had had their fun, a tasty titbit to retail over the backyard walls in the evening. In spite of their long faces and sympathetic glances they were all having a damned good time; fortunately they would soon dismiss this circus, someone would fall under a bus or there would be a local murder the day after tomorrow. Their smug looks irritated him. Death seemed to bring out all that was most sanctimonious in these people – he felt he could go berserk and drive his cab right into the crowd to teach them a lesson, really give them something to cry about.

He calmed down as he drove off. The cab seemed to have a soothing influence, impressing on him a strict sense of his new responsibility. He was no longer angry. He didn't find it in him to hate his father or despise him for what he had done. That had been merely the logical consequence of the way he had spent his life and the period in which he had lived. He belonged to that dead old world whose fruits were decay and ruin.

Oscar Currie had been dead for a long time. This drastic cutting-off of the life stream had merely dotted the *i*s and crossed the *t*s; given the supreme fiat to what was already an unacknowledged fact. Currie & Son was an empty glory anyhow. These last few years it hadn't been a business, just a name. Surely this would be a most suitable epitaph for his father: 'He was a man who lived for his business and died for his name.'

He was only just beginning to realise the change that had

taken place in his own mental outlook. Before, the mode of life had seemed to him damned, but he had, with devastating cynicism, impartially condemned every proposal for altering it without offering any alternative suggestions. Too late he was learning the answers that might even have benefited Oscar. The garage was a closed shop, and he had joined the union as a matter of course, but during the inevitable political arguments he had found his cynicism out of place. His colleagues believed in the principles of trade unionism and envisaged a system of society where even his father, with his specialised knowledge of retail trade, would have found an honoured place. So he wouldn't carry the esteem of being a labelled Currie and the prestige of owning his own business, but he would have a regular job, a five-day week and a living wage. He knew if he were Oscar which of the two he would have preferred, and he wasn't certain that even his father might not have become reconciled to it one day. The world was so big, its needs so enormous, and yet the wastage of human material was still so prodigious; surely a man had the right to live, even if all he could do was to serve in a shop?

This was a nation of shopkeepers, and this a street of shops. He hated to think that all these people were doomed as his father had been, strutting out futilely their hollow little day until war or the cartels and combines obliterated them. Meanwhile they had put up the shutters and were preparing to spend their free afternoons escaping as far from reality as possible at the pictures, at whist-drives, in theatres and dancehalls. The House Traders were closed, too, and a stream of girls oozed through the side door, trickling out like the last grains of rice from a scoop. Pale, taut little slaves, enervated from long bondage at the counters yet chattering gaily like magpies at this happy release that carried them away from the artificial yellow suns and into the free air once more. Kim seemed to recognise one of the girls as he drove past slowly – then he remembered Leah Rothstein. Impulsively he stopped the cab, waiting for her to come up, and, as she drew abreast, he leaned out of the window and called to her.

'Taxi, lady?'

The girl flashed a weary smile at him. 'No thanks.'

'Wait a minute!' He jumped out of the cab and joined her on the pavement as she was about to move off. 'Don't think I'm rude,' he apologised, 'but aren't you Leah Rothstein?'

'That's right,' she said, in a low, cultured voice, 'I am.'

'My name's Currie – Kim Currie.'

'Oh . . .' Her large, deep-lashed eyes opened sympathetically. 'Is it true then, about your father?'

Kim bit his lip to restrain his tears and lowered his head, ashamed of his weakness. He was more moved now than he had been at the very scene of the tragedy, more hurt than when he had trod on his father's blood . . . She had heard already . . . Some gossip had probably mentioned it to one of the assistants, and in five minutes it was all over the store.

'Yes,' he said, 'he's dead . . .' He swallowed hard and adjusted his cap. 'Can I drive you home?'

'No thanks.' She seemed embarrassed, too. 'I live just round the corner.'

'But isn't there anywhere else you want to go?'

'Well . . . I was going to visit my mother this afternoon . . . She's at Hanwell.'

'Right! Jump in, and I'll take you there.'

'But . . .' The girl hesitated.

'Please come,' he said earnestly. 'I feel I've *got* to take you.'

He helped her into the seat and went down to the front of the cab, pulling down the flag. His first fare – a deficit! This was a nice start, but he couldn't help himself; it seemed that only this way could he give expression to the bond he felt between them. It was highly appropriate, too, driving to a small madhouse within a larger one . . . *Wasn't* it a mad world? Could it be sane to kill off parents so indiscriminately? To send an artist to serve behind a counter and a student to the driving seat of a cab? Shakespeare had a word for it, always and everywhere. The Universal Man had nailed down the situation in the last flowering of that gigantic genius:

> In few, they hurried us aboard a bark;
> Bore us some leagues to sea, where they prepared
> A rotten carcass of a butt, not rigg'd,
> Nor tackle, sail, nor mast; the very rats
> Instinctively have quit it.

That seemed to sum it up in a nutshell. The whole world, a rotten carcass of a butt, sea tossed on a flood of wars. He glanced behind him. Leah was crying, and at the sight he, too, was moved again to tears. Quickly he blinked, controlling himself. Camden Town was a dangerous spot; he didn't want to end up this perfect day with an accident. He knew what had happened. It was wrong of him to have accosted her, for his distress had evoked memories of her own bereavement. There they sat, two orphans of the storm, obsessed by their tiny individual tragedies, on the way to a lunatic asylum, while the whole world trembled on a volcano of madness. Surely their tears were wasted on those two puny creatures who had long outlived their usefulness? Wasn't there anything else in the world to cry about? In China? . . . Nothing. In Abyssinia? . . . Nothing. In Spain? . . . Nothing. How easy to tick off these items, each involving millions of lives, at first far away then coming closer, nearer both in space and time. Yesterday Czechoslovakia, tomorrow Poland, the day after, who could tell? Peace and war trembling in the balance, the scales of destruction heavily weighted by one man's lust, yet they found crying stuff only in their small sorrows. And much their crying would help. Hear old Prospero again:

> There they hoist us,
> To cry to the sea, that roared to us; to sigh
> To the winds, whose pity, sighing back again,
> Did us, but loving wrong.

Things couldn't go on like this for ever. Craziness was not enthroned until the end of man. A society was not static by the immutable laws of nature, and this society had killed his father, but it wouldn't get the better of him. Now the dark clouds were gathering for an explosion, he sensed the part he had to play. His father's world was dying, although in its convulsions it might set continents aflame. It seemed too late now to avoid a clash, but probably it was for the best; if it had been better last year than now, it was better now than in three months' time or in six, which held about the full limit of a Nazi promise. He had to look ahead, after the conflict, to see that this never happened again. The survivors, young people, would build a newer, saner world, where middle-aged men were not lopped off like dead twigs because they did not fit in, where violence in private and in public affairs had no place, where prejudice and lies could no longer dim the vision of decent folk. They would establish a society where the whole of life could flower harmoniously, whose fabric would never more be endangered by one shrieking lunatic straddling Europe. Enough of retreating, of whining and pleading; let the dead past bury the dead. No more crying to the sea and having pity sigh back with the wind. Clear-eyed, with a million others, he would stand out boldly in the tempest and shake a fist at thunder.

THE END

MY FIRST THIRTY YEARS

Simon Blumenfeld, 1937

*Author's biography held by
the literary agent John Paradise*

Rough synopsis of my autobiography, embodying too a personal credo. Early rough-and-tumble days in the East End of London, famous people I have met and anecdotes about them; my attitude towards life and literature at thirty. In fact, generally speaking the book might be termed an English equivalent to Freeman's *American Testament* being more or less in the same genre.

Hard times. My father, illiterate one-eyed cap-maker born in Russia, but widely travelled, baker, market man, shoe-black in Constantinople, dock labourer, sailor ending up in East End factory; mother gentle and always overworked takes in washing to eke out a livelihood.

'Grandfather Sold Lemons' – Chapter heading

School. The war. We take shelter in the vaults of the synagogue next door. Formerly a church, the youngsters sleep in alcoves in the walls built to accommodate coffins before burial. My mother loses me in an air raid shelter and is impaled on spikes climbing a gate to reach me. A Zeppelin going down, my father, in the open because the stuffiness of the vaults affects his asthma, pulls out the nervous youngster and shows him a sight he will never forget.

'Calf Love' – Chapter heading

The Country Holiday Fund. De-lousing depots. My first visit to the sea. My mother gets up at four every morning to line up for whisky bought for 6/8 a bottle, sold for £1 or more. The doctor (now dead) in Cannon Street who supplies certificates of ill-health without which liquor is unobtainable.

I save up my pennies to buy a magic lantern. My hoard is discovered and I am rewarded with a pair of new boots.

'Boots And Magic Lanterns' – Chapter heading

The Mission. I am converted. I win a scholarship and go to a secondary school. The Central Foundation School. My brilliant poet friend and classmate who in later life can't resist stealing £100 wherever he works.

I become an agnostic again. The Russian Revolution.

'1917' – Chapter heading

Work. My first job. I am apprenticed to a tailor known in the trade as 'Mad Harris'. Rummaging in one of the drawers for buttons I discover his son is an internationally known crook in jail in Sing Sing, and called the 'Cockney Bandit'. A hold-up specialist, his cockney accent gives him away at an identity parade.

The Victoria Working Boys Club. I box with young Johnny Brown, and there is a particularly pugnacious youth in the gym who calls himself Kid Berg. I give him a lesson in how to block a left hook after a jab.

My second job. The man who collects the rag-cuttings tells us that his son, a violinist, is starting with his band at the Embassy Club. The boy's name is Bert Ambrose. I discover music and the delights of the country. I become an ardent first nighter. I go for a taxi ride with Charles Laughton and discuss his plays. My wife jilts her fiancée and goes to Russia. I marry her soon after her return. We bump into Aldous Huxley.

'Music At Night' – Chapter heading

I become a trader. Markets. Deptford. East Ham.

The Bermondsey Bookshop. Encounters with Louis Golding, John Van Druten, Leon M Lion, Clemence Dane, Humbert Wolfe, etc.

I cross swords with Lionel Britton at Circle House. My friend Dave Freedman who pushes a barrow with vegetables in the East End, and his older brother Barnett Freedman, famous artist now teaching at Oxford. Mark Gertler.

1926. The General Strike. John Goss sings for our local Trades Council at St Georges Town Hall.

The *Left Review* is founded. I am elected on the Editorial Advisory Board with Amabel Williams-Ellis, Ralph Fox, TH Wintringham, Edgell Rickword. Join the Rebel Players. Produce *Newsboy*, *Waiting For Lefty*. Move to various places until they merge into Unity Theatre.

Fascism in the East End.

'Fourth Of October' – Chapter heading

My friends Nat Cohen and Sam Masters caught up in the outbreak of the Spanish Civil War while on a cycling holiday. Nat has been involved in Revolution in Brazil, jailed and deported, but is on board ship for months tossed around like a shuttlecock from port to port being refused admission to every country. Nat, an ordinary tailor, shows a genius for military tactics, is put in command of Tom Mann Battalion. Unsuccessfully tries invasion of Majorca, is wounded, and unable to move without crutches, invalided out of the army.

Sam Masters comes to lunch at my flat with Hamish Miles. They discuss war as Hamish has known it and Sam's Spanish experiences. Within a month both are dead, Hamish from natural causes, Sam on the Jarama front.

'Paging New Leaders' – Chapter heading

My experience with the various writers' groups of the Movement, and discussing the dearth of world figures amongst the imaginative writers of the Left. The necessity for a nucleus of authoritative writers in England.

My wife's health breaks down. We move away from London. Interviews and correspondence with the almost legendary figure of Dr Barnardo's widow.

The crisis. Personal repercussions.

London Books

FLYING THE FLAG FOR
FREE-THINKING LITERATURE

www.london-books.co.uk

PLEASE VISIT OUR WEBSITE FOR

- Current and forthcoming books
  - Author and title profiles
    - Events and news
  - Secure on-line bookshop
- An alternative view of London literature

London Classics

The Angel And The Cuckoo *Gerald Kersh*
Doctor Of The Lost *Simon Blumenfeld*
The Gilt Kid *James Curtis*
It Always Rains On Sunday *Arthur La Bern*
Jew Boy *Simon Blumenfeld*
May Day *John Sommerfield*
Night And The City *Gerald Kersh*
Phineas Kahn *Simon Blumenfeld*
Prelude To A Certain Midnight *Gerald Kersh*
A Start In Life *Alan Sillitoe*
There Ain't No Justice *James Curtis*
They Drive By Night *James Curtis*
They Won't Let You Live *Simon Blumenfeld*
Wide Boys Never Work *Robert Westerby*

LONDON CLASSICS

JEW BOY

SIMON BLUMENFELD

Jew Boy is a novel about poverty and politics in the tumultuous world of London's Jewish East End in the 1930s, where boxers mixed with anarchists and communists, and Yiddish actors and poets rubbed shoulders with gamblers and gangsters. All were united in their hatred of fascism, and were prepared to fight it when necessary. Yet of equal interest is the novel's exploration of the personal lives and thwarted aspirations of young people at this time, both Jewish and non-Jewish. Class means as much to the main protagonists as the older ties of religion and race.

Author Simon Blumenfeld – born in Whitechapel, working its markets as a young man – brings to life the reality of sweatshops and sweated labour, vividly portraying the exhaustion produced by long hours, unforgiving deadlines and cut-throat competition. But this is a story driven by hope, a desire for change, and his descriptions of the exciting culture that existed beyond the workplace help produce a testimony to a unique time and place now firmly embedded in London's volatile history. *Jew Boy* is nothing less than the founding work of what went on to become a unique body of fiction, autobiography and drama – the literature of the twentieth-century Jewish East End.

Ken Worpole, who introduces the novel, is the author of *Dockers And Detectives*, and has played a major part in reviving public interest in the work of Simon Blumenfeld and other Jewish writers from the pre-war East End.

London Books
£11.99 hardback
ISBN 978-0-9568155-1-4

PHINEAS KAHN: PORTRAIT OF AN IMMIGRANT

SIMON BLUMENFELD

Simon Blumenfeld's acclaimed second novel follows the struggles of a Jewish merchant's son, Phineas Kahn, as he makes his escape from the confines of Tsarist Russia to Vienna and then London in 1900, where he settles to raise a large family in the liberating atmosphere but desperate poverty of the East End. Hard-working and wedded to tradition, Phineas never surrenders in his fight to achieve a better life for his wife and children, who along with his great love of music offer solace in the most difficult times. *Phineas Kahn: Portrait Of An Immigrant* follows Blumenfeld's ground-breaking debut *Jew Boy*, and shows the experience of earlier, first-generation migrants.

Based on tales from Blumenfeld's own family history and the lives of people he knew while growing up in Whitechapel, *Phineas Kahn* opens up a window on the sweatshops, slums and synagogues of the area's Jewish community in the early decades of the 20th century. Not only a fascinating insight into what was a largely hidden world, *Phineas Kahn* is also a priceless portrayal – wrapped up in a gripping, warm narrative – of a London now vanished. With *Jew Boy*, *Doctor Of The Lost* and *They Won't Let You Live* it forms a loose quartet that captures the shifting culture, politics and expectations of those who made the East End their home.

London Books
£14.95 hardback
ISBN 978-0-9957217-1-5

LONDON CLASSICS

DOCTOR OF THE LOST

SIMON BLUMENFELD

When young Thomas Barnardo arrived in London in 1866, he
planned to study at the London Hospital before venturing
abroad to work as a missionary. The conditions he found in the
East End stopped him in his tracks. Unemployment, poverty,
overcrowding, alcoholism and deathly diseases were bad enough,
but seeing thousands of half-starved children living on the streets
broke his heart. Inside a year Dr Barnardo had opened the
ragged-school Hope Place and by 1870 the first of his
eponymous homes was in operation. His work continues to this
day. *Doctor Of The Lost* is the fictionalised story of Tom
Barnardo's early years in East London.

Author Simon Blumenfeld grew up in the same streets, his cult
1935 novel *Jew Boy* capturing the magic of the Jewish East End
of the 1930s, and *Doctor Of The Lost* (1938) recreates the area in
Dr Barnardo's day. Drawing on a friendship with his widow,
Blumenfeld brings Barnardo vividly to life, showing the struggles
he faced and the battles won. *Doctor Of The Lost* is set in a
London of rampant industrialisation, when the few became rich
at the expense of the many, and yet this was also a period of
charity and good works, when idealists such as Thomas Barnardo
were prepared to stand tall and fight back.

London Books
£11.99 hardback
ISBN 978-0-9568155-2-1